March of Time and Skin

Tim,

Live, thrive, repeat.

Best

Jeff Stewart

Time and Skin Media
Portland, Oregon

www.jeffstewartwrites.com

March of Time and Skin
© 2008 by Jeff Stewart and Time and Skin Media, LLC.

Cover layout by Mitchell Harris
mharrisd@msn.com

Interior layout by Tatiana deFigueiredo
www.designbytatiana.blogspot.com

Cover photo by Polly Rothwell
www.pollyrothwell.com

Cover model is Roxanne Gregory.

This book is a work of fiction. The situations as well as any similarities to real persons either living or dead are purely coincidental.

All rights reserved. No part of this book may be reproduced in any form without the written permission from the publisher or author, with the exception of short excerpts in articles or reviews, and where permitted by law.

ISBN: 978-0-615-23535-6

Time and Skin Media, LLC.
Email: info@timeandskin.com
Website: www.timeandskin.com

For Meg.

"All truth passes through three stages. First, it is ridiculed. Second, it is violently opposed. Third, it is accepted as being self-evident."

Arthur Schopenhauer

March of Time and Skin

1

I was riding high. I could see the legs of other drivers, the inside of their cars as I passed them. The legs of women. The windshield was close to me and expansive in vision. The first few miles were like driving a spaceship. It was beautiful. I had to pick up my plates and buy new tags. The DMV in Boulder City was closer than Vegas. The dealer had also told me that the lines were shorter. I set the clock above the dashboard.

The building wasn't busy. In the line next to me stood an ugly man. He stared at me. He had this face behind these thick bifocals, which enlarged his eyes to dull brown moons. When I looked back at him he squinted and studied my face. He stepped aside from the line, sat down and watched me. I paid for the plates. I sat at one of the tables and applied the tags to the plates. I figured he was some type of prostitute. I looked out at the van. Dark green. My favorite color. It was glorious. I watched the guy pull on his jacket as I stood. An Army jacket. It was hot outside. He said something to me when I left the building. I ignored him. Outside, I could hear him coming up behind me. I gripped the plates in my hand like a discus, ready to spin and cut him.

"Excuse me."

I kept walking. It didn't bother him. He was used to it. He was used to the treat-

ment. He knew he was worthless but he accepted it, the way someone accepts being born without a limb.
He called my name.
I turned around. He was right in front of me. Then I read the last name above his sleeve on the front of his jacket. He was smiling ear to ear. Something was wrong about it. It was an eager smile, an erection seconds before being mounted.

"That's your name, right?"

"Right."

He threw his head back and wailed. I stepped off a couple of feet. He clapped his hands together and threw his arms open.

"It's me, man! Arthur!"

I stared at him. He spread his arms.

"Hey, man. Give me hug!"

He ran up and hugged me. He smelled like Brylcreem and sweat. I was frozen. He let go.

"Don'tcha remember, man? Grampa? Me? The whole family?"

I got it. He was the son of my father's old man. I remembered them coming down for a visit when I was nine years old. My mother never let anyone stay in contact with that side of the family because she and my father said they were crazy. And I had forgotten them. I remembered why the name Boulder City, Nevada was so familiar. They lived in Boulder City. I shook my head.

"Art. Shit, man. I'm sorry. How are you? How's everybody?"

He shook my hand, hungrily.

"Good, man! Real good!"

My brain scanned itself for memory of these people. There they were, every detail. It came together. Their vacation to our house in Phoenix, our swimming pool, my grandfather's new wife whom he'd met in a nut house, her long armpit hairs which my brother and I laughed about. The two of them at our table, drinking pot after pot of coffee and chain-smoking. The collective insanity of their clan, the three, mutated, screwed up kids and the incestuous feel they exchanged. There they were, one fucked up group. One ugly family. Ugly from the insanity.

I followed behind him. When I glanced at him through his mirror he was smiling at me, and his mirror was full of large teeth. At a stop sign he let cars go out of turn to make sure I was right behind him. I could have made a sharp left and lost him a few times, but I didn't.

I followed him down a dead end street where he parked. The houses were poor and in shambles. Every yard had a broken down car in front. I stepped out of the van and looked around. He was smiling right in front of me.

"This is our cul-de-sac."

I stared from house to house. The clotheslines, the dead autos, the stained clothing drying dead in the hot wind shameless and ugly, the people on their front porches smoking, sweating. I stared at the mailboxes and something came out of me involuntarily.

"Culture sac."

He laughed and clapped his hands.

"Culture sac! Ha! That's a great one!"

We walked onto the front yard toward the door. He stopped and turned. He grabbed my shoulders, out of breath.

"All right. I'll go inside. You climb the tree and when I bring them out, you jump down and yell, SURPRISE!"

"No."

I wiped his mouth spray from my cheek. He sucked his lips and wet them again.

"Okay. Okay. I got it. You hide behind the side of the house and surprise everyone."

I stared at him until the silence broke him. He stepped off,

"Okay, okay. Just wait here."

I waited. An old lady came out of her house across the street and pointed at me. Then she shouted.

"ARE YOU SATAN?"

"Yes." I said.

She ran back inside. Art walked out of the house and leaned against their car. He folded his arms and waited.

The door opened. There he was. Fat, greasy and in his boxer shorts. He studied me. There was a long silence. Then his wife was out there. She wore a nightgown, the same one from my memory.

The old man smiled.

"JEFFERY! MY GRANDSON!

He walked down and hugged me. He stank. His wife smiled at me, and went back inside. I told him it was good to see him again. He looked at my wheels.

"Hey, man! You drivin' that?"

I laughed. "I just drove it off the lot. Art spotted me down at the DMV. I forgot you lived here."

He walked over to the Dodge. He opened the door and sat behind the wheel.

"Good God! This is a great van!"

I didn't know why he was so into it. Something was on the back burner of the collective consciousness of these people. They all shared the same brain, his brain. He jumped out and closed the door.

"Got your plates, huh?"

"I did. Do you have a Phillips screwdriver?"

"Hell yes! Arthur! Get your nephew a screwdriver! Right now!"

"Yes, Dad!"

Art ran inside. The old man turned to me and beamed.

"See that, Jeffery? That's LOYALTY!"

"Have you guys always lived here?"

"Do you know what LOYALTY is, Jeffery?"

"What are you talking about?"

He had no power over me. I was not afraid to leave. He didn't like it. It scared him. He was insane. I told him I had to make time.

"Like hell. Come on in! You can talk to your old grampa for a while."

He put his arm on my shoulder as we walked.

"I haven't seen you for years and years. I'm sorry about your mother. She was a good woman."

My mother had thought that he was an idiot.

Their house was small and hot, and it smelled like body odor. I sat across from him at the table. He looked to his wife.

"Remember Jeffery?"

She coughed up a phlegm ball and swallowed it.

"Yeah. I remember. Hi, Jeffery."

"Hi there."

He glanced out to the van.

"You got insurance for that thing?"

"No."

I had never had insurance, wasn't even aware of it. I thought it was a weird question. He asked me what it was that I was doing with my life. I told him I had left Phoenix and traded my car for the van on impulse after I'd crossed the dam, that I was driving the freeways without aim. He sneered. He said that Art had just returned from Panama, and that his daughter was also in the army. When I asked about his oldest son, he said he was pumping gas for a while then he quit and started living in the desert.

"A place away from it all, huh?"

"No, goddamn it! I mean literally living in the desert. He's a bum!"

"Oh."

His wife coughed up and swallowed another one. Art ran in with the Phillips.

"You okay, mom? Jeff, here's what you need."

The old man stared at the window.

"Jeffery, why don't you go out and put on your plates. Arthur, help him."

I took the screwdriver and told Art I could handle it. Before I made it out the door I heard the old man tell him to make sure they got their screwdriver back. I didn't bother with it. I could put the plates on and toss the screwdriver on the front lawn from the driver's seat. I screwed the plate on the front. I wanted to see if the cassette player worked. I dug a cassette from my backpack and walked around to the front of the van. I went for the key but it was gone. I didn't remember pulling it from the ignition. I felt my pockets. Nothing. I knew I didn't have it on me when I went inside. I walked to the front door.

"Did I leave my key in there?"

He held it up.

"Yeah. Got the plates on?"

"Not yet. I wanted to see if the tape player works."

I walked in to get the key. He told me I could have it when I returned the screwdriver. He was insane. I walked back out thinking about him taking the key. I walked to the rear of the Dodge and fought a rusty screw. The head was stripped. Art walked out and leaned against his car, arms folded, and watched me. It was strange, the whole mood of these people had shifted to hostile. I didn't even know them.

I beat the bolt and worked it loose. As I was tightening down the plate I noticed the number: NIL 741. I thought it had character. I heard a car pull up behind me and stop. Someone stepped out, and I heard the unmistakable jingling of loose objects and hard shoes. I stood and turned, face to face with a cop. He opened his mouth:

"How are you doing, sir?"

"I'm fine."

"Do you have your driver's license?"

"Yes."

"Let's see it."

"What did I do?"

"Your license, please."

"I didn't do anything."

"Your license."

He grinned at me, nothing friendly about it. I stared at him,

"Why are you doing this?"
He stalled. I looked over at Art. He stared at his shoes. The cop answered.
"It's just routine. Strange vehicle in the neighborhood. Just checking you out. Please cooperate."
He ran my license. Then he asked about the van. I told him I'd just driven it off the lot. I showed him the forms.
"I see, well it's all in order. What about insurance?"
"No insurance. I figured I had a little time."
"You figured wrong. I won't, well I *can't* cite you because this is not a moving violation. You will not drive this van another mile uninsured. Tomorrow have your grandfather take you to get insurance. Do you have money for insurance?"
"Yes. How did you know he was my grandfather?"
He paused there, and he was slimy and beautiful, if just for that one moment in his whole rotted life. But he answered.
"Have a good day, sir."
Then he was gone. Art had heard the whole thing, and he was already inside.
I walked in and grabbed my key off the table. The old man yelled at me:
"Now wait a goddamned minute! I did not call the police, Jeffery!"
It occurred to me to flip the table over onto him. The hag coughed up another one.
"Now look, your grandmother's all upset. Come back and have some coffee with your family."
I stepped to the edge of the table.
"You people are fucking insane. Secondly, whatever she is, she's not my grandmother."
Art started to swell on me and stood up. I shook my head at him. The old man told me if that cop saw me driving without insurance he would lock me up. That was the new law. Then he told me the insurance offices were closed until the next day, so I would have to stay the night. I told him I would call Roll's mom and have her pick me up and I'd stay at their place. He buckled. I had two friends in Las Vegas, so he didn't quite have me. But he said it was a bad area where he lived and that someone could slash my tires, and I knew what he meant. He asked me to sit with them. I told him he was a disgusting human being. He pointed to the chair,
"SIT DOWN!"
I did. His wife was on her third pack of cigarettes. I cleared my throat. Art sat next to me. He was smiling again. I thought about how quickly life changes gears. The old man lit up.
"I want to tell you a story, Jeffery."

March of Time and Skin

Art set a cup of burnt coffee down in front of me. I slid it to edge of the table. The old man began his story.

"Have you ever wondered why your mother never wanted you to visit us?"

"Not anymore."

"My daughter, Allison, was a beautiful young woman. Once she even modeled for a Sears catalogue. She was never completely normal. She had a few failed marriages. Then it was fella to fella. One night at a party she met a man, it was in Chicago, I think. Anyway, she fell in love with this man. That night he began courting her regularly. In a few more weeks, they bedded down. Well, to make a long story quicker, he got her pregnant and left her. It was the crushing blow. Wouldn't even talk to her, even when he found out she was with child. She couldn't take it anymore. She lived on the streets and whored herself for money, for a blanket in the park with a bum, for drugs, mostly drugs, for shelter, for company, for anything."

He shook his head and stared at the ashtray sorrowfully.

"She was so out of her mind she convinced herself that the baby she was carrying was either the devil's child or an alien child or some horseshit like that, but that if she aborted it, she would burn in hell."

Art smiled at me. I looked back to the old man. He paused.

"Why are you telling me all of this?" I said.

He took a long drag

"Because. That baby was you."

I looked at the phone on the table. He put out his cigarette. I looked at him.

"What the fuck are you talking about?"

"Hear me out. Haven't you ever wondered why you looked nothing like your brothers or sisters, or, and this is said respectively, your own mother?"

Of course I had. My mother was beautiful. As for the rest of my family not looking like me, I'd pawned it off on luck, for myself and my mother. I had always thought that something was off, maybe more than luck.

He kept talking.

"Now listen. I know this ain't easy to hear. Your father, my son, married Johanna in Illinois, met her at a bar. A bad place to meet someone.

I asked where he had met his wife, since I already knew. The table froze.

"In a coffee shop. Allison happened upon your father a few months after she went insane. Your mother had already given birth to five children, your family, when she met him. Her husband before committed suicide by handgun at their table one night while he was drunk. See, Sonny couldn't have a child of his own and he wanted one. They took Allison in at their home in Peoria and kept her going until she had you. That was her price for being fed and sheltered for eight or nine

7

months. From there she whored around the country. There were two other kids she let go before you, in between marriages. We know of one, a girl. Well, a woman now. Her name's Denise. But it was the last one, the man in Chicago that broke her. So, after years passed Allison showed up here at my door. We took her in, fed her, even got her a job down at a pizza shop doing dishes. We bought her new teeth and cleaned up her act. Then she started complaining about not being able to bring a man here and having relations with him. I told her she was under my roof and that I had rules. Live by them or there's the door. She left. She's still here in the state, in Las Vegas. We know where she is. She's on the street. She's beyond help."
He asked me if I was clear on all of this. I knew he was right. I believed him because he was right. Looking back, I'd felt it my whole life.

"That's why you were not allowed to spend time here. Johanna was too afraid that you would find out."
The old man smiled. I stared at him.

"And you were just dying to tell me."

"We thought you should know."
He lit up. The phone rang. He nodded at me,

"That's for you."

I answered slowly. It was a woman's voice.

"Jeffery?"

"Yes."

"I'm your sister!"

"So I hear."
She laughed. There was a strange and immediate bond with the voice. It was warm and familiar. We made some jokes toward the awkwardness. They stared at me from around the table, more so they glared at me. She said he had been in touch with her for a couple of years and that they had mailed her pictures. She was trying to be tactful in asking me if they weren't insane, if I was close to them or if I cared about them.
I said hell no, and her laugh was wild.

"Me either."

"Had you worried, huh, sis?"

"Yes. Thank God!"

"Yes."
She asked were they at least on the up and up. I said no. She picked up on everything.

"Are there ears all around you right now?"

"Yes."
"Do you have a photographic memory like I do?"
"Yes."
"Good. This is my phone number..."
"Got it."
"Call me back tonight?"
"Impossible."
"Tomorrow night?"
"No matter what."
The old man grew uncomfortable. He grumbled loudly that he wanted to talk to her. She laughed.
"Christ, he sounds like an asshole right now."
"True colors."
"Give me back to him. And Jeffery, I'm going to say this and I hope you don't think I'm a flake, but I love you."
"Right back at you," I said.
I held the phone out to the old man. He snatched it away. In my eyes he saw that he had lost whatever game he'd been playing. I heard him talking to her:
"What's that? Oh. Well, he's about six one, brown hair down past his shoulders, needs to get it cut, especially the front, you know in my day only girls had their front as long as the back of their hair, anyway, he is tan and kinda skinny- what's that? Well sure, whenever he's here I'll have him call you. Your what? No, I think we should feel him out before we give him your address or last name, you know, keep the blood solid. What was that? Sure, I can hold on..."
A moment passed. Then from the ear piece of the phone the whole table heard the sound. It was loud, like a blow horn. The noise jerked the old man's head back. He slammed the phone down on the hooks and cupped his ear:
"SONOFABITCH! I'M DEAF! I'M DEAF!"
The old hag coughed up another one. Art ran to his father's side, almost in tears.
"DAD! ARE YOU GOING TO BE ALL RIGHT?"
"GET THE HELL AWAY FROM ME!"
Art returned to his mother. The old man looked at me, his hand cupped to his ear.
"Loyalty," I said.
He went to the bathroom.

They had a bad schedule. Up around the clock, smoking and drinking coffee.

Art didn't drink coffee or smoke. He just sat there with them. At three in the morning I was still thinking about my sister. I was on the hide-a-bed in the living room. The old man called to me from the table.

"Jeffery, we're going to the El Dorado for coffee."
"You're fucking kidding me."
"WATCH YOUR GODDAMN FILTHY LANGUAGE AROUND YOUR GRANDMOTHER!"
"I'm not going anywhere," I said.
Art jumped up and ran to my bed, his fists clenched.
"Oh yes you are!"
He was shirtless. I looked at his stomach.
"You're fat, Art. A lot of good the army did you.
He looked to his parents. The old hag finally spoke,
"He is not. He's handsome."
She put her arms out,
"Come here, honey."
He walked over to her and knelt. The guy was 26 years old. I looked around the room. I was about to break. The couch was sickening. It smelled like I was laying in a giant armpit. One not unlike the hairs which right now were scratching her son's bare shoulders, her quietly singing to him in between the phlegm balls. I thought about my mother never wanting me to discover the truth, hiding me from these idiots. I loved her more than ever. The old man hissed from the table:
"Get up, Jeffery!"
"Sorry."
Art called from his mother's stink.
"Get up!"
It was a muffled, pathetic shriek. I knew if I left or tried to sleep in the van the cops would be on me in nothing flat. The old man would love to call them. These cockroaches were night owls. I'd have to outwait them. I told them to head out and let me sleep. The old man said he didn't trust me in his home. I could not believe where I was, the point in time. These people. I came from this, these roots. I wondered about my real grandmother, and I wondered if he'd killed her. Somehow I sensed it. He called again.
"Well, Jeffery. We're sacrificing our evening for you. Hope you're happy."
I didn't say anything. I watched them from a hole in the blanket, from the stink of it. Art jumped up, electric and stupid,
"Hey, Dad. I have handcuffs in my room. We can handcuff him to the couch while we go out. He's tired anyway."

I talked from under the blanket," Art, you even touch me and you're history." Everybody started yelling at me from the table. I pulled my shirt over my ears and went to sleep.

It was a few hours later. The sun was coming in the smoke stained window, shedding its golden grace in penlights on that hellhole. The nutcases were both snoring from their room. I grabbed my key from the table. Art was sleeping in front of the front door. I rolled him over with my foot. He scratched his gut and fell back to sleep. Some soldier. I walked out and took my bike from the van along with the forms. I slammed the door and locked it. While I was pedaling up the sidewalk I heard the front door crash open. I looked back. Art in his underwear. He yelled.
"I'M TELLIN' DAD! I'M TELLIN' DAD!"
I rode out into the street, up toward a shopping center. The whole situation was fucked.

I found an insurance office. I had an hour to kill. Next door, I had another key cut, and stuck it in my wallet. I rode around and checked out the town. Nothing. Back at the insurance place I sat in the air conditioning. I stank from the house. I was insured within 15 minutes. I paid the down payment and put the insurance card in my wallet. They would never see any more of my money. I rode back. I had the feeling of a man released from prison, from an asylum. I found a small cafe and ordered a coffee and an egg on a bagel. Bliss. It was hot outside and I was tired. I figured I would make Utah in a while. I threw my bike in the van and locked it. I was afraid one of the nutcases might flatten a tire or break a window. The van was solid. There was something worse.
A man walked out of the house. He was well dressed. He walked up to me and put his hand out. I didn't shake it.
"Hi, Jeff. Remember me?"
"No."
"Uncle Walt. Last time I saw you, you were only seven."
"All right. I remember. How's Rhonda?"
"Hey. You do remember. She's home. We just had our second baby. A girl."
I looked at him. He grinned.
"Let me guess. You went out to get insurance so you can get out of here."
I nodded. He slapped me on the back.
I put my hand out and we shook.
"Congratulations on your second baby. And the first one."
"Thanks. Well, Art's sick. His mother is in his room right now rubbing ice on

his back."
 "Jesus."
 "Do you know why I came over, Jeffery?"
 "I think so."
 "Prepare yourself."
I stepped inside.

2

The old man was at the table smoking. She was sitting on the other corner of the table from him. She glanced at me and took a slurp from her cup. She smoked with her legs crossed. It was my forehead, my facial structure, my features, the same shape and curves of my feet and body. There was my nose. She wore a long bed shirt and men's socks pulled over her calves. Her hair was scraggly. She had no teeth. I looked at her skull. My hairline. Walt studied me. I sat on the couch. He told me he'd picked her up downtown in a park. The old man looked at his daughter and pointed to me.

"Allison. That's your son sitting right over there."
She glanced at me again and chuckled. It was bitter. The old man frowned at her.
"Don't you even want to say hello to your own son?"
She had a hoarse grumble.
"I'm no good at this mothering shit!"
She was right, but I didn't care. I walked up to her, the same way a man would approach another man cut in half by a train, another man dying whom he didn't want to touch or know, but a man he wanted to look upon in order to check himself, to know that he still had life. She looked up at me. There was nothing familiar outside of our blood. She gave me an irritated grunt.

"Okay, here, come here."
She pulled me down and kissed me on the cheek. She stank, a body odor so foul it was almost tropical. She told me she'd see me in Paradise someday. I stood up. I couldn't stop looking at her face, and she grew hostile. She asked me what I wanted from her. I drew back and spat in her face. The old man screamed. She wiped it off and drank her coffee. I spat on her hair. She jumped up and ran out the back door, behind where the old man sat and would sit for the rest of his days. Walt ran after her.
The old man yelled at me.
"YOU SON OF A BITCH! THAT IS NO WAY TO TREAT YOUR MOTHER!"
I picked up the coffee pot and cocked it back. I aimed for his head. He ducked it, and it flew out of the open door behind him. Walt tackled her in the yard. The old man begged me to leave. Not a sound came from Art's room. I walked out of the nightmare and stepped into the Dodge. It started right up. On the passenger seat laid the screwdriver where I'd left it to find the registration forms for the cop. I put it in the glove box. As I drove out I could see Walt holding her on the yellow grass in the rearview. I could now tell any preacher exactly where hell was, give him the physical address.

I drove south out of state and paid for a room in Kingman, because Utah didn't feel right once I had thought about it. I wanted to sleep in the van but I stank, a stink unbearable from the nuthouse, someone else's smell. I got the room and unloaded my things. I didn't want to call my sister until nightfall. I was better at night, more responsive and loose. I showered and changed clothes, found a soft pornography and masturbated. The release of that and the air conditioner blazing against my bed sent me into a long, clean sleep. I dreamed of nothing. I woke up with a hunger. I found the phone book and ordered in. Large, nothing hot, extra sausage and ranch dressing, two sides of ranch, and, if they wouldn't mind, cut it in squares. I turned the television off.
I sat at the table and wrote in the journal. I wrote about Boulder City. I grew bored and read the bible I found with the phone books. Most of Revelation. The imagery, the masterful writing. The terror of those pages. The terror, too, was the people who believed it. I understood it for what it was, it was terror. I closed the book and flipped through the channels. It occurred to me that the same newscasters lived everywhere. Then a knock on the door, a bright blonde with gapped front teeth, and a body. Her hair was fried and high above a tan brow. She fixed her stare on my chin. I rubbed it.
"Yes. Come in."

She did. She said I had a nice bike. I nodded. She put the box down by the book.
"You read the bible?"
"First time." She giggled. It made her human. It made her younger. It was nice.
"I can't understand all those big words in there."
"It's all bullshit."
She giggled once more. I wanted to fuck that giggle.
"How much was it?"
"Oh. $13.50."
I handed her a twenty. She started leafing through her bills.
"The rest is for you."
"Wow. You sure?"
"Yes."
She sat on the table and tapped the delivery bag against her knees.
"What's your name?"
I told her. No, I wasn't from here. I wasn't on my way anywhere. No I didn't go to school. I didn't really do anything.
"A free spirit, huh?"
Something like that. Did she like her job? She did. No, she wasn't married, she lived with her parents. She was once engaged, has one child, a boy, and is trying to move to Connecticut because she'd read they had the best elementary schools. Wasn't she going to get in trouble for taking so long on this delivery?
"I hardly think so. My boss is a real moron. I'll just tell him I had to get gas."
I watched her fingers fan the pages of the bible. Blue nails, long slim fingers.
"You ever get a feeling off of another person?"
She was still looking at the book, like she was talking into it.
"You know, like a feeling that you should know that person from before but you just don't know why you didn't know that person before?"
"Sure."
"You're sleeping in here tonight, right?"
"Of course."
She giggled.
"God. Of course. I'm stupid sometimes."
I smiled. She asked if I would mind if she came by after work. She told me she thought I was beautiful. I asked her what time she was off. Two in the morning. I told her I would leave the door unlocked.

I finished a few slices and lost my appetite. I had never heard a woman refer to a man as beautiful. It spun me, inflated me. It was wonderfully uncomfortable in my stomach. My good luck was maybe returning. I closed the box and dialed the area code and number my sister had given me while I was held over with the freaks. It was a collect call. A man accepted. She was downstairs drawing in her study. I asked him to let her finish and have her call me when she came back up. No problem.

I laid back and thought of Julie. I thought of her naked. She wasn't my dream girl or anything. Yet there was something about her. This simple honesty. An honesty without need. I grew hard thinking of her. I was about to make my move when the phone rang.

"Hello?"

"Where are you?"

"Kingman, Arizona. Don't ask."

I had never been a phone person. We talked for over five hours. She and her husband lived in Wheaton, in a place twenty minutes west of Chicago, and they'd been married since they were teenagers. They both had seven years on me. She had degree in graphic design. Doug was the drummer in a garage band that played bars across the suburbs. His steady job was at the airport, throwing luggage. She had tried to find me for the last two years, on her own. The old man wouldn't give her any further information on me besides my first name. She said it drove her crazy. We talked about our incidental families, and about the strangeness. I told her I would drive out to see her. We hung up. I loosened the door and killed the lights. In the dark I thought about it. My whole life was gone. My father was really my uncle and now I had an extra sister. My mother was right for not telling me the truth. I was grateful for her. She probably would have never told me. She loved me too much. I was her favorite. I could have ended up so much worse, and I thought about her and cried. I cried at her strength, at the shit she put up with during her life. I fell into a steady calm world of darkened plants from another time, a different planet, sounds undefined by this dimension. I fell to sleep.

The door moved then closed and locked quietly. The bedding fluffed, and it sent shots of cold air against my back in the dark. She rubbed my shoulder. She smelled like food. I felt her hand run down my side. I heard each shoe fall to the floor casually. Her breath against my ear made me grow. I turned over and we kissed. She pulled her shirt up so our stomachs touched. I pulled her shirt off. As our tongues worked against each other her pants came down then the rest. It was dark and hot under there. She was on top. It was machinery moving exactly. It had never been that good. Then this banging hit from the other side of the door, a man's fist. We stopped.

"I KNOW YOU'RE IN THERE, BITCH! OPEN UP! OPEN UP THE DOOR! NOW!"

I saw her shadow look at the door.

"Shit." She whispered. I whispered, too.

"Who is it?"

"Tommy. Shit, shit, shit."

"OPEN THE GODDAMN DOOR OR I'LL FUCKING BREAK IT IN!"

She put her head on my chest and sighed.

"Fuck. I'm sorry."

"Your boyfriend?"

"Not anymore. He's a little psychotic..."He was ramming the door.

"Jesus. A little?"

The door started to crack. I sat up.

"Fast. Under the bed!"

She was under the bed. I threw her clothes and purse under there with her and jammed one of the blankets in front of them. I turned the light on and yelled.

"WHO THE FUCK IS IT!"

"JUST OPEN THE DOOR, ASSHOLE!"

I yelled back.

"ALL RIGHT, ALL RIGHT! CALM DOWN FIRST! I HAVE A GUN!"

"BULLSHIT!" I latched the chain quietly.

"WHO ARE YOU LOOKING FOR!"

"I KNOW SHE'S IN THERE, MAN!"

I told him I was alone.

"BULLSHIT! OPEN THE DOOR!"

He rammed again. It was one hit away from a total collapse.

I opened the door and looked out over the chain. There he was. One big motherfucker, with a weak chin. I told him I was alone. His crazy eyes peered in, then around the room. He wasn't convinced. He wanted in that door. Where were the police? I told him I had to get dressed and to just hold on. Then I caught it, the pizza box on the table. Under the bed in one motion. She swore quietly and whispered something about her eye. I threw on my pants and unlatched the chain. He plowed the door into me, knocking me against the wall. He was huge and shirtless. He looked around, ran to the bathroom then ran out. He was at the next door then the next. Finally I could hear sirens. Before I could close the door he was back in the room. He lit a smoke and pulled a can of beer from his pocket.

"Mind if I lay low in here, man? You seem cool."

"I really need to get up early."
He sat on the bed. We heard the cops roll by. They stopped and walked around, knocked on a few doors, knocked on mine. I brushed them off through the chain. He was in the bathroom. They went to the office then they left, slowly. The spotlight was everywhere. I watched it bounce off my journal and hit the television. It shook around the walls then stopped. He came out and sat on the bed next to me.

"Fuck, dude. I'm sorry. She was on foot. I followed her. Could have sworn this was the room." He described her to me.

"Haven't seen her." He started crying.

"I really loved her, dude. I guess I wasn't good enough."

"No one ever is, man." I almost called him Tom. He drank down the rest of his beer. He crushed the can and held it. He sat down and patted me on the back.

"You're a good guy," he said. He got up and flushed his cigarette down the toilet. He came back in.

"I really loved her, dude." He put his head in his hands and started bawling again.

"I mean, she meant the world to me, dude. What the fuck am I going to do now?... DUDE!"

I didn't know what to say. So much for my good luck returning.

"I would have done anything for her, dude. I woulda killed for her and her kid." He sobbed horribly. "I would have married her!"

She stayed cool under there, didn't make a move. And she was under there, naked. But I sat next to him for the better part of an hour. It was war.

He was finally on the other side of the door. I imagined him walking home, his head turned to the street, his hands in his pockets. He would be awake until he heard her voice again. I tried not to think of him. If it wouldn't have been me on the bed it would have been somebody. It was only a matter of time for both of them.

She was smoking a cigarette next to me.

"I hope he's okay," she said, like she had really put some thought into it. I didn't respond. She said she had to get going, that her son was a real handful and her mother worked mornings. She told me she lived in the neighborhood across the street. I watched her fish for her clothes. She was dressed and she looked younger than what she had. She lit another smoke and laid a kiss across my cheek. I watched the door close and stretched out. Then I heard the screaming. I heard him yelling at her, calling her a cunt. I heard him tell her that he was coming back for me. From the corner of the curtain I watched them out there. I was not afraid to fight him but I knew he would take me because he was right. I started getting ready for it. She took off running, and he looked to the room and stalled. He was on her heels in no time. Then they were gone.

I coasted my bike out and opened the van, threw it in with the rest of my things and got the hell out of there. I found a rest stop about 45 miles up the freeway and pulled over and slept.

The sun found a slit in the curtains and sent two yellow arrows directly into my forehead. I opened my eyes. My chest was heavy. I was sweating. I was laying in an oven. I unlatched the backdoors and crawled out. Out there it was hot. The men were walking shirtless next to their wives and kids. It was refreshing to me, almost cold. My skin rose then fell back across my bones. My eyes were burning with sweat. I looked around the desert.

I drove into Flagstaff and ordered a soda. I thought about her. I thought about her selfishness. That big flank of live meat could have killed me, and he would have. All she saw was new skin, vanity. I wondered why I hadn't told the cops that he was in the bathroom. I decided cops were worse than women.

The mountains of Flagstaff were clean and cool. I parked at an overlook and waited off my fever. On the couch in back I fell asleep with the windows opened. I awoke to see the sunset. It was brighter than usual, and colder, because it was a sunrise. I had slept for nearly a day. I drove back to the same place and read the map. Albuquerque looked decent. A young and vicious college girl came into the diner and sat in a booth across from mine. She smiled. I got up and left.

I stopped inside of New Mexico. Never had I seen such a disgusting, dirty, wormed over town. It was horrible. It was a deceased Tijuana in the middle of nowhere. At a gas station I found a drinking fountain that turned out a copper arc. I bought a small bottle of water and a coffee.

The city took forever. I didn't like the look it had. I found a byway going south, and I drove through the Southwest, the impossible mesas, the red plateaus painted far back atop a beautiful brown, deadly, lazy scheme. For the first time in weeks I felt peace. I drove on, listening to an old country station, the songs taking me back to the coffee table of my childhood, to my father drinking coffee and smoking, talking to my mother before the sun came out and he had to leave to roof houses. I was six or seven years old. I admired my father. He was a big man with a long brown beard. My mother would sometimes stand behind him in her bathrobe and pop the heat blisters across his back. I remembered his tattoos. He had done time. The ink was deep green. He explained to me then it was India ink, the kind they had in prison. One on his forearm was an unfinished dagger, another was my mother's name across his knuckles. He was a cool old man, completely devoid of shame yet not without merit. I never thought he'd come to blows with me the way he did when I was seventeen, but then I never thought I would be nineteen and driving aimlessly across the desert, my mother in her coffin, my father completely wasted, a junkie dying away to dust on the streets of west Phoenix.

I drove on for a few hours, cutting through back roads and access roads. For the sheer hell of it, I turned around and took the same roads north, going further up state. I had no plan. I was flying in youth, totally free. A mile outside of a town called Farmington the van died. I jumped out and checked the oil. It was fine. I tried to start it again and it kicked over, made it a few more blocks then started smoking. It rattled and bucked into a gas station on the outskirts. The sun was fading early. I parked on the side of the station and popped the hood. I was as much a mechanic as I was a jet pilot.

An old Navajo walked out of the station eating an orange. I nodded to him and smiled. He said nothing. He stood next to me under the hood.

"What is it?" His voice was angered, aggravated and aggravating.

"I don't know."

"What happened?"

I told him. He walked away slowly and came back with another. He got behind the wheel and cranked it. His buddy stayed under the hood. I walked inside the station and bought a drink.

They were standing over the engine, laughing. His buddy had one tooth in his head. I asked the first one what was wrong with it. He wiped his hands down his shirt and shook his head, smiling.

"It's very bad."

I stared at his friend. He nodded and smiled. I looked at his tooth.

"How bad?" The other one answered. He was the boss.

"Head gasket's blown. Much money."

"How much money?"

"We'll do it for nine hundred."

I only had six hundred on me. I told him.

"Nope. Fix it here or we tow it to the junkyard."

I had the extra key in my wallet.

"All right. Fix it here."

March of Time and Skin

I asked them him how long it would take. One solid day. I took my bike out and rode into town, into that place.

The car lots there were useless. They either had nothing I could afford or anything I would trust. I rode back. They had the van on the lift in the garage. I found the boss again.

"Listen. I really only have six hundred dollars. Can't we do something here, I mean, we're both people."
He scowled.
"You're not my people. Nine hundred dollars. That's a good deal. Somewhere else you'd pay twice as much."
"Well, I don't have it." He looked me up and down.
"Where do you live?" I shook my head. He smiled.
"Maybe you can work here for the money."
"Where?"
He laughed.
"I'll make the call. Job's hard. Very hard. Maybe you'll quit."
I asked him what it was. He uttered one word: digging. He told me I could sleep in the van until I paid it off, but that he would charge me a little extra for rent. I thought quickly about catching a bus, but there was nowhere I wanted to go. I couldn't hitch a ride out with my bike and my things. Arizona was not an option. I told him to make the call. I slept in the van that night in the garage. It was still dark when one of the Indians banged on the door,
"Get up! Time for work!"
I had the sheet of paper with directions and set out on my bike. It was a four mile ride through the dusty roads and paths. I saw the site. A long, long line of Indians on their knees with narrow shovels trenching into the ground, a truck going slowly in reverse with a giant spool of cable they laid carefully into the trench. They were shirtless and moving quickly, and the foremen screamed at them. That endless line ripping a tear in the desert, the line of dark red backs and elbows moving like a long machine. I was my soul after death and I was standing at the gates of hell. I found the lead foreman and told him who I was.
He yelled.
"YOU'RE LATE!"
I tried to explain. He threw a shovel in my hands.
"Three feet deep and two wide. NOW!"
I squeezed in between two big Indians. The foreman ran up and nudged me with his boot.
"NO! You bring up the FRONT!"

He walked me up to the front of the line. It was a long walk. The Navajos peered at me with my shovel, and they jeered me. At the front of the line the foreman pushed me to the lead. I'd had it with him. I turned and held my shovel as to swing at him. He jumped back and pulled out a long blade. I yelled at him.
"FUCK YOU!"
The line burst into laughter. The foreman laughed with them.
"Just dig, white boy. You'll quit before an hour." He put the knife back in his boot and walked away. I dropped to one knee and saw the ditch. I would work the day then sneak out with the van before the Indians came back to the shop. I began digging. The other workers laughed. Their laughter made me angry. I dug furiously for an hour. I made sure to stay in front of them, to beat them with a widening gap. One of them yelled at me to slow down. I heard his friend.
"Don't worry. He'll get tired."
I thought of all the things that sickened me. I found a reservoir of hatred inside my arms. I dug on. Three or so hours passed. It was time for everyone to drink.
It was a long wait for the water ladle. There was a huge steel trough and we all lined up to drink from that ladle. When my turn came I took two or three gulps then another foreman grabbed it.
"That's too much, white boy."
Everybody laughed. They still had ten minutes. They found corners of shade by the trailer and sat. I walked back to the ditch and kept at it. They yelled at me to take a break. The foremen told them to keep quiet, that they were disgusted that a white boy was making them look so bad. I kept digging. I was yards out from them. They had to cut their break short. They were moving as fast as they could, but I had plenty of hatred in me. At one point a foreman blew his whistle and we stopped. He ran over with his tape measure and stuck it in their part of the ditch.
"Too damn shallow!"
A big worker stood up and looked at me. He ran his finger under his throat. I asked him if he was tired, and the line howled. I kept going, faster and faster, delirious from the heat. My skin was burnt.
After the next hour everybody hated me. I didn't care. I would never see them again. We worked until dusk. At the trailer where I had my bike chained the tires were knifed, and they were watching me. I paid them no mind, picked up my bike and carried it on my shoulder up over the hill where they could not see me. Then I set it down and collapsed. I watched the hot and dead sky turn circles over my body, and I remembered the pier in California, meeting Greg, my genius painter buddy from Vegas, and Roll, another genius painter, who had just moved to Vegas from Florida, and they were in town for a week, and we rode our bikes on all day,

practicing new tricks in front of the ocean. I remembered back further, to jumping on a Greyhound bus from Phoenix to Venice Beach, with three hundred dollars in my pocket, the first time I had left home. I liked it there, and I lied about my age to get my first construction job I had found in the paper while drinking coffee in front of the ocean with my first girlfriend. She was six years older than I was, with plenty of neurosis. Her name was Kim and she lived by the beach there in Venice, and in six months she became the enemy, and I escaped her one morning while she was asleep. On that hot dirt, I thought forward from her, to a beach house where I had been a renter, living with an after-hours alcoholic and her lazy eye and her husband, Cliff, who was a psychologist and latently homosexual, which occurred to me on that hot dirt was the reason he always had a pipe in his mouth. I remembered my laundry getting stolen from the dryers in San Diego, and I remembered going to jail in Tijuana and being beaten over and over. But mostly I remembered nothing, and it was supposed to be dusk but the sky wouldn't budge. I heard the rumbling of tires coming behind me. I picked up my bike and kept going. They blew by, yelling, hooting, flipping me the bird, leaving me in a cloud of dust. I set it down and walked it. A mile before the station the two mechanics pulled up in an old car. The boss nodded at me.

"We fixed your van."

I stared ahead and nodded. I felt him look at his buddy and smile, then look back to me.

"See you in the morning."

I nodded ahead. They wouldn't see me in the morning. They wouldn't see me again.

The van wasn't in the garage windows. I walked around back and dug the key from my wallet. I threw my bike in the side door and sat behind the wheel. I could see the last traces of sunlight crashing into the desert. Then it was dark. I turned the key. It purred. They had done a good job. I crawled in back and laid on the couch. The van had no wheels, they had it set upon jacks.

That night I slept on my stomach. I passed out right away, woke up about five hours later. I was stiff and sore. The flesh on my knees was raw. I didn't know when the sun would appear. I found the road and walked. Every step I took my pants would hit the exposed skin on my knees and stick to them. I walked, thinking if this were the way it would have to be then I would show them. I would show them all. I found a strong vigor within that thought. I moved on, and tried like hell to ignore my body.

An old truck coasted past me then slowed to the shoulder. I approached it cautiously. An old Indian with a white ponytail and a cowboy hat. He asked me if I wanted a ride. He lived right near the site. I asked him what time it was. He didn't know. He asked me what I was doing here. I told him. He shook his head.

"Good luck."

There was a pleasant calm to his voice, deep and casual. He lit a smoke and shook one loose for me.

"Don't smoke."

"Good for you. Don't start."

We drove by a billboard advertising the new Jeep Cherokee. He smiled.

"They totally obliterate the Indian Nation then name a fuckin' automobile after it." I laughed. He looked over.

"You got any native in you?"

"Who knows."

"Just a mutt, huh?"

"Yes."

He dropped me off.

I worked the day through. By the end of the week I was adjusted to the labor, and the workers gave up on hazing me. Once or twice my friend would see me walking and give me a lift in. We had weekends off if we chose them. I worked. I found out that I was making minimum wage, which at the time was $3.35 an hour. Weekends were overtime. If I worked the maximum I would pull down around $240 a week after taxes. The Indians charged me twenty dollars a week for rent. I survived on food from the station, mostly orange juice and fruit and candy bars. I bought a battery powered clock with an alarm at a drug store. In bed by 9, up at 3. Walking to work took an hour.

Into my second week I was allowed to ride to and from the site with the boys in the pickups, and that gave me an extra 2 hours a day. My sister in Illinois offered to bail me out, but I could not take her money. I hated the work more and more, but I felt a bond with the desert, with the deadliness of it. At night I would write in my journal and fall to sleep with no trace of sound around me. I tried to take a weekend off, but I fell bored with everything and went back to the ditch.

Payday was once every month, paid to the day the checks were issued. I had started the job on the third day of the new pay period. I came to stand at peace with the Navajos, though we hated each other. I was a symbol of war and death and dominance to them. To me they were just more assholes I had to see every day in order to make money. They were no different to me than anyone else. I was not responsible for their holocaust. I wasn't even alive. They dealt with me the way someone deals with a fly they cannot kill. I found a nice mindset out in the desert, with the job, the boys, the heat, the nothingness. It would do me no good to bitch about it or take pity on myself. There was no time for it. I was a vessel for that cable, for the phone company. I took it, I had no choice.

One day on the job, one of the Indians dug too carelessly and broke open one of the cables. They were fiber-optic lines from the phone company. I learned through another laborer's broken English and hand movements that if you shined a flashlight through one end of a five thousand foot section the light would come out of the other end. He had said it was expensive to repair, something like 400,000 dollars a minute or an hour or whatever he'd meant, for a specialist to come out. We were laying a different type of line next to the fiber-optic that was already in the ground. The guy hit it and cut it open with the shovel. He was called off the line. Work was halted for a few hours. I never saw him again. I remember it because he tried to point the finger at me. I was working in front of him. He was scared. He called the foreman over and nodded at me,

"White boy cut wire!"

I looked at the foreman and shook my head. I kept digging. The worker tried to come at me but I stopped him with my shovel, laid it hard across his shins. Another Indian stepped in and defended me to the boss, an Indian who I had never talked to. I didn't know why he did it. I guess I had earned a shred of respect out there. I was out of myself there, in a certain zone, a haze. Even nailing the Indian with my shovel was in careless slow motion. Everything that happened out there only drifted by with little or no importance, everything that happened was secondary to the ditch.

Payday came. I had not showered in just a few days under a month, saving washing off with the hose at the station. My check was pathetic compared to the work I had done. My rent was 80 dollars -that with the money I owed on the van would leave me with 60 extra. I would leave with a little under what I'd rolled in with. After every one got their checks they had to go back to work. I walked off the site and into town to cash in.

Back at the station the boss opened the register. I told him to get the wheels on before I paid him.

"What? You don't trust us?"

"No."

"Half the money first."

"No."

"He'll put the wheels on. I'll watch you."

"Just put the fucking wheels on."

He whistled to his worker. That's how they called each other. That whistle. I was utterly sick of that whistle. Out back he removed the jacks one by one after the wheels were bolted down. They surrounded me. I dug into my pocket and pulled the money out. They eyed the roll. I held my hand out.

"The keys, now."

The boss dropped the keys into my hand. I peeled off 980 dollars and handed it to him. He looked at me squarely and walked away. His worker following him, and he watched the money over his shoulder. I fired up the Dodge and pulled out, feeling more indifferent than anything. I headed down the same back roads.

I stopped in Tucson. Downtown there was some sort of carnival. I was rugged and dark. I fit right in. For the first time in my life I wanted a beer. I had never had a drink, saving the few times I'd had wine with my first girlfriend. The compulsion came from nowhere, hit me from above. The first barmaid asked for ID, so I went next door. The place was dark and seedy. I sat in the back. It was a dismal bar. The barmaid didn't sweat me about my age, and I ordered my first beer.

I stayed in the bar all night and wrote in my journal. After every beer the words got better. They grew into characters trading lines. I wrote my first pages of dialogue, my first poems. After a few more I couldn't write. Only four men had entered the bar the whole night. After last call I floated to my van and fell asleep.

3

I awoke heavy and wet. My head was full. It wasn't like the small headaches I had gotten from the wine in the past. No, there was weight to this one. Every small noise was amplified grossly. I could remember the old woman bringing me beer constantly. I pissed next to one of my wheels, watching the sun rise. I could hear it rising, crackling. I found my shirt. At a gas station I bought some aspirin and washed them down. Up the highway at a Denny's I drank coffee and got ready to read the journal. It was nice and cool in there. I looked out and saw my van. My head was still pounding from the beer. I felt sick and remorseful for drinking as much as I'd drank, but I also felt a little proud.

I read the drunken pages. After I forced down breakfast I hit a bike shop and got my bike squared away. Thirty-five dollars, over ten hours of digging. I watched my hands as I flipped through the bills. They were darker, larger and hardened, carved throughout with veins and drying cuts. Another feeling of pride.

I drove from New Mexico back to Phoenix automatically, not even thinking about it. Another summer was over but late September was still murder. At my sister's, a large white van was parked on the side of her house. I walked in without knocking. She wasn't anywhere around and I didn't see the kids. One of my brothers sat at the table with his wife. My second oldest brother, Don. I had flashes of him and his wife popping in and out of our lives once in a while when I was a boy. He was notorious in the family for burning everyone for money and consistently breaking his promises. I hadn't seen him for nearly four years, since the funeral, when he and his wife were living in a different van and running cons across the country. They stayed with us for a month, ran up some heavy bills, then he started a convenient fight with my father and they roared off to fuck somebody else for a while. If you were around him long enough you could smell bridges burning behind his back.

    He didn't get up when he saw me. He shook my hand from the table. His wife sat there and made bad jokes. I stepped outside with him while he lit up. Not a minute into his cigarette he asked me to trade him vans. I told him to forget it. He'd been in and out of jail a lot. He was talking about moving to Peoria, Illinois, where my oldest brother Ira lived, and where the family had started. Don worked construction and roofing his whole life. If someone couldn't do anything for him they did not exist. But I didn't quite hate him because I never quite knew him.

They had been sleeping in the van outside for the last two weeks. He said they were pulling out because he didn't like my sister's new boyfriend. It threw me. He told me the guy's name was Duke and he drove down from Peoria, Illinois, to be with her. He told me the guy was an alcoholic. I smiled. Peoria did that to everybody, made them alcoholics. The phone rang. He told me to let it ring. I walked inside and answered. My sister calling from my father's new house. She wasn't expecting me to answer her phone. She asked me if I was all right. I asked her about the new house. She said he was remarried. He'd met some woman who had picked him up off the streets and brought him back to health, and he married her. I didn't say anything. She said that the nutcase from Boulder City called him the day I'd left and told him what a bastard I was, and it started a fight between them. I could tell by her voice that she was worried about me finding out the truth of my birth. Everyone in the family knew but me. Outside I saw their van pulling out of the driveway.

    "That's weird."
    "What's weird?"
    "Don and his shadow just took off without saying anything."
    "He was supposed to leave me money on the table today. Do you see anything?"
I looked.
    "I don't see anything."
    "Surprise, surprise."

"Right."

"Well, I'll see him in a few more years and like an idiot I'll take him back in."

"Listen, I need to get cleaned up."

"Hang around for a while."

I took a shower. In just under two months my father was remarried and my sister had a guy living with her. I stretched out on the couch and watched television and waited on my laundry. The phone rang. A recorded collect call from a penitentiary. If I accepted I was not allowed to use third party calling and the call would be monitored. I accepted because it was my nephew. He asked me where his mother was. I asked him what the fuck he was doing in prison. He said he had gotten popped for petty theft twice then a cop pulled his friend over while he was with him, found a bench warrant and found a gun under the passenger seat.

"Was it your gun?"

"No. But it wasn't his, either."

"How long you in for?"

"Eight to sixteen months. Probably sixteen, though."

"You little dumbass."

"So where is she?" We were cut off. I hung up. No sooner than I put it down it rang again. My third brother, the cowboy.

"Hey, dude. You're back in town." I asked him what happened to Phoenix. He laughed.

"You leave an' it goes all to hell."

"Straight to hell." He said he was doing better than ever. He landed a job sanding down the walls of new houses for the basecoat, and they had a nice place now. He told me that if I needed somewhere to stay I could stay there. I told him choose his words wisely, that I might take him up on them.

"That's cool. No skin off my ass."

I thanked him for the visual and hung up before he could retaliate. It was nice to have some light heartedness to balance such a destroyed return. I stayed the night with my sister and the girls. Her new guy was weird and quiet. He had a beer gut and a thick mustache. He was Peoria. He would leave her in three weeks.

I parked in the back. He was right. It was much better than their old place, which was the guest house in back of her mother's house. Jenny had lost some weight and scored a job at a day care where she could enroll their daughter for free. My place was the couch. I had given my sister a hundred bucks so I was down to just under four hundred. My brother and I agreed that I would pay one hundred dollars a month. I paid for the first month.

I spent the first week sleeping in until noon, driving to my sister's to swim, then riding my bicycle at night in the parking lot of a grocery store, combining single tricks into long combinations. Then it was time to look for a Goddamned Job. I knew I couldn't deliver pizzas in the van quick enough to make any real money, like I used to in my four speed. I bought a Sunday paper and wrote down a few numbers from the coffee table while my brother and his wife drank beer and listened to country music in the living room. A different Venice.

At six in the morning I was hired over the phone as a framer's assistant. The site was twenty minutes away. I bought a tool belt and some basic tools. Seven dollars an hour. My boss was nice enough. I knew more about framing than I'd let on, but the framers there only made a dollar more and they were always stressed out. Due to my experience, my boss's work was faster and cleaner than the rest. After the first week I was raised a dollar anyway, but I couldn't tell anybody. He sprang for lunch every day at the bar across the road and my job wasn't really hard. The hours went quickly and that's all that mattered to me.

When we didn't make the bar for lunch, Marty brought food from home. His wife was Greek and she made good food. After we ate Marty liked to sit around back and burn a joint with the Mexicans. Normally I just passed it, but one day I took a hit, then another, and then I was useless until it wore off. Marty just laughed.

"No more getting baked at work for your ass."

One Friday after work I followed Marty home to Mesa for dinner and drinks with his wife and her relatives who were in town from Greece. I had never been friends with a boss. I think Marty liked me because I was young and hardworking and mostly quiet. At first he found my humor kind of sadistic, but once he got used to my responses about things I think he understood them differently, or at least he learned to relate, or deal with it, if nothing else.

His house was beautiful. He had built a bridge over a small stream in his front yard. He introduced me to his wife as his angry sidekick. She was stout and bushy, dark hair and a warm smile. When he introduced me as such she smiled and shook my hand.

"Great." She had a thick accent. I liked her. She grinned to her husband.

"Is a handsome boy."

I was embarrassed. Marty squeezed my arm.

"Watch your ass, pimp. She's taken."

She laughed and slapped his chest.

"Oh, shut up with you! Come, come! Almost ready!"

Marty put his arm around me, and we walked inside. There were four Greeks on the leather sofa. In front of them on the coffee table were wine glasses cheerfully filled around a long tray of olives and dressings. They were all women. One of them was young and violently attractive. They had thick eyebrows, and the other three were stout and bushy, like Marty's wife. They each stood and hugged me. The young one handed me a glass of wine. The Greeks were good people. They were loud. They saw no point to being another way.

They made room for me on the couch. I was next to the hot one. So foreign, so interesting. One of them spoke.

"Jeff, this is my beautiful daughter." The girl said something to her mother in Greek. The women laughed.

The girl's mother spoke.

"Alexandria says you are a beautiful boy." The girl crossed her dark legs under her white cotton skirt, her bare foot barely touching my pant leg. I downed the glass. The room roared.

Out back we sat under a huge umbrella and ate. Alexandria watched me eat. Never had I eaten more carefully. My glass was always full. Dinner was good, Greek food was more bitter than American food. I liked it. The wine was a perfect balance. Two of the sisters cleared the table. When they came back they brought more bottles. The back yard was full of tall plants. It was modern and medicinal. Marty leaned back and lit a joint. The women watched him. He offered it to me. I politely declined. The women smiled. The phone rang and Marty's wife answered. She yelled from the house in Greek and they all ran inside, laughing. Marty looked over his shoulder and handed me the joint. I took a hit. He finished it off then cracked open another beer. He took a long drink and sat back.

"Well, whadda you think there?"

"You have a fucking great life, Marty."

He laughed.

"Think so?"

I stared out over the pool and the plants and thought out loud.

"Jesus."

"It takes a lot," he said.

We finished the joint and a bottle of red and went back inside. Alexandria was near me at all times, and when she got too close her mother would shake a finger at her. I didn't know how the Greek culture worked with sex. I didn't want to cross any lines. As passionate as they were with kindness, they could be worse in anger. There were heavy and drunk Greek women in the room. I didn't want to step out of line and do something stupid around them concerning Alexandria. Everything that was said in the room was translated to her by her mother.

We sat in there and I listened to them talk. The language was a different color, guttural. Each word was spoken with force. It was intense for the stoned Americans. Marty finally told me I should stay over since I was drunk. He said I could sleep on the floor of their bedroom since the three sisters had the extra beds and Alexandria had the couch. I told him I had a bed in my van. I hoped it made it to her in translation. I asked to use the phone. Marty nodded to the kitchen.

On the machine I told my brother I would not be in tonight, that I was too wasted to drive. I hung up. There she was, backing me up against the counter. She grabbed my shoulders. I started to say something about everybody being so close to the kitchen. She stopped me with broken and uncertain American.

"No time."

She pushed me down there. I pulled up the front of her skirt, and set it in her fingers. White laced over that dark hair and dark skin, a dark and soft and manicured tuft of pubic hair that lifted the front of her panties just barely away from her sex. I pulled the cotton aside and started kissing it. She moaned quietly. I started with my tongue, and brown hips moved into my mouth and my brain spun there, drunken and shocked. The taste was actually sweet, the wet of her fragranced with her smell. She pulled me up and we kissed. Never in my life had I ever...

Marty cleared his throat from behind us. When we turned around he was shaking his finger at her, mocking her mother. She stuck her tongue out at him and walked out. He watched her ass go. He opened the fridge and pulled out a beer. I stood there looking at the ceiling, my arms akimbo. He shook his head,

"Fucking bastard."

Then he was gone. Back in the living room they were watching a movie. Alexandria sat close to her mother now, only glancing at me every so often, playing with my head. I thought, you nasty little fucking Greek goddess. I watched it with them. I saw Greek porn. After a while everyone filed off to bed. Marty asked me if I was sure I didn't want the floor. They said we would have breakfast together in the morning. Alexandria shot me a look from her bed on the couch. A look that made my skin jump up from my bones. I laid in the back of the van and got her out of my mind as quickly as possible. It didn't take long. I wiped off and stared at the moon from the back window. It was high and white, white lace against a dark, exotic sky. At once I hated Alexandria's mother and wished she would die, if just for an hour.

The happy Greek must have died soon. The tapping of her fingernails sobered me. I opened the side door. She was barefoot, clutching a candle. She ducked in. I closed the curtains. Soon after we heard a quiet but steady knock on the side door. Alexandria put a finger to her lips. Each handle was then tried casually. She undressed through the knocking. I kept bouncing from the knocking to her breasts and stomach. It was torture. Then the knocking went on forever and ceased. Alexandria motioned to me like she was writing a note then she walked her fingers in the air. She had written her mother a note saying she took a walk. I hoped for both of us that the note would hold up. We heard the front door close quietly. She lit the candle.

She laid under me and I kissed her everywhere I could. Her body was flawless and smooth and sculpted, her breasts perfect, her ass going beyond anything I had ever seen. That long dark hair all around her. After I could take no more I put it in. The tightest grip any man could ask for. If I hadn't have already came just minutes before she showed up, it would have been over long before I'd even worked her panties off. Her body in that light…

I was fucking a Greek myth, a constellation. She turned me over and put me in her mouth. There was nothing she couldn't do. The only thing she didn't like was my finger up her ass. She would stop me by biting my lip and shaking her head. I turned her over on her stomach and moved with various speeds, massaging her clit with my finger. She bucked and came a few times then I really let her have it. I held off for a long time, maybe an hour or more. She began to run dry so I went as fast as I could and shot the streams across her back. A lot came out, more than ever.

Then something happened. I looked down at her body and got rock hard instantly, put it back in, went for five or six hard strokes, gripping her hips so tight that she gasped in pain, gave her one more hard one then pulled out and shot all over her again.

I fell back on the bed. She moved her hair from her face and laid on top of me. I would grow hard, she would put me in and we would fuck until I was ready, when she would slide off and ejaculate me. We would kiss until I was hard again then repeat it. This happened all through the night and we fell asleep like that.

The sun was out and she was still on top of me. We awoke and did it again. Then again. I was hung over and I couldn't take it anymore. I crawled to the driver's side and got out, looked around and began pissing by the rear wheel. My shoulders shook gratefully. The sun was high and painful and I couldn't face it. Halfway through she was behind me, and she kissed my neck, my ears. She held it while I pissed and she kissed me. Another first.

She was shaking me off. I opened my eyes and glanced over my shoulder to see big mother sitting on the front steps watching the whole thing. She had been awake all night, and she looked rough. Alexandria knew what fuck meant because she sighed before she said it and she kissed me on the ear once more and said goodbye, then walked toward the steps of the house, and she walked it grimly. Her mother stood and they yelled back and forth in Greek. The neighbors awoke and walked out. Her mom kept trying to run at me, but Alexandria was stopping her. Next I saw Marty out front in his underwear. And her mother would break loose for a second and get closer to me, and Alexandria would stop her with all the strength in her body. She turned her head to me from the struggle and yelled.

"GO! GO! GO!"

Marty kept waving me off. The other sisters came bumbling out of the house. I decided it was time to leave.

Back at the house my brother was watching a rodeo on the tube. Jenny and Layla must have been on the east side seeing her mother. My brother asked me where I had been all night.

"Greece."

He asked me where the hell grease was. I curled up on the rest of the couch and passed out.

I wasn't sure if I still had a job on Monday. At the site Marty was drinking coffee on the tailgate of his work truck. He nodded and poured me a cup. I had a seat, and we watched the workers drive in with the sunrise.

"I guess I'm not welcome at your house anymore."

He grinned into his cup.

"You got that right."

"I'm sorry."

He shook his head.

"Fuck man, not your fault. I tried to explain to Big Foot that she had no right to come after you like that. I mean here's her daughter, all over you all night, she corners you in the kitchen and lets you eat her little pussy, -yeah, yeah, yeah, I was watching you fuckers. So what? - Anyway, she sneaks out and jumps in your van with you. I mean, I tried to tell her, which kid in his right mind would walk away from that? And on top of it all you were both drunk. But she wasn't having it, she wouldn't listen. Made for a real fucked up weekend at my place. Just glad they're gone."

"I'll bet. Thanks for defending me."

Though his wife was two towns away, he whispered,

"So, how was she?"

I shook my head at the dirt.

"You wouldn't believe it, man. It was stellar."

"I figured as much. Goddamn it."

I worked the week away and that weekend I drove up to Flagstaff to ride the skate park. It was a good weekend. The ramps were smooth and apart from a few broken spokes and a cracked pedal I rode pretty well. I stayed the night with some other BMXers I had met there and in the morning we rode through town then I left.

Monday morning I was leaving for work when the van started, let out this huge explosion then seized. It wouldn't even kick over. My brother was in the kitchen. I walked in and called Marty's car phone. My brother raised his coffee cup to me.

"You threw a rod."

"Perfect."

Marty answered. I told him I threw a rod.

"Shit. I really need you today."

I told him I'd get there somehow. My brother couldn't give me a lift because he was already late himself. The bus system in Phoenix is practically non-existent. I took my bike in from the back porch and strapped my tool belt around the bars. My brother laughed.

"You're ridin' all the way to Sun City?"

"Yes."

I was coasting up the sidewalk when my brother pulled up next to me in his Bronco.

"Oh, hey dude. I almost forgot. Happy birthday."

He peeled out around the corner. I was twenty years old.

Sun City is where all the old people live. Golf carts everywhere. It's a big retirement community. No one under 55 can live there. We were only there for another month then we had a project in Deer Valley, just minutes from where my brother lived, so I could technically walk to work every morning. Marty couldn't give me a ride into Sun City because it was simply too far out of the way for him. I rode to and from work for a week. I told Marty I didn't want to ride it anymore, and he understood. He figured he could get by for two weeks without me. Anyway, the Deer Valley project was a long one, like a year and a half contract. He told me he'd see me in two weeks.

I was still a few hundred dollars up after rent, but now I had no wheels. A junk dealer came out and towed the van. I signed the title over and he gave me a fifty.

Depression set in. I wanted my own place. I was tired of living with people. I kept in touch with my sister from Illinois. Many letters were written and many calls were made. I borrowed my brother's Bronco one day and drove to the bookstore, bought some poetry and ordered a few scarce books. I laid around for a week and read, or I sat in the park and I read some thick Nietzsche. He was good for depression.

I wasn't a teenager anymore and I wasn't an adult. I was in limbo. I went back to the journals again and updated everything. I wanted to look back on them when I was an old man, read them, relive my life when I could no longer live.

One day I sat in the park and read, and I stopped and thought about Alexandria, about how perfect she was. I didn't miss her or anything. I imagined hunting her down in Greece, her surprise at seeing me again. I imagined more sex with her, and that was all. I imagined being with her would be like any other relationship after a while. I missed my van more than I missed anyone. It occurred to me that a lot of the attraction for Alexandria came with the fact that we did not speak each other's language. The whole thing was so damned perfect, despite the way it had ended, and the fight with her mother almost made it better than perfect.

I was back in a void, back in Phoenix with no way out. I didn't have any friends, anywhere to really go. My brother always called me a loner. I never thought about it, yet I always felt better when I was alone. Nothing really phases a man who likes to be alone. I imagined the strongest and most interesting people were loners. There is a line between a loner and a sociopath, a line similar to the insane and the unsane, a line between the dead and the ignorant. I thought that if a man was an unsane loner neither ignorant or dead then he was all right, though I hadn't seen such a man.

4

I rode to the site Monday morning. I saw the truck. I threw my bike in the back and strapped on my belt. Marty was walking from the trailer with an older guy. He said something to him and the guy split sideways around a pile of lumber. Marty told me it was his brother who had fallen back on rough times. He had my job.

I rode back. I didn't feel like hanging around the house. I rode up 35th Avenue toward Bell Road, since I had resolved to get back into my riding, and I found a large parking lot of a wholesale warehouse. I worked on some new tricks for a few hours then rode to a hot food stand in front of the big doors and ordered a hot dog and a coke. I saw a short guy walk out and rip open a candy bar.

I was back in the third grade. We had this big house across from Acoma Park. I was on the soccer team. My teacher was Ms. Bayard. She was the only teacher who had given me a left-handed ledger. I ran with one kid in third grade, Sean Robles. I remember his parents constantly at work and us at their house, eating and watching television. He had a sister in the seventh grade and I liked to watch her walk around her house barefoot in her socks and short t-shirts. I remembered her getting fat that year, and my brother, not quite the cowboy then, and his goofy friends remarking about what a shame it was:

"A nice piece of ass like that going to waste…"

His family was from Harrisburg and they carried these funny accents. I remember Robles coming to class with a Dorothy Hamel haircut, one of the styles at the time. He was way too proud of it. Soon every other boy in class had the same cut. My father was dime store at heart, and my hair was kept a bit longer than the other boys. Except back then nobody cared much how you looked. What mattered was your position at recess, what you did.

The toughs played football or fast, mean games of tether ball. The sissies played two-square or four-square with the girls. The soccer players were left to themselves. Somehow we had slipped the order. There weren't any bullies at that school. I only had one fight the entire year and that happened in the park with a fourth grader, a kid who tried to steal Robles' kneepads and ball. Soon a circle was formed around us, and the next thing I knew my father and my brother were in the park in their socks, my father telling me to kick his ass. The kid grabbed me in a headlock and cut off my air. I dug an elbow into him, and when he let go I jumped on him and swung wildly. He covered his head so I hit him about the arms and stomach. I remember cursing at him. Then I stopped, jumped off and ran home. Neither of us really won. In the house my father called every one he knew to tell them I had won my first fight. The next day in the park the kid was kicking the ball with us. And that's how it was, a mistake was corrected and forgotten. When my father saw us he called me to our driveway and told me if I didn't hit the kid square in the mouth then I was grounded. I couldn't do it. He hustled me inside and sent me upstairs to my room. My mother heard about it and they fought. She lifted the punishment, which had become a regular job for her.

Robles and I were a lot alike, except he was short. I remember one day, my sister brought home a family of rabbits. I never asked where they came from. My brother and the old man built cages for them in the back yard, and I grew to love the rabbits. Often I would take them to Sean's house and we would play with them. Then when springtime was ending and the heat came, the rabbits got sick. One afternoon the Goodyear Blimp flew close over our house and they were dead. My father told me that the heat combined with the noise of the blimp took them out. My mother went out and bought me a hamster to cheer me up. I had this huge cage in my room with the big running wheel and the plastic see through tunnels. Robles would come over and we would watch him run until our eyes blurred.

Summer came and ended school. One morning the hamster wouldn't move. I called Robles. He said he could save it. I ran it over in a paper bag, and he took a straw and blew into the hamster's whiskers. Then the hamster was stiff. We buried him in the backyard and forgot about it.

We were usually moving. Back to Peoria, back to Phoenix. Once we even lived in the Texas Panhandle, first in a small town, then on a farm about ten miles from it, and it was pure hell. But that year we moved five miles away, which meant a new school, different faces. Robles and I still hung out every now and then. By the time I was in seventh grade we had lost touch completely.

In front of the warehouse, I watched him eat his candy bar. He was working there, wearing the uniform. He hadn't changed much since the third grade. A little stockier, a little less hair. I walked up and stuck my finger in his back.

"Robles. You owe me a hamster, you piece of shit." He turned around. After a couple of holy shits were exchanged we hung out and ate lunch. He still lived at home. I told him I still remembered the phone number.

That weekend we drove down to Mill Avenue in Tempe, the college hot spot. We walked around and looked at girls. Robles was shy. He told me he was still a virgin. He dressed in the latest styles. I wore the usual, jeans and t-shirts. We didn't pick up girls because he was uptight around them. We had grown into complete opposites, yet couldn't bullshit each other because our blood ran so far back. He wanted to get a fast motorcycle and a lot of other normal pussy getting material things. I just wanted a car and some money to leave the desert. He told me the warehouse was hiring temporary Christmas help, people to round up the long metal carts from the parking lot. He said it was only five bucks an hour but the hours were limitless. He talked about the girls there. He had been there for two years and made his way to cashier. He would put the word in to the higher people and I would get the job.

The job was mindless. Pushing carts all day. I worked from early morning to well after dark. They were busy with Christmas. Everyone there liked me because I was always moving. I ate my lunch upstairs with the big burly stockers, listening to them talk about women and cars. I wanted to work with them. I liked their energy, far different from the bullshit humor, which went hand in hand with framers, from the oppression of building under contract out in the heat. The stockers were their jobs. Because of them the warehouse stayed above water. They could fuck with the cashiers and management and get away with it. They walked all over that place by keeping it alive. I really didn't mind the job, partly because I knew after Christmas and New Year's I would be let go. It was a good way to clock plenty of overtime. Robles was right about the girls, though the stockers had first pick. They were the modern day gym coaches. Each of the jobs in there was fast paced. The only ones who had it easy were the homosexuals who roller-skated around the warehouse helping customers and answering questions. They were the butt of every joke in the break room. Gays had it tough in the desert.

After a month at the job we were in the break room watching the news. We were bombing the Persian Gulf. There was a threat that Bush would reinstate the draft. Scared the hell out of me. I was ripe for their picking, twenty years old. If the draft went into effect I was gone. The stockers fucked with me about the war, saying any day now Uncle Sam was coming to get me. I waved them off, but inside I was nervous. We watched the helicopters and planes and ground attacks. I could see myself over there. I would be the platoon misfit. I would take a round right through my chest. When we would watch the young, muscular troops playing football and volleyball in the sand and flashing the peace sign for the cameras I would shudder. It scared me more than the shelling.

Then, after a short while, it was reported that there would be no draft. I knew there were plenty of sheep that had and would volunteer for the Gulf. They would be going over there for nothing. They were the same people who worked their 8 hours, went home and popped open a beer in front of the tube, rooting for their favorite football team, paying their taxes dutifully, financing new cars and wishing for new boats and looking forward to the weekend cookouts, the holidays, working so hard to keep one mighty step in front of everybody they knew, living their lives without actually doing it for themselves, boxing each other in to houses and payments, having kids, watching sitcoms, repeating the same stale routine every day without noticing the way it aged them, dimmed them, killed them. They smiled through it, the children of a lie, spoon fed with selected information to keep them complacent and working for the common goal, the usual deaths, doing exactly what they were supposed to do. They made me sick.

It turned out to be more of a slaughter than a war. Those poor fuckers over there had no chance against a wealthy superpower. Bush kept insisting it wasn't about the oil. When I said to Robles that those countries have been warring upon one another for centuries, and I thought it was hilarious how the U.S. got involved out of nowhere when the oil was threatened, then here's this perfectly slimy little worm telling the blind herd that it wasn't about the oil, and the cattle believed him. Robles didn't care about the Gulf. He was more involved with the new girl at work and dreams of riding her around Mill Avenue on the back of a fast motorcycle. The stockers were gung ho for the American Troops. I no longer wanted to work with them.

Nobody got together for Christmas. My brother was mad at my sister because she refused to open presents at his place. He wanted to be the new king. At night my sister drove over with the kids and they exchanged presents briefly, bitterly, only because it was Christmas and they had to. The girls wanted me to stay over with them but I had to work. I only had until the second of January with my job.

The day before the New Year I was called to the office and offered a full time job with the warehouse. I took it. Out of the seven temps hired for the holidays only myself and one other guy were kept on. Some of it had to do with Sean watching out for me, but mainly it was because I always kept moving and hardly spoke to anyone, and when I did speak it was genial and quick.

I had money again. I figured I would work the warehouse until summer neared then I would take off, and escape the heat, the life, the living past of home. I roped about twenty carts and moved toward the big doors. It was my longest haul yet. I had to really bear down and push the bastards. I looked up to see the entrance so I wouldn't mow over any customers. She walked out and I saw them.

Jeff Stewart

5

Insane, large turquoise eyes, and they did a double take and fixed on me. Long, long dark hair all around them. She was dressed in dark shades of blue, black, dark green. The eyes were claws sinking into my guts. I buckled in there. Everything quivered. I had never felt such a punch. The eyes were drilling into my back. I could feel them. I shoved the carts into place and wrapped the rope around my palm and elbow, watching her walk. She glanced at me and kept moving, her high black boots pushing the earth back. An old man caught up to her. I knew it was her father. She looked back again then her father said something to her and they were walking and talking.

Out there was mine. She was mine. She was my girl. She was different from the rest of them. I stalled. Butterflies in my stomach crashed into each other, fell, and dissolved in the acid, screaming. They were nearing his car. My feet were glued to the floor. A voice in my throat said take it, take it, take it.

A finger snapped in my head, and I blurred myself in between her and her father. He looked at me and kept walking. She stopped. I cannot recall what I said to her. The moment went around me in waves. The car pulled out. In my hand was a part of a torn pink envelope with her name and number. I placed it in a tomb of my memory and sealed the tomb with the blood of her years. I could not believe what had happened to me. I could not stand the hypocrisy in my head. Nietzsche fell over a tombstone and died. I was in love.

That night I cleared my throat twenty times and dialed the number. It was late. Everyone was in bed. Each ring was a paintbrush up and down my chest. She answered.

She was born three days after I was born. She didn't smoke or drink. She said she knew that I would call her, exactly when I would call her. During our conversation she kept telling her friend to hold on. I heard her in the background. Then she began yelling at her friend. She asked me if I would call her the night after. The girl in the background kept yelling at her. I told her I was growing angry with her friend. She said she was sorry. The next day at work I called her on my break. I didn't leave a message. I was too nervous. That night I got her again at the same time and we talked for seven hours, until I had to be at work. She said she would pick me up when I got off.
It was a long day. I was constantly aware of the clock, aware of what I looked like. I didn't eat lunch. It was somehow nearing five o'clock. One of the customer service girls came out and told me that I had a message from Helena, that her car had hit a problem and she was at a garage just across the freeway, that she would be much later than five o'clock, that if I didn't want to wait around work, she would call me at home.
I clocked out and began a steady jog across the freeway. There she was in the parking lot, talking to a mechanic. I made it to the car. When she saw me she smiled, a smile that photographed me. She was driving a red beetle. Inside we sat and waited and talked. It was Friday. We had the whole weekend ahead of us.

I bought her dinner at Denny's. We didn't have much to do in Phoenix. We were both 20 and uninterested in the usual weekend. We talked in her car all night in the parking lot, and we were tired. Back at her place, she made me wait by the door while she ran around and cleaned. Her parents were divorced and she shared the apartment with her father, out of town five days a week. He was a land surveyor for the state and spent most of his time up north.
The apartment was practical. A few of her paintings were hanging about. I smiled. Of course she painted. The smell of burnt incense intoxicated me. In her room she had white sheets hanging from the ceilings, pinned perfectly to where they resembled clouds. I flipped through her music. It was unbelievable. I pulled out an album I hadn't seen since Greg's in Vegas. I laughed.

"I can't believe you have this on vinyl."

She took her shoes off.

"Yeah. Dealing With It was their last good album. I mean, Four of a Kind was kind of decent but I couldn't get into it, you know?"

"I know."

She asked me to pick something. I found one I couldn't go wrong with, one of the greatest. I set the needle down. She laughed from the kitchen.

"Good choice."

The album thundered beautifully from her room. She handed me a glass of juice. She asked me what was next, and we laid back and listened to Nothing's Shocking cave the walls in. She kicked my shoes off. She looked at the clouds.

"Shit. We need candles!"

I watched her get up and walk out. I rested my hands behind my head and breathed.

She lit candles on the stereo and killed the light, and the music danced around the wicks. We listened to the album, and when it ended we talked. I told her everything there was to tell in the world. She swallowed every word. We kissed. Sex was only in the back of my head. She got me off with her hand and we laughed about it. She asked me what I was thinking.

"I'm hungry again."

She ordered a pizza. Before we could eat we fell asleep.

I slept sound and safe for the first time. In the morning I woke up with her arm and leg draped over me, her head on my chest, her mouth sleeping against my neck. My arm was over her shoulder under her hair. I looked around the place and held her. She kissed my jugular tiredly. I fell right back to sleep.

Sometime later I was awake. She wasn't next to me. The room felt darker than before. I hoped I hadn't slept the day away. For the first time, I was mad when I thought about doing that. But I hadn't. I opened my eyes. She was hovering over me on all fours, grinning. I asked her how long she had been there.

"Like an hour."

I pulled her down and we wrestled. I pinned her arms back with my knees and dangled long lines of spit over her head, and sucked them back in. She shrieked and laughed. I jumped off and she landed on my back. We walked to the kitchen that way and I put the pizza in the oven. Back in her room I plopped her on the bed again and we kissed. She wanted to get outside for the day. I told her it sounded good, though I remembered I had already been outside my whole life, I knew what and who was out there. No, I wanted to stay in that room with her, die in that room.

We kissed some more. The oven started smoking. The whole place filled with the smoke. I ran to the kitchen. The pizza was destroyed. She ribbed me about it all the way to Denny's, where I bought us breakfast and coffee and we talked for six hours.

We caught a dollar movie then headed back to her place and had sex. It was the closest thing to religion I'd had. We spent Sunday driving around and thrift shopping. I remember best the way she would walk by and grab me, her head on the back of my shoulder as we stood in places, her hand under my knee as she drove us around. Everything was beautiful, Phoenix was beautiful, the Navajos in Farmington, The jailhouse in Tijuana, the thieves in San Diego wearing my clothes were beautiful.

My time alone was different now. I had this piece of gold in my pocket. Helena worked at an expensive resort in Scottsdale, in housekeeping, and I could picture her turning down the beds, placing mints across freshly scented pillowcases, thinking about me. At work I was more energetic and talkative to the customers, to the staff. When business owners and mothers told me to have a good day I believed them.

She worked from five p.m. to eleven p.m. I had managed to work the ten a.m. to six shift. Either she would pick me up after she was off or I would ride my bike to meet her at the resort. It was a long ride, longer than Sun City, but I rode there almost every night. It made her happy, and it showed her things she never knew.

Her father did not like me. Her mother did not like me. She had four sisters but they weren't too bad. They knew we were young. She was the youngest in her family like I was in mine. Her mother lived in a big house in Scottsdale. It was close to her work, though she lived with her father because her mother chain-smoked and the smell of cigarettes sickened her. As far as her friend, the one she'd had over when I had first called her, the girl was obviously lesbian. Helena thought I was wrong about it, but there is something truly distinctive in gays, a certain flash of eye, a facial structure straights did not carry, something perhaps graceful and more interesting than androgyny, completely designed for their own sex. Then again, I'd never made it a point to hang out with them, or with anything that carried such a required bravado.

Her friend was not attractive. She was Helena's only friend. I figured she had latched on to Helena and Helena simply stuck it out. She wanted Helena. Helena had to have known, but I think she felt sorry for her, and she ignored filtering out the friendship through Gretchen's lust. I remember one night the three of us were driving back from a concert in Helena's bug, when Gretchen got angry at her because she would not drop me off first so the girls could hang out. They were arguing.

She dropped me off first and was back within an hour. We sat in her car out front. She shook her head at the traffic.

"I don't know what her problem is."

"I do. She wants you. Ray Charles can see that."

"Come on."

"Think about it."

She laughed it off. One night I tried to set Robles up with Gretchen. We were at Helena's watching a video. Sean was dressed to kill, gelled hair, shirt tucked in, sixty push-ups before he drove over, the whole deal. I was hoping maybe Helena had told Gretchen what I thought about her and she would have sex with Robles just to spite me since she hated me, and at the same time Robles would lose his cherry. Gretchen wasn't having it. When she walked outside to have a smoke, Robles sat close to us, his palms in the air, his head looking up at the ceiling,

"Why did you two set me up with a dyke?"

I broke out laughing. Helena smiled and shook her head. Gretchen was a few years older, and she had brought some wine coolers over at Sean's request. I didn't like to drink them but they did a slow job. Gretchen cut out right after the movie and Robles crashed on the sofa. The next morning he was gone.

Helena was a contemporary dancer. I would watch her at the underground clubs she drove us to. She was light on her feet and graceful. There was nothing sexual in her dance, but there was aggression. I've never heard a song that compelled me to dance, so I would stand back and watch her. When some idiot would hit on her out there I would smile.

Helena had to go out with her sisters someplace. Robles picked me up and we headed back to his new apartment, a one bedroom near the warehouse. It was a small place, but he was jazzed because he had two girls coming over. The night was moving slowly, creeping past me with Helena's shadow. One of the girls had a hair lip so she was quiet. His girl was short and slutty. They went into his room. He had a lot of wine coolers in him. The other girl and I sat in the living room and listened to his music, mostly modern day rhythm and blues mid tempo garbage. I wanted to walk back, but at the house my brother and his family were asleep and I was the decoy to keep Robles' girl's friend busy while he went for his first. I figured I owed him since he got me the job and through the job I got my girl.

When Robles got nervous his nose bled. It was like that in the third grade and it was always like that. I heard some shuffling from his room and I saw the girl hustle into the bathroom covered in blood. I drank and shook my head. His luck was as inconsistent as mine. She was back in his room yelling at him, asking was he bleeding out of his dick or something. Hairlip looked at me. I told her not to sweat it. Everything calmed down in there, but Robles got nothing. After an eternity they left and he was too drunk and depressed to drive. I stretched on the couch and tried to sleep. I found a muscle and fitness magazine in the kitchen and read it out of pure boredom. It was terrible. Everyone in there so afraid to die, so attached to their flesh. After a while, a quiet knock came from outside. My girl. I let her in. I was never so happy to see her. I told her that. Then I whispered what had happened to my poor friend. We were laughing in his living room, inventing insane situations for him that would make his nose bleed at the worst possible times.

Robles woke up and stumbled out. We walked out the back door and crossed Bell, where she bought us dinner at the same Denny's where we'd first ate. Robles felt lower than usual and we tried to cheer him up. Back at his place Helena took a shower. Her father was back in town, so we stayed. In the morning I was going to sneak away in her car and come back with coffee for us. Her car wasn't out there. I saw her ten speed chained to a pole. She must have ridden it. I was proud. It was at least eight miles to Robles' place from hers. I laid next to her on the floor and held her. I asked her where her engine was. She said it wouldn't start up after she parked it at her place.

"And you pedaled here?"

"Of course."

We made love on the floor but it was cut short when Robles walked out in his underwear. He was on the phone in his underwear and she laughed. He gave us the finger. He was late for work. I dropped him off and we used his car for the day. I had plenty of money in my pocket, and I was off for the weekend. After we dropped off her bike back at her place I drove us up north for the day where we ate in cafes and thrift shopped. It was a good time. I really got off seeing her face when I bought her those clothes, it lit up, bringing light upon a world around me, which had been dark, and full with pain, and people who liked dealing pain. She and I understood where everyone else failed understanding or disagreed with it, only because it was easier to disagree with it.

I was late driving his car back. I figured he had walked home since he lived so close. The door was open. He walked out of his room like a badass. He gave me this grin. I looked at him.

"You didn't."

"Oh, yeah."

I looked around the place and whispered.

"Who?"

"Beth from customer service."

"That new girl you've been talking about."

"Yep."

I shook his hand.

"Goddamn, man. Congratulations. Finally."

Helena shook his hand.

"Good job, Sean. How was it?"

"Oh, man. It was like-"

Suddenly she was standing outside of his door wrapped in a sheet. Her hair was everywhere. She looked like a bitch. She was rough with him,

"Excuse me, Sean. Are you having fun telling everyone about our sex lives?!"

He was stuck out there. He was about to find out what sex really meant. She lowered her forehead and beamed at him. I pinched his ass. Helena broke out laughing. She stepped back in and slammed the door and locked it. He ran to the door and started pleading with her. We walked toward the front door. I called to him:

"Later, Sean!"

We walked up the sidewalk. I took Helena's hand as we passed his window. We could hear her yelling. I looked out to the street.

"And that's that."

Helena squeezed my arm and we walked back across the highway where I called a taxi.

Back at work, Beth told the other girls that Sean was no good in bed, that he was too quick. They started calling him a leaky faucet. This must have hit him pretty hard, especially after he had spent 80 bucks on a necklace for her and had to get some money off me for rent. I tried to tell him that what mattered was he finally got laid, that she had served her only purpose on earth and now he could look for better. About a week later he was laid off from the warehouse due to some new company bullshit. He and four other cashiers got the axe. When he told me this over the phone we laughed. The guy could never win.

Work was kind of lame without him. He lost his apartment and moved back home. He found a job driving for a florist. One day in the parking lot I met a guy who I knew in high school and he told me he had a room for rent in his house. I took it because it was closer to my girl's and because I could have my own walls. Helena got her car fixed and we moved my stuff in.

6

The guys in the house were guys I had seen in school and they were now heavy pot smokers. One guy worked in a junkyard, earning the title Junkyard Dan. The guy next to me was a longhaired rock and roller. He was always fighting with his girlfriend and nursing his old motorcycle that was constantly breaking down on him. Scott was the guy who had the place, the one I met in the parking lot at work. He didn't have to work a job because he'd lost half an eye at a miniature golf place and the company had to pay him eight hundred dollars a month, for the rest of his life. His parents owned the house so he didn't pay rent or have any bills. That was divided up between the roomies. He laid around all day watching soap operas on mute, blasting Black Sabbath and smoking his bong. I liked him.

After I moved in, Helena and I never slept apart. She was at my place when her father was in town, and I was at hers when he wasn't. All the burnouts in the house had crushes on her. Little jokes were made when she was gone. It was a fun house. The floors slept more than the beds. There were always drunken bodies strewn everywhere. I would have to literally step over them to get out the door in the morning. A lot of easy, fried blonde pot head chicks came over but the burnouts never kept one all night. It seemed they escaped just in time, just before they were expected to trade up.

I remember having to pry open Junkyard's door one night because he had a girl in there screaming because he wouldn't let her go until she let him have sex with her. I didn't let her out for her sake. She was screaming, and Helena and I were trying to sleep. I busted the door in and there he was, stark naked with an erection, pointing at her and yelling, completely wasted. He was tall and skinny, goofy with these bucked teeth. His erection looked bigger than his whole body. No wonder she was screaming. I held him off while she found her shirt and scrambled out. Junkyard started to swell on me but I grabbed his erection and jerked it roughly to one side, crippling him to a crouch and eventually to the floor where he curled up and coughed. The girl ran out of the house cursing Junkyard and his mother.

There were parties every weekend and every weekend the cops squashed them. Scott's parents lived up north, so they came down twice a month. The day before they arrived was spent furiously cleaning that place. I always ducked out with Helena on those days.

At the warehouse, I was promoted to a stocker. The hours were from three in the morning to eleven in the morning. I did it for three weeks, hated it and quit. I had a little money left and I got back into my bike riding when Helena worked.

Time passed beautifully slow. I rode at the tennis courts in the park all day, came home, showered and napped. At eleven thirty there was my girl, coming to sleep with me, to be around me. For the first time ever I felt immortal. I had beat the odds laid out by the cosmic assholes up there who thrived on my misery. They were merely children now, annoying gnats buzzing over my head, one by one dropping to their deaths, leaving the last few to flee in disgust before they died.

I had stayed in touch with my new sister, and she was flying out to see me for a week. It worked out to where Helena would be gone the same week. She went to Austin every year at the same time for a music festival. Things just worked out with us. It was almost automatic. The night before she flew out we stayed in my room the whole time. I was glad my sister was coming out in her absence. I would have hated being there, thinking about her. With Helena the word trust was a joke. She would take a bullet before she screwed around on me.

I took a bus to the airport. I stood back behind a column and watched the people come in from the plane. I had only seen old high school photos of her through the mail. I watched them file out. She was one of the last ones off. I watched her walk around the lobby. It was the closest thing I would ever see to myself. She spotted me and ran over.

She was hoping for a better car. They gave her this little red pill on wheels. It was kind of like an egg. Back at my place I put together a backpack and we drove up north. She wanted to stay in Sedona, Jerome, Flagstaff, all of the places she had read about when she read the histories of painters. We stayed in rooms and ate at the finest restaurants. I was concerned about the money she spent. She laughed it off and said it was her husband's credit card, that if she could put up with his drumming in the basement for the past six years then he could afford a couple of grand and be happy about it. We drove through the Petrified Forest and to the Grand Canyon. It was my first time there as well. We checked out the South and North Rims, both of us liking the South Rim better, the one hardly seen in movies, in commercials.

We had a good time, and her time had there had ended. Her favorite painter was Dali. I told her one spring we would road trip down to Florida and see his museum. I watched her plane until it became a little white dot then hopped the bus back home. I was a bit more solid than I was before I saw her. I jumped off at the main stop off of Union Hills and got a haircut. It was the first one since I had jumped on the Greyhound for Los Angeles, when I was sixteen. The barber cut it nice and short, over the ears and a number four clipper around the sides. I felt faster, lighter, more aware. I knew my girl would be impressed.

Helena was back the same afternoon. Just as I rounded the corner of the house, her car parked and shut off. I met her at her door and we kissed. Back in the house she sat on my lap and showed me the pictures of Austin. I carried her to my room and shut the door.

I spent three months and a week in that house. Soon my money was low and I had to look for a job. My sister wanted me to come out there. Her husband could get me a free flight with his airline. Helena and I both hated Phoenix and I ran the thought of us moving to Chicago by her. We talked about it once, and never did again. I think it scared both of us.

7

On my fourth month I sank into another depression. My money was low and I was sick of the jobs around Phoenix, and sick of Phoenix. Then at the house it was ruled that we were all out in two weeks, since Scott's parents were coming back for good. I didn't have nearly enough to get my own place. My sister told me I could stay with her father in Lombard, that there were plenty of places I could work up there and make a lot of money. Helena did not want me to leave, but I told her that I could no longer stay with my family because I was too old. Summer was coming and I wanted her to leave with me, but she had too many things to keep her there. I told her I had to get out. It was decided that I would go up there, work for a month or two then come back, and I would get my own place.

The ticket arrived just in time. Helena cried, she said she could not believe I was going to leave her there. I told her I could not stay with her because it would be too much pressure, concerning her father and all. Our last night there was horrible. I started to back out of the deal. I did not want to leave her. At the airport I boarded the plane, feeling like failure.

I had never flown. The thought of flying frightened me. Everyone said it was safer than driving, but at least in a car wreck you were on the ground. The odds of surviving a plane crash were impossible. I sucked it up and took the fear. It was a flawless trip.

Illinois was worse than Phoenix. Doug picked me up, and the next day I was in Lombard. I called Helena collect and she told me that Robles had come over last night and tried to put the moves on her. I couldn't believe it but I could. We laughed about it.

Nobody wanted to hire me and her father was old and set in his ways. It was a small and religious place, ultimately. My sister was hurt with me because I wanted to leave. And the only jobs that were hiring were minimum wage, and I could make that much back in Phoenix. Helena called me every night and every night I would tell her how much I missed her and what a mistake I had made. I laid in bed at night watching television and missing her. Three weeks passed and I was flat broke. All of the green trees and lush Midwestern backdrops got on my nerves. Finally, I called my sister and told her I was leaving, regardless of how. Doug couldn't get me another ticket. Instead he drove me down to Peoria, to my brother's house in the south end. Peoria, the town of my birth, one heavy town. He wasn't home so I waited on his steps and watched the neighborhood sweat.

My brother Ira was a heavy drinker, a time bomb. Sober, he was the best person alive. But lit up he had violent mood swings. He had been married to his second wife, Sally, for fifteen years. When he came home from the bar she didn't know if he would take her in his arms or beat her senseless. But they had beaten each other, shot at each other. Once she stabbed him in the neck. But they were older and mellow now, and still in love. They had both cut down on the nights out. Peoria was full of small bars and poor people drinking off of crumbs from shitty jobs. The factory across the river wove a tapestry of sour filth, which hovered over the town and stank, turned it yellow. It was always humid there. I hung in the house with them for a few weeks when Helena broke down and mailed me money for a bus ticket.

At the station my brother and Sally each gave me a fifty for the road. The bus pulled out, me in the far back wondering why I had done anything besides end my life when I was sixteen.

The trip was long and degrading. The Greyhound is like the DMV. Everybody is truly equal. You had to sit and wait and deal with the animals. You were powerless against the boredom. Stops were made at every small town that existed. You never quite slept. When the bus became full it took on this musk that you could not escape. The people were losers, like me, and nothing they said could overshadow or rationalize where they were, right there and then at the moment, locked into those seats. A hell of a way to see the country.

I saw the lights of Phoenix. I had not seen my girl forever. There she was. A vision. The quest of my vision. I held her against the noise of the station, against the past six weeks of being without God. We kissed and she wept, her tears burning my face like holy water.

The next few months were rough. I stayed at her place when her father was gone. He never knew. I ran into Scott my second day back, and on the days when Helena's father was in town, I stayed on the floor of his studio, which was almost worse than being homeless. I found a job washing dishes in a Japanese restaurant. It was a temporary job for minimum wage and I was released after four weeks, released with crumbs.

The relationship was getting tense. I worked at a thrift store in the day and closed this fast food place at night for a while, got fired from the thrift store, quit the burger joint. A pizza place hired me and I lasted for two weeks before I got mad and quit. To make it all worse, Helena's lawyers finally settled a car accident she was in over 4 years ago. I wasn't about to ask her for money, I still had some soul hanging.

There was talk of Gretchen letting me move into her extra room but she wouldn't do it. She would want nothing more than to have me out of the picture. Helena saw something in me that no one had ever seen. She had faith. I began to get paranoid. There were plenty of men who would have killed to have her. It was all in my head. She had gone through so much for me. She was all I had left.

From her place one day I called Robles to see where he was working and to see if he could get me a job. I hadn't talked to him since I'd left. He answered and I spoke.

"Sean, hey man."

He hesitated. I looked at Helena and she grinned.

"Are you there?" He lowered his voice, trying to sound tough.

"Yeah. I was just out back lifting some weights."

"Yeah?"

It was hilarious, because if anybody else had tried what he had I would have reduced him to liquid. With him it was all right. He was totally innocent. He told me that he had to tell me that he tried to kiss her. I told him to forget about it. He said he had no job. I let him go because I knew he was uncomfortable. I could imagine him driving home from her place that night, laying in bed and sweating bullets of shame. I knew him. He had already paid.

I found places to stay here and there. Summer had ended and I was now into fall. Helena's mom let me rent out her basement. I had my own room and a shower down there. It was weird for Helena. She got me an interview with the resort. It was for a fruit boy, someone to wear that sissy ass uniform and deliver fresh fruit to the rooms. I was hired, barely, and I started the next day. I would often see her at work, in her own uniform and we would laugh.

The job was simple. I hauled around this big plastic cart with fruits and knocked on the doors, waited, then shoved the key card through and replaced the fruit. Five bucks an hour. Two months passed. I met this Englishman who was over for some college work exchange and we started hanging out. He was a heavy drinker. During my time there we worked a lot of hours, and he would come over and hang out with Helena and I at night. He constantly flicked us shit about the American accent so I gave it back to him by pointing out his bad grammar. He would bitch about America to get at us. One night we were drinking and he said we were inferior. I assaulted.

"If you guys are so fucking great then how come you lost the Revolutionary War?"

Helena slapped my arm. He waved it off.

"Piss. We let you have it."

"Yeah right. You dainty little fuckers just sat back sipping your gay ass tea and whining. You guys sound like a bunch of turkeys gobbling in a field, in a field about to be slaughtered by American bullets."

He broke out laughing.

"That's it. Fucking great. A great lot of bullshit!"

After we broke each other in we became buddies. He was staying with another guy from Sheffield, who worked in another hotel on the same program. They were there for a year. One weekend we drove to the Grand Canyon with their buddy from Los Angeles. Helena had to work. That night was my twenty-first birthday. Helena had already taken me out the night before. I would be back in time for hers. I didn't have much money so I thought I'd take her to a movie and we could camp up at the church where I had once slept on the way to Vegas, to see Greg and to stay at Roll's, and I slept there then, on the steps of that condemned church, the stars so close and set in stardust they were like flies swarming in smoke, and I wanted her to see it.

The Grand Canyon was beautiful, again. We stayed with some waitresses that Ray'd picked up with the accent. It was dark by the time we got to their place.

They built a fire and they drank and smoked weed and cranked loud music. They danced around the fire. I drank with them, and at one point I remember riding on the hood of the rental car while we sped around the dark. I was wearing my boxers. Ray cut a sharp left and threw me. I landed in the dirt and rolled. The watch Helena had got me for my birthday broke off. I stood up and they were cursing at me and speeding back toward the fire. I thought I was cut up pretty badly. I looked for the watch forever and gave up. Ray met me halfway back on foot.

"What is it, mate? All in good fun."

"It's not that. My watch."

"Shit. Come on. We'll get it tomorrow when the sun shines."

Back at the house they had their waitresses and I had the couch.

In the morning my elbow was stuck to the cushion. I peeled it off and had to run to the kitchen to sop up the blood. I had lost skin everywhere. Nothing major beyond the elbow, just these little scuffs. Soon the house awoke and I set out to find my watch. Ray came to help me.

Outside it was brilliant. We were surrounded by these orange walls, which reached up into the sky like fat, disfigured fingers, and they stole your breath. We followed the tire tracks. Then I saw it shining. I stood over it. My skin shook. I was calm by fear.

"Found it."

Ray came jogging up.

"Jolly fucking good, then. Now we can..."

We stood frozen. The watch was sitting less than an inch away from an edge that dropped for half a mile. We stood there and looked at it. I picked it up and shoved it in my pocket. Neither of us spoke for a couple of minutes. Back at the place Ray never mentioned it so I never mentioned it. Sometimes when I saw him at work we made jokes about the watch.

I ended up taking Helena to a movie for her birthday but we never made it up north. I bought a bottle of wine, and we sat in a park and drank on a blanket. We fell asleep there until a cop kicked me awake and moved us on.

I wasn't liked by security at the resort. One night I shaved my head into a Mohawk, after Ray had bet me twenty dollars that I wouldn't. I came into work with the top combed back. The sides were bald. After a few days I was in a room and I found a money clip holding thirty-five dollars. I called down to make sure the room was vacant and I told them there was money in there. I put the clip on a shelf in the cart so the maids or the mini bar stockers wouldn't steal it. The next thing I knew there was Vic, the head security prick, dressed in his civilian clothes with a walkee-talkie. He was proud of himself.

"Let's go, Jeff. Now."

I was fired for theft. It didn't matter that I had reported the money to downstairs. The fact was that I had *removed* it from the room, thereby instantly terminating myself. It was a good day for the bastards. Helena had been there for two years and everyone knew I was her guy. It made her look bad, even though they knew it was a chickenshit move on their part.

I moved out of her mother's place because Helena and I couldn't be natural there, and because it felt right to leave. Ray gave me a ride to a house with a room for rent, after I had talked to the landlord over the phone. I set my stuff on the front porch and knocked. It was a low part of town. There was loud, modern country music coming from the house. No one answered. I rode to the gas station to call the number. It was busy. I walked inside the station and bought a soda. As I walked out I bumped into my father.

Jeff Stewart

8

I unloaded my things and looked around. He had moved from his new house into an apartment. It was far on the west side in a bad neighborhood. I rented the extra room. My father got me a job tearing off roofs with him at Luke Air Force Base. He got fired for threatening our foreman during my first week and I had to pedal to work in the morning, like 7 miles. This new situation was so insane that I could not even think about it. Here I was in this tiny room, my father was remarried and Helena was so far away I could only talk to her on the phone. I saw her maybe three times every two weeks. I was losing her.

One night I hopped the fence to the grocery store and bought a magazine for something to read. When I hopped back over I was face to face with two large, young black gangsters, dressed in dark blue. One of them had his hand in his pocket. I could see the chrome of the pistol. The other one spoke:

"What you claim, bitch?"

I didn't know what to say. I didn't say anything. I was about to die. I looked at myself. I was wearing a red flannel and I was white. I saw Helena's face crying. The other one nudged me. I didn't know what to do. I was not part of this bullshit. Nothing I said would have helped me at that time, that year. I went into a bad English accent. Their faces softened.

"Hell, man. Where you from?"

"England, mate."

They started laughing. The smaller one took his hand from his pocket. He rubbed the top of my head.

"You was close, cream. But we gotta take that flannel."

I quickly gave it to them. They laughed. The other one mentioned that he knew Englishmen liked to drink. They implicitly forced me to come back to their apartment around the corner and drink with them. They were so taken in by my being from another country. I couldn't get out of it.

The place was crowded. There were two other thugs there, a lot of weapons and a skinny white girl who mothered one of their kids. I was never clear on who the father was. She and the baby had the room with whomever and the others shared the second room, one got the couch. I remembered Ray's take on American beer when one of them offered me a can. I responded.

"Ah, American beer. Pisswater. Couldn't get a queer loaded."

They roared and high-fived each other. We finished the case and I stumbled back. I was loaded and I made noise coming in. My father heard me struggling with the lock and let me inside. I made it to the room and contemplated my death until I fell asleep.

I slept until the late afternoon. My father was in the kitchen. I told him if any thugs in the complex asked about me, I was British, then told him why. We had a couple of beers and talked about life, and he told me that his wife didn't like me, and I told him that road went both ways. He was in a hard spot there, and I understood what he had been through to gain the little ground he had gained with her, and I said I would move out that day. It was a brutal conversation for both us. I looked in the paper and found a room for rent two miles from there. The room was small and cement. I could barely fit myself and my belongings in there, but it was cheap and without a deposit. The people who lived there were burned out ex-addicts and the whole place smelled like cat piss.

One morning I took a bus back over to where I came from and landed a job as a short order cook in a bar. It was a good 20 miles to the west side where I basically now just kept my clothes and slept when I had to. I would work for 12 hours, stay awake at Denny's across the street drinking coffee and come back. Helena told me that we should not see each other or talk for a couple of weeks, that she felt we needed time apart so I could get my life together. So far it had been one week.

I rode my bike to work with my backpack one day and ended up staying gone from the west side for a week. I would work, find a spot behind a store and bundle up and doze off for a few minutes here and there. I never told my boss about my problem. One night at the bar I met a guy who lived with this girl a few miles away. They were only roomies. The next night I met her. I gave them free food because they had a day until payday and they wanted to drink. The next night was Friday and I was off at nine. They came in and tipped me a fiver each. They told me they wanted to drink with me when I was off. I called Helena at work and asked her to meet me there. She said she was going dancing. Back at their table they poured me a glass. I was tired. I stared at my hands around the glass. Something was dripping on them. Dave shook my arm.

"Hey. You all right there, man?"

I realized I was crying. It was embarrassing. After a few more pitchers I was drunk. His roomie, Sarah, asked me where I lived. I was drunk enough to tell them, to tell someone the whole story.

They shared a nice place. My things fit perfectly on the bottom shelf in the closet. I was on the couch. My rent was two hundred a month. The place was nice. Helena came over and saw it. We went to Denny's and talked, where I told her that I still loved her and that I was sorry for being such a damage case the last few months. I told her she was all that mattered to me, and I meant it. And I footed the bill, drove us back to the apartment in her car where I picked up some overnight things and we went back to her place.

Dave got me a job where he worked bussing tables at this five-star restaurant just a block from the apartment. I was making good money. The rich tipped poorly, but there was a high turnover of them. Helena gave me a ride to pick up the rest from the west side. When she walked in and saw the floor on which I had slept, the ex-junkies and the squalor, I could sense her breaking. She had no idea. The bare survival had checked her, and out in the car she kissed me. I was back in stride, I had showed those assholes above one more time who they were dealing with.

9

I was high class now, living in a condo in Scottsdale and working at a world-renowned eatery. One night Sarah told us she was moving out to live with her boyfriend, thereby breaking her lease, thereby leaving Dave and I to the wolves. I had some decent money saved up, so I went looking for a place.

I found an apartment up the road, and Dave got the living room. I was staying at Helena's again on the weekdays. Her resort was only six blocks from my restaurant, and it worked out perfectly. After three loud music violations Dave brought upon the apartment when I was out, they gave me an eviction notice. Seven days.

I ended up living in a nicer apartment with two other guys I'd met through the paper. I had the big room that hung over the pool, my own bathroom and a nice alcove. I gave Helena a key. The restaurant cut me off because I was the newest hire and because they had slowed for the season. I had money, so I hopped a bus to Vegas and stayed with Greg and his girlfriend, Stephanie, for a week. They had been together since high school, and I had been thinking about him the day I was let go. They had rented a nice little house off of Cholla on the east side, and I saw Greg's latest paintings and we rode our bikes hard that week. And when I got off the bus back in Phoenix, Helena picked me up at the station and I had a new take on life.

Time was with me again. I found a higher paying job, still bussing tables. But it was a looser atmosphere, and I grew a goatee. I made some crazy friends at the complex where I lived. One guy was Jared, from Seattle living with his buddy Grant, also from Seattle. Jared was the one who'd landed me the job. Our boss was a six-foot tall gay Asian guy with a Texas accent. He was utterly insane. My main roomy was a guy from Redondo Beach named Tim, and he was a lady's man. He dressed sharply, and he had a tattoo of a moon on his shoulder. He was white and rich, but tried to talk black and poor, and I would call him on it. He was a good guy and he took it. I would find out later in life that he died only a few years later at 24, from drowning in the Salt River while he was tubing drunk.

I was making good money and was saving again. Helena loved the place. She had seen me rise and fall and rise again. Living there was the best six months of my life. The apartment was beautiful and my girl was always there. And something about the people who came over all the time was good, Tim's friends, his groupies, people I worked with. I mostly remember Helena being there, watching me take a phone call, watching me stand in the kitchen listening and talking to Tim about his latest conquest, me watching her read at the kitchen table from my couch, watching myself sleeping soundly under her skin, the warm fall sun outside, streaking wonder about the balcony, at night sitting outside in the hot tub with Helena. Nothing could touch me.

One day on the tennis courts I broke my foot while riding. I had no money for a doctor, and I had to bus tables walking on the inside of my foot, until the foot no longer worked, and I had to leave the job. I became bitter. Sitting around shook me. Helena was kind during all of it. Tim always had girls over and for some reason Helena became jealous. All of a sudden we were fighting constantly. I would hang out mostly at Jared and Grant's. She would find me there and we would fight about nothing. One time I had Tim and one of his girlfriends drop me off at a minimart by her house. I called her and told her where I was. She and Gretchen were going shopping for a wedding in Gretchen's family and Gretchen wouldn't pick me up. I hung up and walked home. Something was wrong. If that would have been a year ago she would have dropped everything because I was a mile away. When I got home hours later she was waiting for me, writing me a note. I asked her what happened. She was crying. She told me that I had gotten mean, that she was looking at old pictures of us when we'd first met and that my eyes were different, that they had fizzed out and became hardened. This insulted me and I walked off. In my room she said that she didn't like all the girls around. I didn't reassure her because I was too sore from walking back with a half healed bone and I was angry with her. She came by a couple of days later and we hashed it out, sort of. I had missed her, but I was too angry to tell her.

On my 22nd birthday we fought. On her 22nd birthday we fought. I loved her as much as I ever did but there was something I wasn't doing right and something she didn't approve of. I couldn't figure it and she wouldn't tell me, and that just got to me worse.

Our lease ended and I was healed. Tim was moving on and the other guy, who had been a no-show for most of the lease paid his last month and decided to move in and marry his girlfriend. I would have married Helena in a minute, if either of us believed in marriage.

I found a room to rent across Hayden Road with these sports fans in college. It was a boring neighborhood. Helena and I had lost touch for a few days. When I called her once she was short with me and when she called me back I hung up on her. I couldn't believe how we were treating each other.

She came over one day. We had this strange sex in her car. Inside my room she told me that she had met someone else. I thought it was a joke. I mean, we had hit some tough times, but the words coming from her mouth were impossible. She said she had met him at a car wash, where he parked his car around back and sometimes slept between double shifts, saving money to travel overseas. He was a few years older.

I was in shock. She said that she needed to get away from me, that we had become unhealthy for each other. I didn't get it. She was crying. I completely lost it and broke apart right there. After a few hours she left.

She was coming by every night for a while though it was over. I wouldn't accept it. One night I called her and she was gone. I tried all of her sisters and her mother. I was awake all night with a knotted stomach. I went through my things. It occurred to me that I had hardly written in the journals since I'd met her. The things I had written were few, written in blank spots when I was alone in my room, and the writing didn't say much. I had almost forgotten about it. The next afternoon I borrowed one of the sports fan's cars and drove to her place. She was out front doing something to her car. I walked up.

"Where were you?"

Her eyes welled up. She looked away. I had never seen her in a turtleneck before. She told me that *Steve* and his parents took her on a bus trip to Laughlin and he had just dropped her off. I softly pulled down the sweater. Her neck was covered with these ugly red Marks from his lips. I fell back against the car and threw up. She was crying and trying to talk to me. I fought her off and drove away. I had lost her, I had lost everything.

Back at the house I called Ray's to see if he could give me a small loan. Actually, he owed me twenty bucks. He had just left for back home. Jared had moved to Seattle and I was supposed start a new job on Monday. I kept seeing this guy kissing her, touching her, her allowing it. I kept seeing her walking across the grass toward me, her long hair shiny in the light, a hole in her jeans just over her knee. I stayed up all night vomiting yellow nerve acid.

I borrowed the car and drove toward my sister's. It was a different kind of tired, this sick fatigue I had never felt. The earth was not solid. It existed in waves. Every fixture was a sign of grief. Every animal, every walker and driver took on postures of liquid. My stomach was on cold fire. My heart had split and stretched out to a dripping string, wrapping my ribs and spine together to where they bowed in the middle.

What I saw next was pure insanity, a gift from the devil himself.

At a red light I saw a sign that read UNIVERSAL WASH. Under it was this creep leaning into Helena's car and kissing her. She was laughing. I went into shock. The heartstring tightened and everything snapped at once. The odds of me seeing that were impossible. The cosmic assholes above reached down and wriggled a slimy finger in my ear. A car honked behind me and I turned around right there in the intersection, nearly caused an accident, and flew back to my room.

I counted my money: $216.00. I packed a small backpack and got on my bike. I pedaled east across the state until it was pitch black and I collapsed from fatigue.

I woke up just outside of Mesa. I called my brother and he came out. I asked him to pick up my things and take them to my sister's. I gave him my house key and told him to take the bike. After he loaded it I had him drop me off at an on ramp by the freeway. I stuck my thumb out. After an hour a jeep with Iowa plates stopped. The guy was an older neo-surfer type and he asked me where I was headed. I told him I was going to Iowa.

10

I was quiet in there. He was nervous because I was quiet. I was up for days and looking rugged. I had turned out to be big. I wasn't skinny anymore. I had no body fat but I had filled out. This hit me when the surfer half jokingly asked if I was going to kill him. My mental image did not match my physical image. I told him that I was out of it because I had lost my woman. He sighed and shook his shoulders,
"Nothing hurts worse than a broken heart."
I looked out the window. The buildings and desert and fences and lines blended together to make an ugly face, scowling at me. He reached his hand over.
"James."
I told him my name and shook it.
"I'm not gonna say anything to you about it, brother, because I know how it feels."
"Thanks."
He pulled out this yellow pack of cigarettes with a blue eagle on it and shook one loose. He held it between his teeth and shook one loose for me.
"Have a smoke. It'll calm your nerves."
"I'll be all right," I said.
"Don't worry, man. It's a natural cigarette," he laughed, "but I know, it's still suck-

ing the corporate cock, regardless."

He lit up and shot out a cloud against the windshield. It hit the glass and divided into two arms that reached out of the windows and vanished. He looked at his lighter and set in on the dashboard.

"Fuck it," he said.

We drove through a lot of the night. Somewhere in Texas he pulled up to a drive-thru and ordered. He looked at me.

"You hungry?"

"No."

He got the food. The smell sickened me. I hadn't eaten in days. He was fumbling his burger, trying to shift.

"Son of a bitch. Hey, man. Do you have a license?"

"Yes."

"Drive a stick?"

"I'll drive."

We parked and switched. On the freeway he ate and kicked his shoes off.

"Don't fall asleep."

"No chance."

He leaned back in his seat.

"I know what you mean. Thinking about what she's doing, about the fucker she's with, wondering why, fishing for reasons. Your stomach's all goofy, your mind's racing, part of you has been torn out and frozen. Fuck! I'm so glad that's behind me now."

I smiled, "To make everything you just said worse, the day after it ended I saw her kissing the guy from her car."

He closed his eyes and clenched his fists,

"AAAUUUGH!"

"And the fucker had a ponytail."

"AAAUUUGH!"

The road was dark, feeding the white lines into my forehead. He put his feet up on the dash and looked over.

"Hey, man. I got two words for you: Fuck her."

I didn't say anything. He dug in the paper sack.

"Here. Have a fry."

I took it and had a small bite. It screamed all the way down to my stomach. It bounced back up and almost came out. I fought it down. I chucked the rest of it on the freeway. We had just crossed into Oklahoma. James signed off.

I drove through the night alone. I couldn't get my mind off her. The world now was cold. I was thrown back into an ordinary place devoid of beauty. I could not fathom how she could flake me off and give herself to another guy so quickly. Everything was a black and white newspaper and it was dull and sorry. I grew hateful. I found an off ramp and jumped out at a truck stop. James stirred awake. He looked out from under his blanket.

"What's up?"

"James. I'm sorry. There's something I have to do."

He looked around the truck stop and laid back down.

"Okay."

It was windy out there. Inside I got change for a ten. I dialed her number back there. It took a ton of change. I got the machine:

"I just wanted to tell you that I'm back on the road. I just wanted to tell you that you've destroyed me. I just wanted to tell you that I thought you were different. I just wanted to tell you that with you I had the-"

She picked up.

"Where are you?"

"Oklahoma," I said. I was bitter. She started to cry. I spoke slowly.

"You will never see me again."

"Please stop."

I heard the guy in the background tell her to just hang up on me. She knew that I heard him and she gasped. I told her I was replaced quickly. She started to break down, "Please don't do this."

"I just wanted to tell you that I love you. You were everything. From this point on, count me out. You've really proven yourself."

She sobbed and pleaded with me. I hung up.

Back in the car, I quietly closed the door. James spoke from his position.

"What did she say?"

"Nothing."

I felt a little better. I still couldn't shake the thought of him in that apartment with her, him sitting under her paintings and clouds. Somehow she could let his torso touch hers, and she didn't feel covered in slime.

The lights of Tulsa were ahead. I was hungry again. James sat up.

"How long have I been out for?"

"A total of four hours."

He stretched and spoke to the roof. "Feel like stopping for a minute?"

"I'm hungry."

"Good."

Inside I ordered some wheat toast and hot tea. I didn't have a jacket so I sat there wearing one of James' ponchos. He was eating a tuna melt and a baked potato. I finished one wedge of toast. I had to put her out of my mind when I chewed and swallowed. It wasn't happening. I watched James wolf down his food. I was envious. He sat back and relit. He grinned at his cigarette:

"Get this. I met this woman in the flea Market. She owned an Indian jewelry stand. She was really spiritual. I thought she was the best thing since sliced bread. She gives me her number and I call her. I go to her place. Turns out she's from Minnesota. I have an uncle up in St. Cloud. We start talking. She makes me this weird ass middle-eastern food. She begins to tell me that there's this force in the universe that guides everybody, that the force brought us together."

I watched his eyes, two tired spots of blood, and they jumped to keep alive.

"Now, I'm totally blown away by her, right? So we hang out for a few weeks and decide that we can't live without each other. She drives back home with me and we drive my things from Iowa to Mesa. I had a little money saved. I was just coming out of Santa Cruz when I met her. She had me believing that whole universal bullshit because I was gassing up and walked into this flea Market place strictly from road hypnosis. I don't even fucking like jewelry, you know? Anyway, I get us into a place and start working the stand with her. It was great. We made money and we had this nice place."

The smoke burned down to his knuckles and bit him. He hadn't smoked any of it. He cursed at the smoke and crushed it, lit another and inhaled deeply.

"The relationship gets deep. We go to sweat lodges together. We shave each other's heads. We have sex in the strangest places. We can read each other's thoughts. It's heavy. We drive down to Mexico and have a mock "spiritual" wedding. Six months or more goes by. Summer hits. The business dies down. I take a job driving a bread truck. She gets a job as a D.A., you know, a dentist's assistant. Something she went to school for but quit when she invented the whole jewelry stand idea... So, I'm busting my ass on this delivery route. After a while she starts acting weird, like everything I do is bad or stupid. She starts telling me that she wants me to go to school and learn a trade or specialize in something that offers a career. She starts wearing make up and these half-assed corporate outfits. Then there are these "get-togethers" she drags me to at the "doctor's" house, so I go. All of these faceless assholes. I tell her that we do not belong there. She freaks on me. So time goes by and one day I crash the bread truck. It was a Saturday. I go home and she's not there. Strictly on a hunch, I drive over to the fucking dentist's place in north Scottsdale and there's her car. The front door's open so I sneak in. She's walking from the bedroom to the kitchen wearing one of his shirts. She sees me and screams. I bust out of there. She's in my rearview jumping up and down, her tits flopping out of the shirt. He runs out in the street and tries to calm her. I see her fight him away and run inside before I turn. I speed home and start packing."

I thought about it. I even thought of Helena.

"Man."

He nodded at me.

"Yeah. And what makes it worse is that she came home before I got the chance to split and I actually let her talk me out of leaving. I actually took her back. That's how fucked my head was. She had me totally convinced that it was MY fault she slept with him, that I wasn't making her feel special anymore. Then-get this- I even APOLOGIZED to her that same day."

He looked at me apologetically, "I'll bet you think I'm a chump, right?"

"No."

"So, after a week I have a new route, well, a double route. An old man who had worked there forever dropped dead and they gave me his route, which was only three stops in Paradise Valley, then I had to do my usual route."

I leaned back and grabbed another wedge. I found I could eat so long as he was talking.

"Now, my only condition of us staying together was she quit her job right then and there. So I'm driving this dead guy's route and I see her car in front of the dental place. Stupidly, I think she must be there to pick up her last check. At about four in the afternoon I call her from the truck phone and ask her how she's doing, what she did today. She says she slept in then turned the phone off and laid in the backyard and read all day. I let it go. The next morning was Monday and my only day off. She booked out to the mall, or so she said, and I left her a nice little letter and moved my things out into storage, found a hotel and stayed there until I got an apartment, worked the job for about a year longer, shipped my things back home and jumped on the freeway, where you were standing."

He stared out to his jeep. "I only saw her twice after that, driving somewhere or inside of a store. Once she saw me and started towards me and I walked away. Fuck her, man."

Back on the road I was driving again. James looked over at me.

"Iowa, huh?"

"No."

"Well, come to Iowa anyway and you can stay with us until you figure out a plan."

"Thanks."

"Shit. It's nothing."
He yawned.
"You're a good guy. I can always spot an asshole a mile off. You're just lost right now." He pulled his blanket over his shoulders and tried to make out the dark hills, tracing what he could make out on the window with the back of his finger.
"Believe it or not things will get better or change, one or the other. At least shit will be behind you. You'll move on. I know right now that sounds like bullshit, but you'll find out."
He faded into sleep. I wanted to be tired but I wasn't.

We made Des Moines. It was grey outside the entire trip after the night passed. I didn't know what time it was or what day it was. All I knew is that it took forever and he was out the whole time. James sat up and looked at the town.
"Jesus Christ, man. We're here. I'm sorry. You must be exhausted."
"I'm all right."
He laughed, "I'm wide awake. Who ever said hitch hikers were dangerous?"
I told him I'd let him live on a whim.
He waved me off and gave me the directions. The Midwestern neighborhoods were all the same.
He reached over and honked. A girl ran out. She looked a bit heavy but pretty. I would have to be drunk, or else not have Helena crouching on my brain, digging her hands into the worms of it and ripping it apart, nerve by nerve. He smiled when he saw her. I talked to my hands on the steering wheel.
"Your sister?"
"Yeah. That's April. Don't even think about it, motherfucker."
"Shut up."
He jabbed me in the arm.
"Come on, let's grab our shit and get out of this coffin."

The house was huge. I could tell by the furniture that it had belonged to their parents. Three others shared the house, as his sister told me, but they worked and went to school. He asked her about someone named Tim. She said he had joined the Army, and James called him an idiot. They set me up with my own bed in my own room. I stayed awake until nightfall due to stress. Every time I walked by the phone it tried to suck me in. I kept noticing the time, figuring the difference from Arizona and placing Helena somewhere in her day. Right then she was sleeping, that creep next to her. My stomach would twist and I would have to stand there and fight it.

The sun came out and I was drunk with fatigue. His sister made lunch and asked me why I wasn't eating. James gave her a look, so she backed off. We sat in the living room and watched television. I was bound to that chair. I was catatonic in a moving world. Night came again. I laid on the bed, my heartbeat out of sync with the grandfather clock that tormented me. I passed out. My body took over, sending me into endless nightmares of Helena to which my mind was prisoner, but my body had put its foot down on my nerves. In one scene I was talking to her father on the phone, him telling me she was staying wherever she was staying. In another her and the ponytail guy were kissing, he moved to her neck and she turned and laughed at me, her whole head dark green, her hair like blades. The blades jumped at me and cut me. I flew out of the bus window and rolled. I reached out to grab the watch and I fell with it, for miles. I was supposed to wake up before I hit, but I landed on my feet and ran.

Then I was flying over her car on Bell Road. It turned off and I flew into a window where I landed on a long couch. I sat up and there was Cliff, smoking his pipe and masturbating. The scene blurred me onto a highway where I hit and rolled.

I rolled forever. It was painful. Suddenly I hit something and stopped. A gravestone. It grew higher and higher from the asphalt, shadowing me, dwarfing me. I tried to move but my legs were broken, the bones sticking out from the tops of them. The ends of the bones turned into orange embers and receded, crackling down to my feet, searing my legs to ash until they dropped off. The gravestone crumbled at the base and began leaning toward me. I couldn't move. I looked at my stumps and screamed. They were wiggling violently but they wouldn't get me anywhere. The huge stone snapped at the base and came down upon me. I put my hands up and screamed at the stone. It hit me and came apart like rain.

Helena was on all fours over me. She smiled so lovingly, tossed her hair back and spat on my face. The spit rose and grew into a light that took her away and I was freezing. Two large callused hands picked me up from the road, stumps and all, and quickly pulled me toward the sky. I jumped awake sweating.

There was a note on the table downstairs. On the backside a map was drawn from the front door to the bar. I wasn't going to go. I sat in the living room, fidgeting. The house started to come in on me and I stood and grabbed the note.

I looked up. A neon PBR sign. Inside they were in a booth. James called my name loudly. I sat down on the end of the booth, next to him. He whistled the barmaid over. I ordered a house draft. The whole table stared at me. He must have told them. There were two guys and a girl. James' sister sat next to him. Hands were shaken all around. I felt like I was wasting time. The barmaid plopped the glass down. His sister took care of it.

I told them the next round was on me.

"Nonsense," James said, "you need all the head start you can get."

"Thanks."

I picked up the glass and finished it. James nodded. Soon another came then another. Soon we were all buzzed. The clock read 9:30. Right now she was turning down beds at the resort. Her creep was in his car wondering about his good luck. There I was, drunk in the Midwest with strangers. I was a fool and a madman. No, I was a fool.

The beer helped my mind. My flesh loosened. I had slept for 16 hours and it suddenly hit me that I was now in Iowa, far from her, far from grace. I lit up. At the table they asked me about Venice Beach, about Vegas. I told them about the towns, the differences. I was the youngest person at the table and I had done more than any of them. It made me feel low. They had their lives, they had direction. I had no major skills. No interests. I thought of my bike back there. I thought of the last five years. People to me were vehicles. With or without them I felt no different. These people were nice people, but if they each died tomorrow I wouldn't flinch, wouldn't ponder it. It made me feel worse.

To avoid myself, I made conversation with them. During the night I had let James out to go to the can. So, I was between them. I knew that his sister and I would end up having sex sooner or later, despite how I felt about everything. Everyone at the table knew it. James withdrew a bit and when I went to use the bathroom I came out and took the aisle again.

We closed the bar. In the living room James came out with a case of Bud. We drank and listened to music. James sat close to his sister. When the beer was gone I stood, and shook his hand.

"James. I'm going to bed. Thank you, thank you, thank you for the hospitality."

I could see he felt a little bad for playing the plantation owner. He was clairvoyant enough to understand my situation. And in the room I locked the door and stripped, I fell on the bed and stared up into the darkness, the darkness spinning. I heard the knob being tried quietly. I refused to get up. I counted backwards from one thousand on my fingers. Then I was out. That night I prayed for the first time ever. I prayed that I would not dream. Instead I had more nightmares.

I wasn't too badly hung over. I felt different in the morning. April didn't have a job or go to school. I sat at the table with her and drank coffee while James went through the boxes he had shipped out from Mesa. She asked me about my parents. I told her they lived in Wyoming on a farm. She made breakfast, and I ate what I could. I walked to the store and bought a map. Every step, every leaf in the gutter, every car and cloud took me back to my girl.

That night I had a course planned out. I would hitch straight east to the coast then make my way to New York City. James made a good point when he said that it would be winter soon and that I didn't want to be stuck somewhere in the cold. It was already cold out. I didn't want to go back west. Any kind of warm light would bring me back to her and I would suffer. James took a break and watched me run my finger along the atlas.

Rent at their place was cheap. I was hired up at the bar as a short order cook. It was easy. My boss was a good man named Gus, with one eyebrow, and he worked the bar constantly because he was convinced that everybody was a thief. But I could tell he had to be there. That place was like a lung to him. He could manage without it, but he needed to be there. He needed to know it was his place. It got hard to imagine the two of them being separate things. He had the bar and he felt safe with it.

The snow hit. One by one the roommates moved back to their homes. I had a bigger room. I hadn't seen snow since I was a small boy. I didn't see much of Des Moines. My whole life revolved around a three block radius. A couple of months passed. Helena was on my mind constantly. Back there it was warm, orange. We would be outside walking around in it. Now I was in Iowa, cooking for drunks and writing compulsively in my journals. It was the only thing I did that made me feel any better.

11

It was now 1993. The big ball came down in Times Square from the television at the bar. The Village People had performed there. The bar was full, and everyone cheered the New Year. I took off my apron and punched out, sitting with James and the crew at their table. He had been working in a sheet metal warehouse. James was impressed with me because I paid my rent on time and ignored passes made by April. She hadn't had a boyfriend the whole time I'd been there.

In time there were a couple of girls. I had them, though for some reason I felt guilty over it, like I was somehow cheating on Helena. I told James about it. He shook his head:

"See, man. That is so fucked up."

I didn't say anything.

"I don't mean you're fucked up, bro. I mean it's fucked up how you still feel that way and she probably doesn't think of you one way or the other."

It made sense to me. Sometimes it took someone outside to get to you. His words were healing, but she was still in my head, if only in the back of it, but still a heavy presence. When one of my girls from the bar would leave, April was a bit cold toward me. She wasn't unattractive. She was the first girl that I had considered having sex with after Helena, and thereby under the power of association, I thought it was wrong to give in.

March went and took a lot of the bad weather with it. It was still nasty in Des Moines, though it was bearable. I had enough saved for a cheap car, but I wanted to wait until the weather was fully broken. I worked four days on and three off at the bar. One day I walked in from the bookstore and saw James on the telephone. He was talking seriously with somebody. He hung up. He was yellow.

"My ex-girlfriend's father. She's dead."

"What happened?"

"Lake Pleasant. Boating with the dentist. Collision. Over the back and into the motor blades. Plus, she was hopped up on pills."

"Oh, man."

"But it wasn't that. When she hit the water a jet skier had to fishtail to miss the other boat. He hit her and broke her shoulders. She couldn't make it out, bled to death on pills under water."

"James. I'm sorry."

He shook his shoulders, "Fuckin' weird, man. I feel fuckin' weird."

He looked at my new book on the table: Death on the Installment Plan.

"Fuck, dude. I'm gonna be sick."

He leaned over the sink and let it go. I turned the book over. I waited for him to finish. He looked at the table.

"I need to be alone."

Up in my room I laid across the bed. Downstairs I heard him tell April about it. I thought about how losing Helena would be easier if she had died while we were together, realizing I could cope with her death better than I could her leaving me for another guy. It hit me and mortified me. I was mortified by my selfishness, as honest as it was. I didn't necessarily wish her dead, it was the thought of her leaving me for that guy that brought it on. Suddenly I wondered if I felt that way about her if I really ever loved her, or if I were bitter and broken that she'd left me first, though I would never have left her. For the first time ever I confused myself and discounted a big part of the situation. I felt fifty pounds lighter for the moment.

Later that night, James knocked on my door and asked me if he should go to the funeral. I thought about what I would do. I told him if I had the means then I would probably go, even though it would be strange. I told him I would definitely see the stone. He asked me if I would drive to Arizona with him. I told him I couldn't. My demons were still alive.

He went. While he was gone, April came into the bar and got loaded. I was standing by the bar in my apron waiting for my after-shift drink. Some big, dumb looking guy sat next to her and started making his moves. I drank and watched them. Hours passed. I'd been drinking a fair amount since the end of my shift. He leaned over and kissed her. She paid for the drinks and tried to get up but stumbled back off the stool. He caught her and looked around like a gorilla. He told her he'd get her home. I walked around the bar and cut in.

"All right. That's enough. Come on, April."

I walked her to a booth and sat her down. He was right behind me, breathing down my neck. I nodded over to Gus and he reached under the bar for the billy club. The big guy tried to scare me.

"Hey, what the fuck. I said I'd get her home, motherfucker."

I looked at him.

"I'll bet you would. You need to move on."

The redneck in him came out.

"You don't tell me I need to be movin' on, son."

I took off my cap and set it on the table.

"Sorry, dad."

He swelled up. I wasn't afraid of him. He was big but he was soft.

He pushed me. I pushed back verbatim. He postured himself like a gorilla, and it sickened me. Then he took a swing. I ducked it, and he lost balance. Before Gus could make it over the bar I was on top of him, landing blows directly in his face. I blacked out. Rage took me over. His face was that creep kissing Helena, his face was the watch resting on the edge of a canyon, his face was my stomach twisted for the last four months, not to mention Tijuana or Farmington or Boulder City, or the nightmares. I felt his bones moving down there. I heard women screaming. Gus had to choke me with the club to pry me loose. He pulled me in the back room and yelled for everyone to exit the bar. He left me in there and walked out and locked the door. The gorilla was unconscious. Gus leaned over him, cracking his Roll club over one of his hands until he was satisfied. He grabbed me by the shirt and pulled me back in the room. He held the club and looked at me.

"This is going to hurt."

"Stay the fuck away from me, Gus."

"Listen, I have to break your nose, bud."

"Like hell."

"You want to go to jail? You want to get locked up for assault?"

"Why would I go to jail? He started it."

He pointed to the door and whispered through clenched teeth.

"That prick's gonna need plastic surgery! I couldn't stop you for about two minutes. You want me to get sued?! You want to go down for a felony?! Fuck you! Now put your arms down and take your medicine!"

His words frightened me. He walked out of the room and called the cops. He came back in with a bottle of Ten High.

"The pigs are on their way. Here, take a swig, a nice long swig."

I grabbed the bottle and took a long swig. I handed it back over and looked at Gus.

"Do it."

The club came quickly. It wasn't so bad. What really hurt was the sound and my eyes filling with water, my gums pulsing. Gus then punched me in the eye. He tossed me the bar towel from his pocket. I walked out behind him.

I sat in the booth next to April. I looked down at the guy. I heard the sirens. He was all blood. I held the bar towel to my face. My nose was definitely broken. The towel was full of red and yellow. April buried her head into my arm so as not to have to see the guy. My knuckles were cut up and splintered and they stung. The cops were knocking violently. Gus let them in, and some paramedics jogged past them with a stretcher. The cops moved me to the other end of the bar. Gus and April told one of them that the guy was getting aggressive with her and I'd stepped in to make peace when the guy swung and broke my nose and that I had to keep fighting him off of me. He wrote down their statements. When they tried to question me I told them the only thing I remembered was getting hit in the face and defending myself. They were utterly pissed off that they could not arrest me or trip me up with a different story. It was worth taking the pain to see them writhe. The gorilla was coming around. One of the medics called an officer over.

"Hey, Frank. He's carrying."

The medic was holding up a baggie of weed. The cops forgot about me and raced to the gorilla. He was on the stretcher.

"Hey, now! That ain't mine! It ain't mine!"

Then he started yelling death threats. Gus nodded and smiled at the threats. A medic was finally sent over to me. "How are you doing?"

"I think he broke my nose."

"He sure did. Do you want a ride to the hospital?"

I looked at Gus. He was shaking his head, rubbing his first and second fingers against his thumb, indicating money.

"No," I said.

April interrupted,

"I'll take him."

After everything was over, Gus sat in our booth and had a shot. I was gauzed up and throbbing. He told me to make sure I got to the hospital so everything would be official. He also told me I owed him for a quarter ounce of weed. He bumped me up fifty cents an hour and told me if I ever did something that stupid again he would kill me then fire me.

April was still drunk, so I drove her car. A doctor checked me over and gave me a prescription. We swung by a 24-hour pharmacy. Back in my room I popped the codeine with some coffee so it would dissolve faster in my system. I undressed in the dark and lay down. Soon I was floating amongst the greatest men who had ever walked, and everything in the world was fine, just fine.

April came in and sat on the bed. I pulled the covers over my middle. She was still drinking. She could barely speak. Her question barely made it out,

"How are you?"

"Ethereal."

She finished the bottle. I could smell the alcohol on her skin. She threw the blankets back like they were bothering her, and she rubbed my stomach. At once she was down there, her head bobbing. I was powerless against the feeling, the feeling of her mouth, the smooth motion over me, the codeine, the bridge of my nose humming a deep, steady ring. She was going at it, and I was in afterlife, weightless over the wars and destruction. I saw coastal lines sink in the ocean, the perfect hand of God reach down and splash the water over continents of filth and waste and lies and greed, making them clean again, young again. It was a cleansing by nihilism. I was up there, I was up there, I could do no wrong. She finished me off and walked out. I succumbed to the codeine.

I woke up late in the afternoon, feeling heavy and guilty. Downstairs she was at the table, drinking coffee and holding her head. I felt bad about the night before. Mostly I felt bad in the way that I had betrayed my buddy, let his sister go down on me after I had proven myself to be impervious to her. I could have stopped her if I had really wanted to, and I remembered not locking the door. I poured some coffee and sat down. I was about to say something about it. She spoke.

"Dear God. My head."

"You were putting them away last night like Kool-Aid."

She held her head and moaned.

"Ugh. Don't make me laugh."

I drank my coffee. She looked at me through her fingers.

"How's your nose and your eye?"

"Not bad. There's some pressure."

"Thank you for watching out for me. I was so drunk."

"Forget it."

"No one's ever done that before, you know, looked out for me. Except James, of course. Can I ask you why you did it?"

I thought about it.

"It was his greediness. He had the look of a weasel in heat. He made me sick." She wrinkled her brow.

"Is that all?"

"No. I didn't want to see you wake up with that mistake."

She smiled. I didn't want to add that last part but I didn't want to leave her hanging. She started to say something but she stopped.

"No. What is it?"

"I have a question for you. But I don't want to insult you by asking it."

"You won't insult me."

She thought about how to say it.

"Last night. Did we, well, do anything? Wait- did I do anything to you?"

I was relieved. Either she really didn't remember or she wanted to see what I thought about it. I looked truly puzzled.

"No. I mean, not that I remember. I was so whacked out on codeine. What are you thinking?"

She blushed and giggled.

"Oh, it's nothing, it's stupid. Never mind."

I sighed, inwardly. She really didn't know.

I still had a full prescription. I decided to take the throbbing and let it go away naturally. Those pills were magical. I could use them later, to get to sleep in other places that weren't as easy as this one.

That night I went to work but Gus sent me home. He told me to take two days off, that he'd closed the kitchen for the weekend. He told me he'd pay me for it. That night April and I played scrabble. It was an easy win for me, but it was something to do while I was on the mend. We played for a while, then she leaned over and kissed me. The phone rang. She answered. It was James. She told him the story about the bar fight. He wanted to talk to me.

"Gus broke your nose, huh?"

"Yes."

"Thanks for what you did, man."

"Well, now we're even. You gave me shelter and advice and I saved April from The Hulk."

He said we weren't going to be even for long since he needed me to wire him four hundred dollars to fix his jeep. He was stuck in Kansas and needed a room and money for the repair. I asked him what happened.

"I don't fucking know, man. Something about the bearings blowing out and the tie rod being bent all to hell. They can't fix it until morning. I'm stranded."

"I'll go wire it when we hang up."

"Thanks, man. I'll get you back with my next check."

"At least it blew out near a garage, look at it that way. How was the trip?"

He told me the funeral was closed casket, of course, and that he'd made peace with everything, that going there alone was a good move. I watched April run upstairs. I told him something arose there at the house, that his sister had just kissed me and I wanted to see what he thought about it, that if it was going to in any way make him think less of me or feel weird around me then I would cease-fire. I also told him I'd mail the money no matter what, so not to say anything he truly didn't mean.

There was a long pause.

"Wow. You know what, man? She's twenty-four years old and her own woman. You know I like you and I damn sure know you're honest. Two things: if you two decide to do anything please do it safely and from the time you do it, don't bring any other girls home with you. I know you don't have any real feelings for my sister, but if it has come down to this, to where you talk to me about it, sex must be getting unavoidable. I'll give you one thing, you have balls."

I told him I was clear on everything, and that I was on the way to a Western Union. He said April would know where to go. I started to hang up.

"Wait. Let me give you the town I'm stuck in first, well I guess it doesn't really matter, it's all in the same computer, still it can't hurt."

I wrote it down. In the store I wired the money and bought some condoms.

Before we had sex I made it clear for her that I didn't want a girlfriend. I would be leaving in a while and it would only be sexual. We would have fun with each other and play it lightly. She was with it. She had a nice body out of her clothes. She wore baggy clothes and I was surprised with how solid she was. We were good in bed with each other. The next couple of days felt kind of weird, but it became normal. Her only condition is that we didn't sleep with other people. I knew that was out anyway because I was staying there. I didn't mind. She always right there when I needed it and my whole take on the situation was primal anyway.

The next night Gus called with some heavy news. The guy whom I had exploded on had a lot of hillbilly friends and they had been calling the bar, looking for me. He also said that three of them had just walked out after interrogating a few patrons. He told me that I might want to lay low for a while. He said the boys weren't fucking around about killing me, that the guy's family was deeply involved with the Klan, so that would explain their mentality. He let me know that he told them I had split town after the fight, that I was scared, that I closed the place last night, robbed the safe and skipped out. He told them he was looking for me, too. He said they bought it.

"Just lay low, bud. Don't worry about your job. I'll survive. My nephew can cook all week and I'll still keep you on the payroll."

I hung up. James was back on Monday. I heard him come in. April was in the shower. He walked in my room and sat on the floor.

"Fuck."

"Long trip?"

"Well, it's over." He nodded to the sound of the shower, "How's everything going back here?"

"Don't worry."

"Cool. I wasn't worried."

There was a loud knock on the door. James went downstairs. I looked down from the blinds. Four big, bald men. I could hear the southern accents.

"You used to work down at Elliot's?"

James immediately picked up the ball and ran with it.

"Let me guess. You're looking for the fuckin' cook, right?"

"Thas' right. Heard he lived here. We got no hash with you, mister."

James sounded angry.

"Well, I got a little hash to settle with his ass."

"Meanin' whut?"

"Meaning that he acts like he's protecting my sister in a fight down at Elliot's, he brings her home, fucks her, comes home from work late the next night, cleans out our valuables, and fuckin' takes off! I just drive home from a fuckin' funeral in Arizona, my jeep breaks down on the way back and costs me a shitload of money, and I walk in the door to find my sister crying and all of our priceless family shit gone!" He slammed his elbow against the door.

The rednecks cursed me and shook their meaty heads. They were excited. One of them chimed in:

"An' the motherfucker robs the safe at th' bar before he cleans you out!"

James looked shocked. He was good.

"You're fucking KIDDING me, right?"

"Nah, no sir. Ah wouldn't kid 'round bout somethin' that suhveer."

James shook his head at his feet.

"That son of a bitch."

"An' he beat the hell out of one of the brothers."

James shot them some irony from his door,
"Your friend, was he a big guy?"
"Well, as big as the rest of us."
"Did the cook have a weapon?"
"Nah, no sir. His bare hands."
"Well that hardly makes sense to me. He was no where near your fellas' height or size."
The main redneck looked around at his buddies.
"Really, now? Darrell sayin' he was a big fella."
"Not like you four. I do know that Darrell broke his nose for him and busted up his eye pretty good."
"No shit! Well, Darrell wuz probably too blitzed to 'member that."
"Well don't go thinking I'm defending the bastard. I still want a piece of him." The big redneck put his hand out.
"Wellsir, we won't take no more of yer time. Shit, we drove all them miles fer nothin'. See, we live in the country. Darrell wuz just gettin' outta jail an' he was bar hoppin'. Don't know how he ended up way over here. Crazy sumbitch, I'll tell ya. Now he's gotta go back IN jail. Fuck- we really wanted to find that cook. We wuz gonna do us a killin'."
James nodded at him.
"Well, the fucker's long gone by now. Probably half way through Montana. We'll never see him. Don't worry, he'll get his. What goes around comes around."
"You right. You goddamn right."
"Sorry you fellas didn't have any luck."
"No. We are sorry bout yer valuables an' yer sister. "
They shook hands again. James stepped back in the doorway.
"It's too bad you guys didn't get a hold of him. I would love to see that."
"Well, like you said, he'll git whut's comin' to him one day. Sorry to trouble you, mister."
"God bless, fellas."
He closed the door and locked it. I watched them walk down the street. Four big, dangerously stupid human beings. James walked back into my room and leaned against the door and looked at me. I nodded at him, "Smooth."
He cast his bloodshot eyes on my bandages.
"Your week must have been as bad as mine. Wanna come downstairs and have a drink with me?"
"Yes."
We sat on the couch and drank rum and coke. April came down, drying her hair.

She hugged her brother.

"Who was that at the door?"

He told her. She asked how they got their address. James said it was a small neighborhood, that somebody was bound to talk. I knew he didn't want to ask them because he didn't want to sound afraid of them. April sat next to me on the couch with her drink and told James that she had a new boyfriend and laughed, then elbowed my ribs. He stared into his drink.

"Great. That's all I need. A fucking hitch hiker making it with my little sister."

We drank to it and played music in the living room until well after dark.

I laid low for the hell of it, and resumed cooking on the next Friday. James paid me back and I bought a car. The next month the weather broke and I bought a new bike. It was expensive, but I didn't want to call my brother for my old one because I didn't want anything that reminded me of Arizona, let alone that period of my life.

April was softer than I was, and she started developing girlfriend traits: bitching at me here and there, buying me a shirt, writing me letters and pointing out my flaws, getting upset when I would go ride my bike or watching me practice from her car, thinking I didn't know she was watching. She would get moody and pout if I went to the bookstore without inviting her.

James had a new girlfriend by now and he'd moved her in. I think seeing them together influenced April. One night I came in after dark from riding, and April came into my room and started bitching at me because I'd missed dinner. I was still sweaty and in my zone from the session. I pushed her out of the doorway with my finger and locked it. She stomped down the hall and slammed her door.

Downstairs in the kitchen she stood next to the counter while I brewed some coffee. She told me I was being inconsiderate. I raised an eyebrow at her and grabbed a mug from the cabinet. She slammed the cabinet shut in front of my face.

"Listen, you're making me feel really fucking trapped here," I said.

That hit her hard. She looked confused. She wasn't expecting it. I had never cursed at her before. I continued solemnly,

"I've been nothing but honest with you. I told you I did not want a goddamned relationship. I understand if you have developed other feelings for me, but make no mistake, I don't have those feelings. I do care about you, meaning that I wish you no particular harm. I am attracted to your body and I like hanging out with you, but I'm severely fucked in the head and I could never love you. What I can do is leave you. I can leave anywhere in a matter of seconds. Believe me, this wouldn't be the first time. You have been making me feel trapped for weeks now. I thought we

laid out all the cards before we started this, and I've upheld my hand. If you need a boyfriend then you're with the wrong person. If you have naturally developed deeper feelings for me, you don't know how sorry I am that I cannot return those feelings. This has nothing to do with you as a person. I think you're amazing, but I would not miss you if I left. Now, if you'll excuse me, I'd like to take a shower."
I left her there. I thought it went rather well.
I ran the shower and stepped in. I had cuts on my shins from riding and the hot water stung them. I always loved that feel. It was progression. April stepped in the shower with me. Nietzsche had said that every woman, good or bad, wants to be beaten. While April and I kissed in the shower I knew he had it wrong.

It was getting time to leave Iowa. I'd quit Elliot's, and was waiting on another final check. Whenever I thought of the west I thought of Helena. She really had me. Not as bad as before, but she was there, even though I could sense that I was nothing to her now. I wondered if I would ever get past it. I spent the next week having sex with April. Every time she brought up my plans she cried. I knew that I would be gone and some other guy would eventually come along and I would be a memory, if even that. If I could be a memory to Helena then I would be a ghost to this one.
James tried to hide it, but I could tell that he thought, even if indirectly, that I was burning his sister. I thought that was interesting since our fate was so random. If he had driven past me on the freeway, none of this would have happened. Yet I was never ungrateful. I think he forgot how we'd met. I did consider him a friend of mine, the same way I considered Marty a friend of mine, or Ray a friend of mine. Or a better friend than both of them, but I saw nothing special in anybody anymore. It was a sick learned conditioning that I had but nobody else that I knew had.
Helena must have had it. Maybe losing her was in some way paying my dues for something else, but I could rationalize anything like that. No. Life was not so reasonable. It was good and bright, but it was hard and it hurt. All I could do was become harder and push back, though I knew that life never folded, and unlike a lot of people I had met, I took full responsibility for mine.

I drove east. My plan was to see every state in the country. For the next two years I hit every state east and south of Iowa and wrote in my journals. There were different girls, a lot of jobs and a lot of rooms and apartments and parking lots. I found romance in staying in those rooms above a sidewalk, writing in the journals and occasionally getting drunk. I liked to drink when I drank, and when I did I drank until I dropped, but I could only do it maybe once a week. I was lucky that I didn't carry the alcoholic gene. I did not quite love the taste. Instead I just dropped in on the devil, I didn't pal around with him.

I went through nine used cars. I slept hidden away in parks or abandoned yards during the lean times, or sometimes I would walk around until I found something to get into. Some of the south was all right. I hopped a train once, but it wasn't like I thought it would be. I did not like New Orleans or any of Mississippi. I liked Savannah enough to stay for a season. Florida made me sick in parts, and only some parts were truly southern, toward the top, and I was surprised with how much rain it took in. Miami was a wavy drug. I only drove through Alabama and Arkansas. I mostly worked construction. I learned that without an education all you could really work was labor or a delivery job or food service. Or worst of all, telemarketing. What drove me away from the south more than anything was the humidity and the slow mannerisms of the people. They were too relaxed, possibly wiser than most. And I liked certain parts of the East Coast: Myrtle Beach, The Carolinas. I only spent 2 days in Manhattan and I didn't sleep. I liked the energy of it, the danger. It was a different kind of decadence than Los Angeles, it was more lethal and real. You made it or you didn't out there, cut and dry. No grey areas. I would walk down 2nd and hang around Tompkins or I would catch a band on A or B. It was expensive to drink there. The city didn't quite overwhelm me, but it didn't welcome me, either. I learned that East Coasters complain a lot.

I only saw Boston from the freeway. After Manhattan, every other city appeared kind of sickly and weak. Most cities from the freeway looked something like a block of New York. I drove up into Maine and turned around. Then, like everybody else, I went back home.

12

I was older now. There was no way out of it. My mind had changed to different thoughts and I had traveled alone for years. I was neither proud nor ashamed. Crazy shit that happened to me now was common place, like the guy who held the gun to my head in Tampa and took my wallet, like the breakdowns on the highway, and bad cops and court dates for speeding tickets, or failure to appear for such tickets, twice resulting in harsh arrest. And I had read the so-called giants who used to glorify the road and the trouble, and I knew they were liars. I would be twenty-five that year, but everything really started when I was sixteen, when I had seen my mother die of an acute heart attack in front of me. She died from nowhere, right in the living room. There had been states and cities and towns, two oceans and several other bodies of water. The jobs were all the same jobs, the same feeling. There had been good women and bad women and women and girls and buddies and enemies and assholes. I did not care about my life but I did not want to die.

I rang the doorbell. This time my sister answered. I hadn't seen or spoken to her in nearly three years. I stepped inside. I wasn't tired or worked over this time, but I looked older than my years, and I knew she noticed it. The girls were tall and my nephew had gone back to prison after being out for two years. He wouldn't be released until 1999. She asked me where I had been. I told her I was traveling. She said she was jealous. She had no idea. I asked her if I could stay for a week until I found a place. I had never asked her before.

I met a girl named Brandy. I didn't like her name. My car blew out so we drove hers around. She was four years younger. I needed three hundred dollars to fix my car. She got a job stripping for two nights and had it fixed. We ran together for six months. One time, things got rough and we both lived in her car for two days. She was an adventuress with rich parents. She thought I was something special, and that she was even more so. She stripped again for a few more days and moved me into a room and had my car repaired again. She was all body. It took her six months to realize that I was an asshole, whether she meant it or not. I never cared about her. In fact, deep down she repulsed me.

I landed another delivery job. I knew the area well. I remember one night this address looking awfully familiar. As I drove there with the pizzas it hit me. Helena's old apartment. I made the famous right turn onto Beardsley and parked. Of course, they no longer lived there.

I held the slip in my hand and remembered the torn pink envelope with her handwriting. There was the door, the porch I had waited on anxiously while she cleaned. My skin was frozen down my arms. The curtains were open and I could see the hallway that led to her room, so many good lifetimes back. Now I was just a shell.

Some fat guy answered. I stepped in while he wrote the check. The ghosts of her rushed me at once, floored me. Everything came back to me in one devastating blow of loss, of anger. I drove back to the shop, punched out and quit.

I was living in this hot little brick room in Tempe. My roomies were nice guys who were older and worked day jobs. I barely saw them. I was without a car again and working at this Mexican/American eatery off of Mill Avenue for six-fifty an hour. I worked four to close. I picked out a waitress, a blonde named Kelley. Totally not my type, but there was life in her. We had sex a few times back in my room but nothing ever came out of it except her hating me.

13

On my break I met a girl who was into speed metal. Her name was Ella. She had piercings everywhere and a tattoo of a skeleton reaching out of the skin on her forearm. She was a cool one. She had been staying at the Allen House, a midway point for junkies and half-wits. She would walk over and talk to me every night on my breaks. I never had sex with her because her blood was stained and getting worse. She had to take her medication every three or four hours, and you could smell it on her breath. She had holes in her throat because she couldn't give up smoking. I asked her about it.

"They try and tell me to stay positive. How ironic is that? They say that I am living with it, not dying from it. It's a joke. I'm fucking dying from it."

When she wore make-up she could almost hide it. It took a lot of make-up. One night she drove me home. She said she had escaped from the place for good. I gave her some floor space for the night. I went into the kitchen and poured us some orange juice. She said citrus burned her throat, so I drank hers. By this time I had boxes of journals filled front to back. They were in order from the beginning until the present, the only sense of organization I'd had. She asked about the tablets. I told her. She wanted to read. I figured it couldn't do any harm.

No one had ever wanted to read them before or else I wouldn't let them or else they didn't know I kept them. I asked if she wanted a glass of water. She didn't. The phone rang. I knew it was for me since everyone else was sleeping. It was my sister in Illinois. She was calling to tell me she was pregnant.

I talked to her for a while. It had been a few months. Back in my room Ella was turning the pages. I sat on my mattress. She looked at me and shook her head.

"Holy fucking shit. This is good. No. It's great."

"Come on."

"No. I'm fucking serious. Look at me. I'm dying. Why would I bullshit you?" I thought about it. She really had nothing to gain. She folded the journal and held it on her lap.

"Listen, have you ever thought about getting a typewriter?"

"Not really. I just write in those things for myself. Nobody would be interested."

"What do you mean? That is such bullshit!"

"I'm just surprised you're able to read my handwriting," I said.

"Is all of this true? I mean, these aren't just made up stories or anything?"

"It happened."

"You need to type this shit out. People need to read this. These poems, these stories..."

She read aloud from one of them. It was embarrassing.

"Ella, please. Nobody gives a shit."

"What are you talking about? Have you looked at yourself lately? Haven't you put it all together yet? I mean you even *look* like a fucking writer."

"Go on."

"I mean, you've traveled, you've fucked up countless times, had your heart broken, gone through hundreds of jobs and you, my dear, are completely insane, out of your mind. Read this shit. How much more obvious does it have to be? I mean, seriously. Open your eyes."

Every word she said bounced off the walls but would not escape. Instead they hit me right in the chest and sunk through, and my heart was soaked by them. She shook her head at me.

"What time do you work tomorrow?"

"What's tomorrow?" I asked.

"Wednesday."

"My one day off."

"I'm driving you out tomorrow and we're getting you a typewriter."

She went on and on. I told her that if it would shut her up I'd get a typewriter. I tossed her my sheet and a pillow and fell asleep with my clothes on.

During the night I would turn over every few hours to see her on her stomach under my candle turning the pages. I thought she was mental. I can only sleep in the dark, but she really liked reading what she was reading. It was the first time I'd seen her actually relax and not chain-smoke and think of death. I thought it was interesting, the way she thought all of those things that happened in there were exciting, romantic, or worthwhile. I only kept the journals because they made things better for me. They were personal. I didn't mind her reading them, and that was only because she was dying and any way she took it wouldn't last long.

It was sometime after noon. We were in a thrift store in Phoenix off of 7th. Ella was looking at clothes. There was this grimness to it. It was hard to not picture the clothes she was fingering on her body in a coffin. I couldn't watch anymore. I found the typewriters. The place was much cheaper than the typewriter store we had gone to by the mall. I couldn't afford their machines. I went through them, settling on this ugly brown one that was louder than it was ugly. An electric. Ten dollars. I liked it. Next door at the drug store I bought some paper, and we hit the typewriter place on the way back to by a pack of cartridges. While I waited for the old man to bring them back from his stock, I thought of her words last night in my room. On the freeway Ella looked over at me fingering the dead keys in my lap, and she smiled. I thought it was strange how I never saw her again.

I set the machine upon the desk and plugged it in. I ran a sheet through. I walked around the house thinking about what to write. I would go into the room, see it sitting there and walk out again. I sat behind it. I flipped the lever on the side. It started like an engine.

I typed my first sentence ever, in capitals:

HERE WE GO.

I liked the feel of it. The bricks around me gave the words heavy acoustics. I didn't want to start out by copying the journals. I had never written them for others to read. I was not some fucking hungry young writer on the road. Instead I just wrote things which came into my head right there. I made many mistakes. For a while I practiced the keys, finding the quickest ways to correctly write a sentence. Then I began my first short story. It was about a loser waking up in a stripper's hotel room, his tongue in the ashtray. It went on for about four pages. It was magical. It was not like handwriting. I was actually there in that hotel room. I saw the whole scene through the black keys. I had escaped my life and lived in a better world of better tragedy, without the senselessness. I created the sky and the clocks, the curves of her body and the universe, molecule by molecule. I realized I could live forever through doing this. It was purely beautiful. I finished the story. She had dropped him off at a bus stop and drove to the night club. He had nine hours to sit there.

I sat and typed poems, poems for the years long since wasted. I remember those poems, the life they gave. Some of them were dark ones about Helena, about the nature of women. Mostly they dealt with the people and the jobs and the nights without escape, the days which promised nothing. The words made me see things differently, more clearly. I wrote poems about places and people and jobs and parks and dogs and sunlight and children and handguns and everything.

I needed nothing else from that point onward. I needed a room, some caffeine and a typewriter. I typed furiously, sweating. I couldn't roll the next sheet through fast enough. I'd never felt so useful. It was happening, thundering away, bending the walls downward. I sat there all night and typed to my music. Angels circled above and around my room, protecting me, allowing me to move and move. I was in love. It was all action. It was all mine.

I sat back and rested. I had a thick pile of pages piled next to the machine. I stretched out and looked at the clock: 6:23 p.m. I jumped out of the chair and ran to the phone. I had nearly missed two and a half hours of work. I was hoping that I didn't get Rob. I hated Rob. A different manager answered. I played it dumb, asked him if I was supposed to work today. He didn't really know for sure. He'd just go check the schedule.

"Yesiree. Supposed to be here at four."

"Shit. I'm on my way."

"Take your time. Not like you haven't already."

I had to be graceful. He could have been an asshole about it.

I walked to work every day because it was only eight blocks. Only this time I was armed. I had the pages I had written in my backpack and they were heavy with substance. Back in the kitchen on Thursday was always slow. As I walked to work I wondered how the guy in the next room had slept with me hammering away all night. He was a short, skinny guy named Peter. Peter worked in an office for the phone company. I would sometimes see him when I stumbled in late on the weekends with a girl. Sometimes he would see me walking to work on his way home and nod at me. I thought he was a little frightened of me. He woke up early, showered, shaved, made breakfast and wore a suit. I was just the opposite.

I read my things on my break. I had typed out all of it. I was proud. I watched the people outside walking with each other, with their spouses to see a movie, with their kids and their tucked in shirts and pressed pants and perfect hair. I finally felt like I had one over on them. I had finally discovered an edge.

By the time I closed I was dead tired. I wanted to write but I was tired. I felt young again. I hadn't pulled an all-nighter since Manhattan. I fell back across the mattress and read from the pages until my eyes blurred and I fell asleep, long and blue and without dream.

That Friday I was let off early because the fryer went down. I had never seen the inside of the house at eight o'clock. The only car there was Peter's. From the hallway his door was open, and I heard The Dead Kennedys blasting from his room. I didn't think of him as the type who would like them. I knocked without looking in. I told him it was me.

He was sitting on his bed reading Trotsky.

"Peter, I hope the typewriter doesn't bother you. I know you work mornings."

"No. I like it. I didn't know you wrote. What kind of stuff do you write?"

I shrugged politely. I didn't know how to answer that. He moved his feet back.

"Here, man. Wanna sit down?"

I sat down and looked around at his posters, mostly nautical maps. I listened to Biafra scream.

"DK's, huh?"

He nodded from behind the book, "You like them?"

"Very much."

He called over the book, "Your favorite lyric?"

"Tomorrow you're homeless, tonight it's a blast."

"Ah, Riot. Very nice."

I laughed. We were connoisseurs of punk. That night we drank and talked. He was loosely strung. It challenged my perceptions of the suit and tie guy. I liked him, and I didn't like very many people I had to live with. He was just dealing with things in his own way. At least he got it.

For the next 2 months I wrote and worked. I was barely riding my bike anymore. May was approaching. I had been working with this new guy named Fin. He was a young smartass. He had these buggly eyes that laughed at you. I remember one day, one of the token homeless hippie kids from the park came in. They lived in the park and bummed spare change on Mill. They called it "spanging." I hated them.

I had never once in my life asked a single soul for a handout. I was out there in my youth, really traveling, facing adversity. I had to bust my ass working, and I didn't always have a warm grassy park or a car to sleep in. They walked around all day bumming change and playing hand drums, wearing expensive clothes and fresh tattoos. They made me sick. The kid asked Fin and I if we would cook this tofu burger on our grill for him. He was with his little girlfriend. Every one of them had these dumbass nicknames and weak, white boy dreads:

"Hey, brother. Would you cook this for me on the grill, man? I can give you some pennies..."

I smiled and told him I'd take care of him.

"Heeey. Thanks, brother. You're all right, man."

I walked back to the kitchen and looked around. Fin tossed me a wad of pork, and I placed it carefully in the middle and cooked it. We were laughing.

I looked at Fin.

"Buns."

He tossed me a hamburger bun and I plopped it in. I handed it to the kid and we watched him stand out in front of the window and eat it while he talked to his girlfriend. Then he took a huge bite, swallowed it and puked on the sidewalk. They looked inside at the dripping flesh. He heaved again. His little girlfriend ran in the door and yelled at me.

"YOU ASSHOLE! CASPER HAS NEVER DIGESTED MEAT HIS WHOLE LIFE! NINETEEN YEARS! YOU'RE A FUCKING MONSTER!"

I picked up a handful of shredded beef and heaved it at her. It hit her neck and slid down slowly. She put her arms up and shook it off, running in place and screaming. She was crying, sobbing something about murder. She reached into her large, stupid hemp purse and came at me with some mace. Fin and I were throwing meat at her, and she was spraying this mace in circles over her head. Her boyfriend ran in and held her. We let the meat fly until the trays were empty. It was just after opening and Rob was in the back. He heard the hippies and ran out. He rounded the corner, right into the cloud of mace. The girl took off screaming, her boyfriend running after her.

In the office we sat across from his desk. He was using one of those eye flushers. His eyes were beet red, and Fin sat there laughing at him from across the desk. For me, the moment was too great for laughter. He began.

"Normally, I would have to write you guys up for this, but due to the blatant disregard for food cost and rudeness and the outright hostility for the customer I'm afraid we're going to have to sever all-"

"I quit." I said. Rob looked up from his rag.

"WHAT?"

Fin laughed, "Yeah, I quit, too, man. No room for growth here."

Rob sat forward in his chair.

"No, no, no. You're fired!"

I stood up, "Too late, Rob. Anyone calls you for a reference, which they won't, you have to say we quit. Try to say we were terminated and you're fucked. And yes, it's a threat."

Fin stood up and followed me out, "Have a good day."

We punched out in turn. On the way out, Fin made a good point by mentioning if we would have let him fire us then we would, by law, have to be paid within 72 hours. I thought it was worth waiting another week to see Rob's blood boil. Fin dropped me off at the house.

I had rent covered already and if I was careful I could cover next month's. I spent one solid week writing in my room. I didn't step outside once. There was nothing out there anymore. I could not stop. Peter asked me casually to let him read a story of mine. I let him read one about a nineteen-year old kid stranded in Hollywood who let this older guy masturbate him in an X-rated theater for bus fare. He read it and came back into my room. His face was shocked.

"You should do something with this shit. You're good."

I didn't agree. I had years ahead of me before I would even be close. I knew it, and I knew it would be a long haul. I was not good enough for my own standard of writing because I hadn't lived enough, and for me that was the only method, and this was only practice. It was frightening to see it that way, but anything real is never pretty once it's absorbed.

Fin popped in one day while I was writing. He looked around my room.

"Man. This place sucks."

"Thanks."

"I wanted to tell you about this job, working on a boat in Alaska. They need people. I did it last year. A summer at sea and they pay you like a thousand bucks a week, man."

"How many hours?"

"A shitload. Like eighteen a day. But you can't spend your money, and when you get back on land you're fucking rich."

"You've done it?"

"Oh, hell yeah. I had an easy ass job, though."

"How do we get there?"

"We take the boat from Seattle. It's cool."

He gave me the address in Seattle. I wondered why he had bothered to come by. Maybe he figured we were friends because we had been fired together. I had to type this woman a letter of intent. I did, and a week later she called me and hired me over the phone. There would be a physical and a drug test in Seattle. One month away. Fin left me his number on the page and I called him. We had both forgotten about our final checks so I told him I'd meet him down there.

He filled my glass with his pitcher. Next door at the eatery Rob was doing his job and we weren't allowed to go back, ever. He handed us our checks from the entrance. They screwed mine up somehow. I had an extra day's pay on there. Fin leaned back and read his check.
"Those fuckers!"
"What is it?"
"They charged me fifteen bucks for two shirts. Fuck that place. I should burn it down."
"Do it."
"Right."
I asked Fin how he was getting to Seattle, since I was taking the bus.
"I thought you were going with all of us."
"Who's all of us?"
"Shit, man. There's like seven of us road tripping up there. I thought you'd ride along and split gas with us. We're leaving in two days, taking a few weeks to get there, two cars and a truck. It'll be a good time. We'll play it loose."
I thought about it. He refilled my glass and told me that three of them were meeting us at the bar. I didn't want to meet them, but he had been buying the drinks and I didn't want to walk out on him.

They were loud and obnoxious jocks. They were good kids, but they were loud and obnoxious jocks. Their leader was a big guy named Vincent who still had a baby face. He reached back and slapped the head of one of the others around Fin.
"Hey, Mahoney. Gimme a buck for the jukebox."
That guy moaned, "Ahh, maaan. You didn't bring any money again?"
"Just give me a dollar, faggot."
I stood up, walked to the juke and fed it a fiver. I quickly picked out old Willie Nelson and Don Williams and Gordon Lightfoot and some Sabbath. I was having a decent time, and I did not want to listen to any drum machines or loops or samples or keyboards or girls or mainstream rap bullshit. I put another fiver in and played more music. By the time my songs were over I would have made plenty of time to escape.

The leader sat across from me. He was barely old enough to drink. I looked into my glass and absorbed Whiskey River from the speakers. Fin told me that Vincent had just come off "the road." I looked across to him and asked him from where. He suddenly became old and wise. The table listened to him tell his story:

"I was driving my mom's car back from Colorado. I was half a mile from Cortez when the car just shut down, man. It's a new Merc, man, you know, all electrical. So it shuts down, man. The car phone only works in the cigarette lighter and since the whole car's dead I couldn't call anyone. It was still early so I set out on foot, down the freeway. I walked half a mile into town and called my mom. I had her credit card so I got a room and she had the car towed. They fixed it by dark, but I was too tired and pissed off to drive so I stayed there. One of the guys shook his head at the table,

"Man."

I looked around the table. I thought he was joking. But he wasn't. He was scarred. I downed my beer so I wouldn't start laughing. Then we started talking about the trip. Vincent said he wanted to rough it for the three weeks up there. He stared across to me. He was trying to look rugged.

"Whatta you think there, man, you ever roughed it on the road?"

I gave him a loose smile and told him it sounded like a good idea. I drank until my songs were played out and I laid a twenty on the table for the beer.

"My share. I'm heading out."

I told them I'd be at the meeting place in two days.

I went back to the room and wrote for a while. I had nothing to pack.

The next morning I awoke and rode my bike around for hours. I was feeling soft from the writing. I knew I couldn't take my bike with me on the trip. Peter let me borrow his car that night, and I drove to my sister's and locked it away in her garage along with the journals and my typer. I spent the next day walking around Tempe. I climbed a mountain and sat there on a palm shaped rock, looking out over the towns. The whole world was something, or it was supposed to be, and the faces were supposed from something, but everything had fallen short because the two of them were tangled together and helpless now. I walked back down the path and bought a new Walkman and some batteries. Back home Peter asked me why I'd needed his car. I told him. The landlord lived up in Prescott and I asked Peter to tell him to keep the three weeks rent I had left over for the sudden move. I gave him my tape player since I could not take it and since I had forgotten to load it with everything else the night before. The next morning I was awake early, had some coffee and walked down to Farmer where the house was.

After a couple of hours, everyone who was going was on the porch. I counted seven of us in total and one girl, a hot native spiritual. Before she showed the boys were betting on who would lay her first. I watched her but I knew they didn't have

March of Time and Skin

a chance. And they wouldn't let her out of their sites, she was locked in their crosshairs for weeks. I felt sorry for her, and I knew I wasn't part of the group, either. I was the older freak with whom they had nothing in common. I hated sports. I hated sportswear and radio music and Mtv and light beer. I hated parties. I had no interest in dropping acid on Haight/Ashbury or stopping off at the Grateful Dead show with them in Nevada. They had forgotten which decade they lived in, all of that shit was dead now, just a ridiculous idealism behind a slick corporate image. Everything they wanted to do had long been exhausted. I sat away from the circle while they discussed the big trip. I was riding along to save money. It was Vincent's idea to stop in Nevada and sell peanut butter and jelly sandwiches to the hippies outside of the concert. He'd made a ton of them.

We set out. I was crammed into the back of the truck camper with my music. I liked it back there. I could sleep and look out the window from time to time. Nobody else wanted that spot. In one of their new backpacks next to me a book stuck out. I flipped it around and read the title: On The Road. I grinned bitterly. How pathetically uniform that one of them would have this book on the trip. I had never read the book, never read anything by him. I remembered once reading Capote, who wrote that Kerouac didn't write, he typed. Still, I never took a stranger's word on anything. I didn't open the book because one of the guys owned it and I did not want to be involved in any way. I had tried to read some of the other "Beats" but I just couldn't get into them. Something was phony about it. To me, it was self-serving mumble hiding behind plastic open mindedness and homosexual undertones. I could take it no longer, and I plucked the book from the backpack and read.

I didn't like it. It was whiny, boring, and obvious. More homosexual undertones. It was almost like he wanted to make out with his buddy. I thought the travel was weak and that the way he was getting money sent from home made him sound like a pussy. I reached over in the cooler and swiped one of the sandwiches. I unwrapped it and dug in. Of course! It was *creamy* peanut butter. Crunchy was the only way to fly.

We stopped in Lake Mead. They wanted to camp and get stoned with the hippies. I wanted to remind them of the piss test less than three weeks off, but I kept my mouth shut, because I was hoping some of them would fail.

I had never liked hippies or the Dead. I've never liked sorry history or bandwagons of any type. They were simply dirty football fans and lawyers. Every thirty seconds a hippie would walk by and try to bum food from me. I was at the truck alone, sitting on the tailgate, reading and eating oranges.

"Hey brother, can I get an orange off you?"

"Hey brother, can you spare an orange?"

"Hey brother, how about giving me one of those oranges..."

They were young and a little older and each full of shit. I took a walk, a long walk. Their dogs had shit everywhere. They were mangy and sick looking creatures. I thought it was cruel how the hippies took care of them. They didn't take care of them. The standard smell of patchouli and armpits unnerved me. I was sickened by their slovenliness. The old hippies I could deal with. I respected anyone who could survive like that for 30 years, regardless of their taste in music or ignominious methods. The young ones bugged me. They walked around with their fingers in the air. Soon the same finger would be in the air, hailing a taxi on Fifth and 48th, in a hurry to get to the office.

In the parking lot at the concert they were there, in droves, those fingers up there. I learned it was up there for a free ticket to the show. I always thought it was great how the tickets were so expensive. The free ticket was called a miracle. It was hot in Nevada. I wanted a cold wave to come through and lick me up from that place, landing me behind a desk by myself with my typewriter and my music playing, a full stack of typing paper and a cold coffee. That would be a miracle.

That night I asked Fin where they were staying. He didn't know. He said everyone was meeting at Slots of Fun on the strip the next afternoon. They were going to stay there for a while since they had only made six bucks from the sandwiches. I wanted to tell him that hippies don't pay for food, but I didn't care. I bummed a ride from one of the boys and he dropped me off just inside of Las Vegas. Stephanie answered. They had gotten married last month and they were living in a house off Maryland Pkwy. She said Greg was out with the guys playing pool but he had to come back in an hour to take her to work. I hung up and walked toward Maryland for an hour. I called back, and he answered.

"What's up, man? Are you stranded?"

"Yes."

"Where are you?"

I told him and gave him a quick summary of everything. I asked him to bring me in.

"Keep your sorry ass put. We're on the way."

He had a beautiful house. One of the guys joked about coming over after they had moved in and there was Greg, on the wood floor on his knees scrubbing every inch with a toothbrush. We sat out back and drank. It felt like home to be around the old crew. I told Boyde about the sandwiches and the six bucks. He laughed.

"So it was a business trip."

March of Time and Skin

He asked me about the job in Alaska. I told him.

"Man, you're gonna be hatin' it after the second *hour*."

Greg tilted his bottle at me.

"Fuck it, man. This motherfucker's a trooper. High Plains Drifter."

We laughed. It was damn good to be there.

The next morning Greg woke me up by blasting a Victim's Family album. He was standing over the back of the couch.

"Heavy metal sunrise. Wake up, man. I won't see your crazy ass for four more years."

We drove down to a cafe where they hung his work, and we sat outside.

"Now it's Alaska, huh? Fuck man, I was just telling Stephanie about how I wondered when and where you were going to finally plant some roots. Not that it matters."

I opened my journal and handed him my pen.

"Draw me a picture."

He began drawing. I sat back and watched his left hand move, and I watched the pen, creating fat cartoonish things from all points of the paper. It was a guy who looked like me, an ace card in his pocket and his thumb out, on a thin highway with two girls kneeling, holding each leg. It was amazing.

At the casino we parked and walked around. Hippies everywhere. We walked the carpet past the machines and tables. Greg was disgusted:

"What do hippies have against a flat stomach? They all have to brew the biggest gut."

I laughed. It hurt my hangover. He mentioned something about the girls not shaving their armpits or legs, then he attacked their breasts:

"And another thing, why don't these chicks wear bras? I don't want to see some unshaven bitch with saggy-ass tits walking around. You can quote me on that one."

I had to slow up and laugh. It had been a long time since I had been around someone in my element.

I saw the group. Fin told me that they would be outside in a few minutes. Greg and I sat outside in view of their cars. We talked for a bit and then they filed out. Greg saw them walking.

"Shit, man. Good luck."

He gave me a hug and took off. I waved him down in his rearview. He looked back out his window as I jogged up, my hand in my pocket. I told him I'd forgotten to give him something. When I made it to his window, I pulled my hand from my pocket and punched him in the back of his shoulder, really laid it in there. He held his shoulder and cursed me, steadily. I smiled.

"That was for '89. Roll's front door."

He laughed and drove off. When I could no longer see his car, I turned and walked toward the group. They were by the cars playing hacky-sack.

Everyone piled in. I got the camper. We stopped for gas, and I handed my share to Fin from the sliding window. We drove up Sahara and got on 95 north. We were back *on the road.*

I leaned back and played my music, staring at Greg's drawing. I thought back to when I had first gone to Vegas, seeing him outside of Roll's parents' church-like house in Green Valley. It was the first I'd seen Greg since the pier, and he slugged me on my arm right when he walked up. Sure, once on the pier, I had pedaled up behind him at full speed and kicked him in his spine and he fell off his bike, but that was the game. And there at Roll's, my arm was throbbing, and I was tired from the drive, so I vowed to get him back later. And I looked at his drawing again and thought about the years between the drawing and the camper, and I saw the vein-work of lives and it was hot outside. The breeze coming in from the windows barely helped. I was sweating a lot because I was hungover. The cars kept honking at each other, racing each other. I blasted my music and passed out. It was eight hours to Reno.

I slept the whole way. We ate and cut over to Lake Tahoe where they lost their money and had to get their parents to wire them more money, which they also gambled and lost. I had lost some, but I called it quits before the fever overwhelmed me. I took the loss and walked out, fighting every urge to turn around and try to win back the $30 I had lost. The fever took them by storm. They were each low on money. They were bitching because they only had a few hundred each. I had left Arizona on the trip with half of that. They were back on the phones, getting more sent out. That night they chipped in for a couple of rooms. Over dinner, Vincent reached his hand out for my share. I told him I didn't want to pay for a room, that I would sleep outside or else stay in the camper. We had sleeping bags and everybody but me had a tent. I didn't see why a room was necessary. Everybody wanted to shower, he said. I told him I was sorry, but I wanted to hold onto what I had in my pocket, that I couldn't call mommy for money. The table froze. No one had ever talked back to him. I was getting annoyed with him the entire trip. He looked coldly at me, but he wasn't fooled, he knew I could take him. He knew I had nothing to lose. I grew bored with his face and stared to the kitchen, watching the cooks drive the wheel and stress, and I knew Vincent was staring me down in front of his buddies, so I looked back at him and took it to reality.

"Go ahead and say something, big man. Call me out. Let's see how tough you are."

The native girl looked at him and smiled. Everyone at the table got off on seeing him humbled. He shook his head.

"We don't need to get all stupid here, man. Let's just get a room tonight and from here on out we're camping."

Against myself, I chipped in for the rooms, though they ended up bothering me with their talking and watching sports, and I slept in the camper anyway.

In the morning I went into the room and brushed my teeth. Outside after they showered something felt different. I though about departing and making my own way, but the job started in two and a half weeks and who knew what would happen to me between there and Seattle. Everyone was quiet. What I had done to him at the table made them lose respect for him. I saw him by himself tying his duffel bag by the tailgate and I began to feel bad. He really hadn't done anything to me, except to get on my nerves, and I wanted to think that I'd called him out because he was young, with the natural opportunities which were stripped from me when I was young, and that I was maybe a little jealous of him, but I wasn't jealous of him. It was a simple case of putting up with too much in a short amount of time. But I walked over and shook his hand and apologized for being ruthless. I knew he would tell everybody that I apologized, probably because I was afraid of him, and though they wouldn't fully buy it, it would restore part of their fear.

And I liked their idea of roughing it- expensive campsites up the California coast, cooking expensive steaks and drinking expensive beer. We stayed in the Redwoods and up at some guy's house in Santa Cruz. I thought of James and his sister, and I wondered how they were doing. My favorite part was watching them in San Francisco, watching three or four of them walking around on acid. Haight/Ashbury was desolate and there they were, walking around on acid.

I sat across the street in Golden Gate Park and thought of Vollman's Rainbow Stories and talked to Maka, the native. She was good company, the only one in the group my age. She was going through a heavy break up and we talked about that. I knew nobody on the trip had a chance with her. She was too smart. Sometimes I would talk to her over the campfires when everyone else was asleep. When they were awake, they talked about girls and parties and sports and fighting. I would walk off into the woods. Whenever Maka and I started talking late at night, it was inevitable that one of the testosterone brothers would wake up and sit with us, if not all of them. She was beautiful and I would have been on her in a minute, but she was a real woman with real problems and she wasn't interested in anybody. She just wanted to talk to someone. She was the one piece of sanity I had with the group.

During the campsites, whenever she would walk off with somebody else or she was missing with a couple of people, the remaining frat hounds would stare around: "Where's Maka, where's Maka?" Then they would hunt her. I started to wonder if I could take two more weeks of it.

We stopped along the Oregon Coast. It was devastating, by far the most beautiful place in America. I didn't want to leave there. It was breathtaking, the jade backdrops with their lighthouses set to the side of ocean atop the grey rocks, the cliffs that ran down into the beaches, the way everything moved and melted together with this carelessness, this ease of nature's face smiling back and forth through time, and it would there long before and long after my own life. I broke away from them and walked the beauty.

In Portland we stopped and drank. I liked the downtown, it had a good feel, and the people had a good feel about them, or the ones I had seen so far had a good feel about them because they were survivors. I walked the downtown alone and watched the bar fronts and sidewalks, it was dark and clean and I had the feeling that I was in a different country for the first few hours, until I met up with the ant tribe, and we drove a ways west, and there we stayed with a jock's sister, an uptight girl surrounded and controlled by her rented environment, her shiny, expensive, synthetic comfort, and her faceless fiancée.

When we made Seattle we had a week left. One of the other boys in the group also had a sister, and she shared a house with a pair of sisters in Ravenna, just north. Downtown Seattle was a tight fist of buildings set to a side of water. We flew by it, found the house and unloaded.

That night there was a big party at the house. All of the girls were in college, and it was wall-to-wall frat boys and bad music and cheap beer, dyed blonde squat college girls in tight jeans, with eyes like pigs. I couldn't take it in there, and I walked out with my backpack, headed toward the city. It was a long walk and I was twenty bucks away from being broke.

I walked up the roads closest to the freeway, and I made Capital Hill after a healthy amount of time. I was tired and it was getting late. I found a park behind a Texaco and walked far back in the darkness and slept.

I woke up alone, alone. It was beautiful. There was a sting in the air but I wasn't cold. I rolled up my sleeping bag and bought a cup of coffee. I sat under an umbrella on Broadway, and watched the people. It was early in the morning. The street was still asleep. I walked down Pike, and into the famous market. There I remembered Jared and Grant. It had been four years. I didn't know if they were still there or not, or if Grant had even moved back. He was listed. It was still early and I didn't want to wake him. I walked around the market and down First to a peep-show joint, where you could slide a dollar into a slot from a private booth and watch live girls dancing in front of the one way mirror, or a two way, if you wanted them to see your face. And they would see the light come on over your mirror when the money was put in and they would dance over naked and spread their sex apart in your face. It only cost me three dollars before I finished, then I walked up to Pioneer Square, turned around and took a Ferry across the bay to Bainbridge Island, only because I had never taken one before, and I walked from the terminal there and drank Italian coffee from the edge of an old pier, and smaller things than ferries floated by, and I watched them on the water. They pushed through a patch of flotsam, and floated out of mind. And my mind was with them.

Back in the market I called the number. I woke him up. I was surprised that he remembered me as fast as he did. He gave me Jared's number out on Whidbey Island, where he was staying with his girlfriend at his grandparents'. I called the number, and he told me to meet him up at the Streamliner on Mercer.

We sat and drank. Jared asked about Helena. The name ran cold under my skin. I told him. He shook his head. He knew I would never do better. I told him about the trip. His girlfriend was nice, but I could tell she wore the pants, even if Grant wouldn't have told me anything earlier. They took me out to Whidbey where the house overlooked Useless Bay. I saw my first Bald Eagle. I liked the island. It was quiet and I was among friends. The next day we laid on the beach and drank, at night building a fire. I asked about the date. Tomorrow was orientation for the job and the drug test. I had almost forgotten.

Sylvia let me borrow her car. I drove off the ferry and followed the directions. Her car was nice and black and fast. I pulled down her sunglasses from the visor. They were big and pink. The day looked better wearing them. I passed a lot of industry and then I was there, pulling into the gravel lot of a big warehouse. There were about fifty people out front. I saw the group from Tempe playing hacky-sack by the truck. They watched the car speed into a spot. I was blasting some old metal and her speakers were loud. When they saw me step out they were speechless. I hadn't said goodbye to them when I'd left the house in Ravenna. I stepped out and nodded to them:

"Gentlemen."

Inside the woman who did the hiring warned us about the job, before we signed the contract. When the contract was signed, that was it. Once you stepped on the boat you were theirs. You were a body, completely stripped of autonomy and distinction.

"You will not be alone up there. You will have no privacy. It's not a place to get away. There is no alcohol or drugs allowed. The hours are long and hard. If you decide to quit then you will be helicoptered to land and charter planed back here. You will be reduced to four dollars an hour. You will be charged for board and food, otherwise free, charged for all transportation and if you haven't made enough to pay us back, then your next job will be garnished until you do. If anyone wants to walk out, now's the time."

A couple of sissies left. She talked to us one by one and showed us a video of boats going under and people dying. She gave each person a chance to back out, and it was almost like she was trying to get them to back out. I couldn't wait to get out on the water. She gave us the address for the drug test and the physical. I took care of it right away. It was easy. Lift 70 pounds, carry it to here, squeeze this handle, jog in place... I pissed in a cup and took off back to the island.

The next day she called us in one by one from the waiting room. She told me that I had passed my tests and that she extended the offer for employment if I still wanted it. She would see me the next day for the signing of the contract and a safety demonstration.

Everybody got the same spiel. I wondered if she ever got tired of it, if she ever changed the words around to make it more interesting for herself. Everybody got hired except for Vincent and his little buddy, Mahoney, who both tested positive for marijuana. But she was a cool boss, and said since they driven all the way from Arizona they could retest the next day. They would go out and buy one of those drug screen packages, drink a lot of water and vinegar and carrot juice, piss the whole day and pass the other test.

The next morning we signed the contracts and practiced jumping in and out of the safety suits, which were heavy, and when activated, swelled up around you and sent forth a red flashing bulb. Hypothermia would kill you within twenty seconds if you hit the water, and the only thing exposed beneath the suit was a narrow slit for vision. The suit would float forever...

She went into more rules. Then she covered the sexual harassment parts. I looked around. There were only a few girls there and they looked like men. The next day we were to meet in Ballard at the docks where we would set out. A nine day trip.

That night Jared and Sylvia and I drank in the bar downtown where Grant worked. Then we drove out to Lake Sammamish where his brother sometimes lived. It was a nice place with a balcony and the lake was right in the backyard. We built a fire and drank. I had to be in Ballard by three in the afternoon. I drank there with friends, happily altered, and we talked about Arizona after Sylvia fell asleep.

I grabbed my backpack and jumped out. Sylvia tossed me a mixed tape and a pack of batteries. I'd gone broke just in time. We didn't need money on the boat, and there was a small store there that sold pretty much everything and it would be deducted from your pay. I looked up at the boat. Jared reached across her and handed me a silver flask.

"What's in here?"

"Ten High."

Sylvia was eyeing the boat from her seat. I thought about where she was sitting and what she was thinking. It only made sense in part. I gave her a big kiss on the cheek and shook Jared's hand behind the wheel.

"Thank you guys."

He called me a landlubber, and they drove off. I took my last steps on solid land for the summer and walked up the ladder.

We sat in the galley at the long tables. I found out that Maka had backed out the night before after talking to her ex and he put her on a bus back home. Everybody ate. We had a five star Chef and the food was incredible. I watched the boys eat and laugh. I felt like I was in an old movie. We got our bunk assignments. There were six racks to a room, and the rooms were just big enough for six racks. She had put me in with the Arizona guys because she figured we were all buddies. I took the rack furthest from the door and closest to the ground.

The boat was just less than two hundred feet. It was crowded. You never walked more than ten feet without going up or down some stairs. They were taking volunteers to on-load supplies. I was the only one from our group who volunteered. I wanted to make as much as possible, and I figured I was already there so what the hell. I helped load and got a nice twelve-hour start on my check. Our room was on the top floor. They had left me the bottom bunk in the far back corner. I laid down and slid the curtain shut, turned on the nightlight and read a book Jared had bought for me as a floating away present, Journey to the End of the Night. I had already read it, but I didn't say anything. I fell asleep before Bardamu enlisted.

14

I awoke rocking up and down. Something was wrong. I sat up from the rack and hit my head against the top bunk. My stomach was jelly and my flesh felt green. I couldn't swallow. My head was full of heavy liquid and my brain was floating in it, bloated and green like my flesh. I put my hand over my mouth and ran for the bathroom. I was off balance in the hallway. I stumbled into the walls, the vomit spraying out between my fingers. I had anvils resting on both shoulders and a solid steel box on my head. I ran into the bathroom and found a silver toilet on the platform. I grabbed the sides and let it go. It was horrible, pink. I stared down at it,
"Oh, God."
Here came more. I went, until I was dehydrated. I straightened up and flushed, sat back against a sink. I ran the faucet and washed my mouth out and drank. As soon as the water hit my stomach, it bounced back out against the mirror. I hopped back to the toilet and threw up the rest of it. I repeated the cycle six times.
It turned out that all the new blood on the boat was seasick. All but Fin, and he'd once bragged to me in Tempe that he was the only one last year that didn't get sick, that he had the perfect equilibrium for it. I made my way outside. From the railing I could see the trees of Canada. The fresh air made me feel better. Fin was the one who had a different room. He was out there, smoking. He smiled at me.

"How do you like it, man?"
I nodded and threw up over the side when I smelled his cigarette.
"Go see Kurt. He's the temporary medic. He'll give you some pills."
Down in the dry room the lifers were in there smoking. They were at sea eight months out of the year. They were older. I walked in and asked them where to find Kurt. They laughed at me. I held onto a locker and cursed them.
"Yeah. It's really funny. Motherfuckers."
They stopped laughing. I didn't care. One of them studied me for a while. He got up and moved on me. I couldn't let go of the locker. I watched him coming. He was shorter but full of muscle and tattoos. He had a shaved head. I put him at about 32 years old. If he knocked me out at least I would rest. He put his arm over my shoulder and took the smoke from his mouth and held it. I would learn that his name was Stu, and that he was a real nutcase.
"Look, man. Kurt's gonna lay some pink pills on you or give you these Wonder Woman bracelets to wear. Don't take them. Go back to your rack and fight it out naturally. Do not take the pills. Let yourself adjust."
He looked around the room. He had a gruff, hoarse voice.
"Am I right, boys?"
They agreed. One of them spoke from behind a chili dog,
"Every new fuckhead on this boat is taking his drams. They will become dependent on that shit until they hit land again. Be a man. Take the pain."
Stu pulled on my chin hairs.
"And we wouldn't want you to be sick so we couldn't kick the shit out of you later, honey."
I knocked him away. They roared. Stu slapped me on the back.
"I'm just fuckin' with ya. Jesus. Here man, seriously."
He put his hand out. I looked around and took it slowly.
"See, there ya go. Sleep it off, man."
I walked back through the galley toward the stairs. Their laughter rode upon my back all the way to my bed. I laid back in the dark. Every few minutes someone from the room would get up and run out to the toilet. I closed my eyes and went with the movement of the boat.
I woke up sweating a day later. I was soaked. Every ounce of my body was thirsty, and the room smelled of vomit. I walked out into the hallway and looked around. I jumped up and landed. I spun a fast circle and stopped suddenly. I stuck my mouth under the sink in the bathroom and drank. I was totally normal. I walked outside and inhaled the sea air. It tasted fine. It was dark out. Down in the galley I wrote in my tablet. I was aware of Stu watching a movie on the VCR but I

didn't look at him. I began a paragraph about the Canadian coast.
"Watcha writin' over there, Bob? Memoirs or something?"
"What?"
"That's my nickname for you, man: Dinosaur Bob."
"Why?"
"It just is."
He walked the bench and plopped in front of me. I closed the tablet.
"How you feelin', Dinosaur?"
"Sound advice. Thank you."
I shook his hand. He was pleased with himself. He asked me where I was from. I told him I had grown up in Arizona.
"No shit? A desert rat."
"You got it."
"I was fuckin' a girl from Mesa. You know where that is?"
"I've been there."
"Is it nice?"
"No."
"Huh. Neither was she. A real whore, you know?"
He looked around the galley and spoke quietly.
"Hey, Dinosaur. You ain't got no herb, do ya?"
"No."
"Shit. You struck me as the type."
"I get that a lot."
He reached into his pocket and pulled out a couple of small spray cans.
"You wanna have some fun, Dinosaur?"
I read the cans: FART SPRAY. I knew he was testing me, he wanted to see how uptight I was. I thought about everyone in their racks tossing around, their bodies feeling heavy and green and glued down.
"Sure."
He took a side of the hall and I took a side. In turn, we sprayed every room and closed the doors, every room except mine and his. One by one, each person got sicker and ran for the toilet. He grabbed the can from me and ran out the back, chucking them over the port side.
We sat out there. He told me that this was his twelfth season out. Fin came out back and asked him for a smoke. Stu had already given him a nickname while I was sleeping. Stu saw him and laughed, "Heeeey. Creepy. What's shakin', Creepy?"
Fin rolled his buggly eyes at me. I smiled at the pack as he pulled one out. It turned out that Fin was assigned to Stu's room. I thought about it. Stu was too

intense to room with. I thought about Fin being in bed worrying about getting some little fucking prank pulled on him while he slept. Stu smoked his cigarette fast and ran inside, just like that. Fin watched him go.

"He's sleeps directly over me and he jerks off constantly and talks to himself while he does it."

I laughed.

"I thought it was funny, too. For the first five minutes."

I pictured the whole scene. It was good.

"And he calls me baby and honey pot and pinches my ass. I need to move out."

He asked me if I wanted to trade rooms. I said hell no. We went back inside and sat in the galley.

After a few days the people were coming alive and eating slowly. I made friends with Andy, a long, long haired ex- Mormon from Tempe who sang and played guitar. There was Ben from Hudson, Wisconsin, who had red hair and played the harmonica. Then there was Ian, a chunky, balding kid with a pony tail who could balance anything on his chin, and I mean anything. There was Reggie, who really went by Ricky, who was an older black guy and who cut hair on the boat for extra cash. He was my favorite. He was always cheerful. He had a big stomach and a cigarette burning constantly beneath his mustache. It was impossible not to like him, especially when he asked one of the Tempe jocks for a smoke but refused it because it was a light cigarette. He said only pussies smoked lights. I sat back and thought about it. He was right.

On the sixth day out the Chef named it Caribbean night and made Caribbean food. I had heard horror stories about those boats. I was told we had the best one. I was lucky that I wasn't stuck with a group of hardened criminals and rapists. There were boats like that. This was a younger crowd, apart from the lifers who were not going up there to work with us. We were to hook up to a bigger processing ship which had already been out for four months and work with them, on the actual company boat. Our boat now was the boat of the lifers. We were just staying on it for that particular season. Stu said we were all lucky, that no other boat had a soft yogurt machine and daily showers and a big television. He was proud of the boat and his life. I thought that if I were someone like Stu I'd be proud as well. He was a walking, angry cartoon.

The next night was a talent show. The first prize was one hundred dollars. Second and third got nothing. Ian was taking bets on his victory. I sat down to watch the show. The Chef announced they were one contestant short. The other 49 of us were quiet. Stu's hoarse voice came over the crowd and found me like a bullet. He was shouting.

"Hey, Dinosaur Bob! Read us some fucking poetry!"
I sat still. Stu jumped up on the table and pointed at me.
"Dinosaur's a writer! Come on, BOB! Don't be a pussy!"
Everybody was egging me on and cheering. They really wanted the show to happen. I shook my head. They started booing me. I liked it. Even the Chef and the Captain were yelling at me to join the show. Stu ran upstairs and ran back down and tossed me the tablet he had seen me writing in. I'd had on my bed, and he told me that if I didn't read for the show, then he would find a way to make me regret it. Everybody laughed because they knew I had to either cave in and read or endure something disgusting. I wasn't afraid to stand my ground against Stu, but I didn't want to have to worry about what kind of sick shit he would pull on me, either. I only had six pages or so written, about the trees of Canada and the trip from Arizona that brought me to them. I knew I didn't have a chance at winning the money and I also knew some people would be mad at me if I read it.

The show started. Ian bombed on his last balancing trick when the chair on top of the chair on top of that chair kept falling down. He really wanted to win, well, he kind of had to now. He'd bet a lot of people. I wondered if the judges would cut him some slack since he did his whole act at sea while the floor was rocking. Stu and one of his buddies did a Bugs Bunny/Elmer Fudd hunting skit, where Elmer shot and sodomized the rabbit. I wanted that one to win. Andy sang a song about the boat and strummed his guitar. He was good. I wasn't expecting him to be good. It was my turn. The Chef was the announcer and he said it was time for some culture. Stu suggested loudly that Andy play guitar while I read. Everyone cheered. He sat behind me. I looked back at him. He put his palms out. I shrugged at him and shook my head. He laughed. The room settled down. I read the story slowly. Andy picked up on it and fit the mood exactly. Every now and then I would glance up and see the faces. They were most serious. Some had their eyes closed, trying to picture it. The story ended and everybody was silent. Then they grew into an orchestra of applause. It rose and rose and they yelled. Andy smiled and nodded at me.
Stu was screaming for more:
"Fucking encore that shit, Dinosaur!"
I couldn't take it. I put my arms up and sat down. There were a few more people. The Chef and the Captain and Kurt were the judges. Andy sat next to me,
"Jesus Christ. I didn't know you could write."
I looked around.
"I've never read out loud like that."
Andy won hands down. I actually came in second. Ian took sixth and it de-

pressed him for days. I never thought I would get second place at a talent show in the middle of the Bering Sea. I couldn't help but feel proud. Then the storm came.

The boat was rocking so bad you could run up and down the door frames. People like to imagine the ocean as being blue and beautiful. I used to imagine it that way. When you're that far out at sea the water is black. Day or night it is black and deadly looking, like obsidian in slow motion. Black as far as you could see. The boat was small, anyway. We were going side to side like the boat was plastic. Everyone was grabbing their survival suits. Some were crying and some were scribbling down their wills. I laid in my rack and drank from the flask. Let them fire my corpse. I sat back and thought how it figured that I would end out there. I masturbated one last time, emptied the flask and closed my eyes. If the boat capsized then their survival suits were useless. The boat crashed through the swells and you could hear the waves roaring into the sides. My last thought before I made myself sleep was Helena.

It was calm and dark. I didn't know what to expect. There was no light or movement. I heard nothing. I reached out and pulled the curtain back and stood in the dark. Then I felt it, a gentle rocking beneath my feet. I walked to the door and went outside.

It was warm out there. I was shirtless. The sun sat dark red on the horizon and it was huge. You could look right at it. The black water stretched out far to reach it. I breathed in and held the handrail, watched the horizon melt around the sun. How small we were against the grace of the heavens. Our petty dreams, our need for self. Our weak assurances.

I was the only one out there. I saw a whale emerge from the water and twist out there in front of the red. It hung there upside down in front of the sun, it hung there careless and lazy, totally oblivious to us, to the human refuse of the boat, sacrificing our luck and lives for a goddamned dollar. It went back through and my heart swelled in my chest so fast that it cracked my bones. Something happened to me which I could not understand. I wept. I stood there and wept at the beauty of what I saw. I wept when I thought that the moment was meant for me and me alone, as I so badly wanted it to be that way. I so badly wanted to be chosen by God there, to be pulled out amongst the clean cold blackness of the water, to stand naked on the back of a whale before the harmlessness of a sun which was now trained for damage. I wanted that scene, I wanted to be transcended into that scene forever. I wanted everything to be beautiful again. I wanted to be beautiful again.

I never told anybody about the whale. That day we circled the Aleutian Islands and headed inward over Alaska's horn. It was the first land we had seen in over a week. They were dead, white capped volcanoes atop small isles. It was unlike anything I had seen in the contiguous states. It was a completely different planet. We were up there now, during the six months of light. We were on the southern end of Alaska, so the sun would only fade out for about 40 minutes, then jump back up. It was strange to see broad daylight at three in the morning.

The boat slowed into the bay and set anchor next to the processor. A plank was drawn and secured. That day in the Galley, the lady who hired us was choppered in and she introduced us to the main foremen. They were both young with attitudes. They had already been at sea for four months and they were salty. Their eyes sunk into us like dirty teeth into clean food. We had to walk the plank and sit for the main medic's lecture, listen to him spew out bullshit about him being able to recognize us by our coughs within a week. He talked about how filthy the fish were. He said that if a scale would reach into a slice on our fingers then it was possible to lose the whole hand. A lot of what he said sounded dramatic. I didn't like his eyes. They were beady and they peered at you over a fat, hairy face. He went on about the billions of tons of salmon:

"Never will you see so many fish..."

The time was kept by military hours out there. Everything was O' this hundred and O' that hundred. There were three shifts: B, C, and D. The first day we were observed to see what we were best at doing. The top floor of the factory was the slime line, where the fish were sucked up through large tubes from the small catching boats and dumped on a conveyor belt, which fed them into the first couple of workers who straightened them out and stuck them on pegs, before they went under the front of the machine that cut the heads off. I didn't want that job, having to stand across from the same person, doing the same thing they did. I made sure I did a lousy job. All of the machines were loud, right in your ear. The machines were everywhere.

After they were decapitated, the fish moved down to the workers who stood on both sides of the belt and sliced their bellies open and pulled their guts out. The guts plopped into gutters, which tubed down to the next floor to be sorted through for the eggs. After the fish were gutted they moved down the line where more workers held these suction tubes shaped like spoons and scraped the spine and sucked it clean. At the end of the line before the chute that sent them down, two or four more workers sucked the spines again. At the end of that hell stood the fattest man I had ever seen. Frog.

The fish dropped to the level below where they came out in bulk. One guy had to set them head first down that belt, which ran opposite of the slime line. Down that line the fish were graded. We were shown how to spot an A, B, or C fish, by the water Marks and damage. Slot D was for the mutilated fish and the chum. At the end of that line, the fish were weighed and dropped also according to weight. Usually, the weight and the grade were similar. Any of the huge King Salmon picked up by the nets were saved for the meals or Captains. I would see one eventually. It was the size of a small shark. Back away from the scales was the roe table, where the guts came down and you had to quickly separate the eggs from the rest of the guts. One side, the sperm sack, heart, liver, all of it, was tunneled down into the grinder for fish food, and the other side was for the eggs, where they were gently tunneled down into the egg tent on a smaller boat and mixed softly by hand.

Once the fish were graded, they were dropped downstairs to case-up, where they were set upon trays in racks that were carted to the walk-in freezers. Once they were frozen, they were pulled out for two guys who stood in front of the line down there, banged the frozen fish loose and sent them down another belt which moved in the same direction of the slime line two floors up. Two people stood in front of an air machine and held the plastic bags in front of it to open them quickly and they bagged the fish. Workers on both sides of the belt had scales and they had to place a box on the scale and fill it to a certain amount specified by different cards that were displayed, describing which grade were coming down and the size. When you got the weight right, you put the box back on the belt. Down the line it was checked and marked and weighed again before it was set on a different conveyor belt, which ran up the side of the boat and out onto a deck, where the off-loader had to chimney stack the boxes on a pallet, net the pallet, then finger bang the crane to take it away, over the rail and onto our boat. From there the Japanese took what they bought.

You had to double shift one job, and then for the remaining hours, go somewhere else until you were released for your six hours off. You had a few 10 minute breaks and two half hour lunches, when you had to strip off your four layers of gloves, your raingear, your boots, sit down and eat then run back to supply for new earplugs and gloves. One large pain in the ass. There were no such things as Sundays or sick days or anything up there. As long as the fish were coming you were hard at it, and there were billions and billions of tons of fish. You could not be sick unless the medic proclaimed you as being sick, which meant you had to be nearly dead and unable to move.

We went back to the boat and sat in the galley. They would have our schedules done by the end of the day, and some of us would have to start immediately. We were free to walk the other boat in the meantime. A lot of them were shelter kids and trailer park people, and they were basically hateful. There were a lot of teeth missing on the other boat, a lot of chewing tobacco and creeps.

Andy, Ben and I walked the work boat. It was like crossing over into Gallup from the Petrified Forest. It was a human jungle. We were the new guys from next door, and the entire 60 of us would have to be placed in their pecking order. Their galley was dank and dark and it smelled like mold. The whole boat had a lingering taste of urine. We walked around in our shorts and t-shirts and watched them. They were there, waiting for us. These were our finest hours, when they couldn't touch us. Andy and Ben threw their attitude back at them, but I would walk by and nod to them. Those two didn't realize they'd pay.

Three hours later, a Japanese tramper set anchor next to our boat. I learned that Japan was mere days away by water and we were working for the Japanese. They paid millions for the product. A pallet of the eggs alone cost them 35 grand. There I was, seven miles from land I could barely see, sandwiched between Japan and northern Texas.

I sat up on the top level outside and watched the Japanese scurry about their boat. Stu was down in the pit under the open deck, stacking crates of ropes and nets. He spotted me:

"HEY, BOB!"

I waved to him. He scampered up the wall and ran to the pole and climbed it all the way up to where I was sitting. No stairs for him. He was hanging by both of his hands from the high ledge where I sat. He looked up at me and smiled, beneath him was a long drop, at least to a broken leg. If I would have left he would have been fucked.

"Gimme your hand, Bob."

I pulled him up. He hopped over the rail and sat next to me, and we watched the Japanese. He shook his head,

"Hardcore little fuckers, man."

He pointed to them, "Those pricks are out for two years sometimes. They live for this shit, it's like their fucking duty or some shit."

"Really?"

"Oh, yeah. Some of them even turn to each other for sex out here. They live and breathe and sleep and eat and shit the industry."

"Insane."

He put his palms together and bucked his front teeth, "Much ah, honor, Dinosaur

March of Time and Skin

Bob, son."

He reached into his pocket and pulled out a silver rope which he had made into a wristband. It was heavy and thick. I looked at it.

"You made that?"

"Oh, fuck yes. I sell these."

"Nice."

"Five bucks."

"Impossible."

He spun it around his finger, "I gotta ask you something, Bob."

"What?"

"There's this girl. She lives in Kansas. And I got his thing for her. She has this dorky ass boyfriend. I want to send her a letter, you know, a sexy letter to make her hot, to show her who her daddy is."

I fought back the laughter. He breathed and continued.

"But I ain't too good with words, you know what I'm sayin', so I thought if-"

"I'll do it. Just give me her name and a rough outline of the relationship."

"I'll give you ten bucks."

"Make me one of those wristbands instead."

He liked that.

"Hey, there ya go. My talent for your talent."

He told me the story. I said I'd have it ready in a while. Then I said not to worry, that no one would know. He told me I was all right. He handed me the wristband. I told him I wanted a new one, one made especially for the trade.

I crouched against the wall in my rack and wrote his letter. I kept it under two pages because I knew he would have to copy it. I kept it basic and dark and shocking and psychotic, with an edge of latent obsession. I was through with it in about ten minutes. I took a nap.

In the dry room I found his locker and stuffed the letter between the vent holes. The schedules were posted. I had to work immediately. They made me a grader.

I was in the back straightening the fish as they piled down. Once in a while I got one they had missed, the head snapped and twisted, an eye dangling, the orange flesh breaking out of the neck. Soon I was covered in it.

The clock moved slowest in there. I would look at the clock and look at it again an hour later and it had only moved three minutes. I stood there for five hours, shuffling fish. We got a coffee break for ten minutes. I walked outside and watched the bay. It was one of the few moments when it was dusk and all of the lights of the boats in the bay were flashing. There were other processors out there from other

115

companies and a lot of catching boats. The lights illuminated the bay and made it look like a small city. The boss blew his little whistle and we were back in there. I felt sorry for him. He was a little man with heavy bags under his eyes. His job was to stand there and watch us. In that room was a large window in which the quality control people sat and sometimes the higher-ups when they choppered in. They would sit in the office and drink coffee and watch us. It made us feel low.

The sunsets up there were devastating, unreal. Colors that can not be described. They were so beautiful they looked fake. I felt like I could reach out and poke them with my finger and they would crumble down into the water, revealing the usual ugliness. They didn't last long where we were and I felt that my breaks and lunches were timed for them.

We never quite slept. Everyone in the room had a different shift, so there was always some disturbance. The wake up calls were the worst, this fat laundry girl from the work boat making sure I was awake before she left.
"Get up, now, get up, come on, you're not up yet..."
One day during a break I talked to her outside. It was a plan of mine to ask her to skip over my rack. Wake-ups came twenty minutes before your shift and I had an alarm clock. She was fat and ugly and mean. She liked to wake us up. The talk did no good.

I worked my double as a zombie in the grading room and spent my remaining hours folding boxes in an open room on the offload deck. They would call up for boxes from a chute in the room and I would send them down. I watched a redneck load the pallets. He wasn't wearing raingear and he could listen to music. It was nice out there, sunny and warm. Fin had lucked into the egg tent with a few of the Arizona boys. They stood around and talked, swirling their hands around the barrel. That was their job. Andy was on the top deck outside, sorting through the fish that came out of the chutes from the catching boats, organizing their size for beheading. Ben was just inside of him, on the slime line. They were given boring jobs, working inches from the guys to who they'd thrown attitude. When I would walk by during my lunch and see them in there I would laugh at them. They threw me hostile looks, and sometimes the finger. During the few moments when we would cross each other's path, or got lucky enough to catch a break at the same time, we would talk about what we were going to do back in the world. None of us were sure. Ian was one of the pounders who shook them loose downstairs. The other Arizona boys worked the scales down there.

After the first week we were hardening, getting mean. One time the wake up girl came in and told me to get up. I told her I would get up if she left. She was getting loud with me and I was tired. I could see her silhouette after she yanked my curtain back. I slept naked in my rack because it was the only way to keep my sheets somewhat free of the smell of fish. She looked me over quickly and told me to sit up. I closed the curtain. She jerked it open again and started barking commands. I reached around and found my shoe and held it back. She turned and began waddling toward the door. I thought the hell with it and threw it. It hit her big ass. She shrieked and bounced out. I laid back down. The guys in the racks above and around me laughed tiredly.

I punched in two minutes late. The two foremen were in the dry room. They asked me why I was late. They were punks. They only worked twelve hours and they had their own rooms with televisions. They had these smiles. They didn't have real jobs. They walked around. One of them told the other that he thought I would like tank diving. He looked at me. I liked the way it sounded. Tank diving. I thought of diving under the water in full scuba gear, doing some kind of repair or freeing a snagged net, touching sea life. The youngest one nodded at me.

"You're tank divin' today."

"Sure." I was excited. It pissed them off.

Tank diving. Rubber pants up to your chest in the hole of a catching boat shoveling rotted fish into the grinder. Up to your hips in them. It turned out that the youngest foreman was fucking the laundry girl. I knew I'd find politics out there sooner or later.

I quickly understood why we had such a good cook. The best food was needed for this job. Everything you owned smelled like fish, regardless of where you had it on the boat. You never completely got used to it. Dreams on the still water were different, more supernatural. Life on the still water was still abnormal, since the ground was always shifting. Two weeks passed. Then three weeks. I began to think that this was my new life, that I was never getting out of there. We all thought that. We had 45 days of work left.

I became close to people on the boat who back in the world I would never consent to know. We looked out for each other, covered each other. When I had to work the slime line next to Ricky and his hand cramped, I took on his share. Downstairs when I was off a pound for my weight, Ben would toss me a rotted fish from the floor and I would seal the box quickly. We all found ways to duck the order and work in different areas. As long as we were working fast. There were so many workers, yet the two punks had me singled out. They were on me constantly. The Japanese were everywhere, watching you move. They were compulsive. The machines were louder and louder. In most factories when a machine broke down you had to stop. Not there. You immediately found something to do otherwise you were tank diving.

Frog took a fondness toward me. He was such a fat blob. When he sat in the break room his stomach pushed out and hung over his knees. One day after I had accidentally spit on the heads of the foremen from the top floor I had to work the slime line all day. Frog and I sat in the break room and drank coffee. He was the king of the slime line. He truly took pleasure in watching his workers suffer. He mostly left me alone. We sat and rested. He nodded to me.

"You're a good worker. Keep it up, I started out just like you."
I nodded back, "But you also ended up just like you."
Frog's game was trading punches. He was all blubber, so you couldn't hurt him. He hit me hard. I held my arm and called him a fucker. He leaned back and tightened his arm, "Come on, come on. Show me what you got..."
I brought it up from the floor and hit his arm with everything I had. He tapped his arm, "Not bad."
He blew his whistle and everyone outside ran for the line. I was reaching down for my gloves when he really let me have it, in the same arm. It dropped me to one knee on the floor. I looked up to see him padding out the door as fast as he could, cackling. I couldn't get him back until we were off the clock, but by then I didn't care.

One day I was folding boxes for the boys downstairs when the older of the two foremen came out and sent the redneck to a catching boat. The other foreman came out and they talked and looked at me with much evil.

"Hey, Stephen King! Get over here!" One of them said. They laughed.
I walked over. I looked them up and down,
"You guys are good. You should take that shit to the stage."
They had these perpetually stupid looks on their faces.
"That's enough. You think you can offload, Hemingway?"
They laughed again.I shook my head at them,
"You two are hilarious. How do you land on your material?"
"Look, freak. Can you do it or not?"
"I can do it."
"Good. You're an off-loader. Startin' tomorrow. Until then, tankdive."

Sons of bitches. They made me tank dive through my lunch. I got the last laugh, though, because the substitute off-loader was on B and I was on D, so after his double shift, that gave me four extra hours to sleep.

I loved the job. I wore my street clothes and I was outside all day. I listened to music. It was considered the hardest job on the boat. Boxes full of frozen fish off the belt and in your arms quickly. The belt had various speeds and after my first two hours I was doing a better job than the redneck. I was full of bruises from finding a method, but once I found it I ran with it. I was loading the pallets faster than they could throw them on the belt. I could have a pallet loaded before the crane operator swung the boom back over with the old net.

This bothered the moron brothers. I would have five minutes in between the loads. They started having the workers set the belt speed for maximum after the belt was full. I just picked it up a bit and went faster. This gave me even more time between hauls. Word had already gotten around to the main men about my speed and the foremen had to go back to the way it was before with the conveyor. They still had me after my double shift. It was the slime line or the tank. Then I talked to their foreman, a partner of the company, into letting me switch onto the C shift, when the foremen were off during my remaining hours. I had to pull a triple shift to match the time difference, but it was worth it. Now I would off load and walk right over and fold boxes. But I could feel them devising plans against me behind my back.

A lot of people were sent out to fold boxes while I worked. I liked it when Ricky or Ben were sent out there. We would actually get to have some fun. But usually, the foremen would send a grubby little spy to watch me and report back to them. Whenever they sent a mutant from that boat to fold boxes I worked even faster. Time went by fast out there. I had it made. I now knew how the toughest prisoner felt in the yard, how it felt to live in the coldest layer in hell.

We had two weeks left. Ricky had been having a fling with an older laundry lady on the work boat, and he was more cheerful than ever. One day I was bitching to him about getting busted back to grading since the foreman gave the redneck his job back offloading, after he started a fight with one of the Hawaiians on their boat. I was bumped back to the D shift, and I was back in their clutches. When I tried to duck the slime line and head down to the scales they made me tank dive. I was bitching to Ricky endlessly over lunch. He put his arm around me.

"You wanna know what I think? I think fuck em'. I'm makin' money."

He was right. I felt stupid for getting mad over it. It was only a week more. I could take anything for a week. I went to my locker to put my tablet away. Next to my boots sat the wristband Stu had owed me for weeks. I wanted to ask him how he got past the lock, but I didn't care. I put it on and went back across.

Time was a blur anymore. One hour or eighteen hours held no differences. I was down in case-up one day when we heard the whistle from the staircase. It was Stu: "EVERYBODY WHO' S STAYIN' ON THE SPEEDWAY PUNCH OUT NOW! WE PULL ANCHOR IN TEN MINUTES!"

I looked at Ben. The Speedway was our boat. We were leaving. The mutants watched us run up the staircase. They had a three week trip back. One of the engines on the work boat had blown.

We ran up and looked for Andy. He was already gone. I punched out and ran by Frog, delivering a hard hit to his arm. I got him. He wasn't ready. Everybody on our boat was cheering. Over on the workboat the mutants stood against the rails and watched us. Eggs began flying at the work boat, and they hit the mutants and broke onto them, and it gave us back a few things that were robbed from us. The eggs came from the Captain's room. Stu. He didn't work for anybody over there. They couldn't touch him.

We had a new Captain and since he was lacking his Celestial license he had to stay within a certain range of the coast, which meant the trip back would take a few extra days. Because of the way my rack was facing, I was now rocking side to side. We all had a long sleep and the side to side motion wasn't bad because it was different. The trip back was boring. I mostly hung out in Andy and Ben's room and we played cards. After the first week we were climbing the walls. I caught up in the journals and I was now writing in them from day to day. I missed my typewriter. I missed my bike and I missed having sex. I missed having options. I still missed her.

I decided I would buy a van and head down to Phoenix. Andy wanted to ride with me. Ben was going to stay in Seattle for two weeks. The days at sea wore on and on. Soon it was getting dark again. Soon it was the trees of Canada.

Ben was waking me.

"Get up, man. We're here, we made it."

I ran out. There was Seattle, off in the water. We had to wait for an hour on a drawbridge repair. We were seeing cars and buildings and highway again. The city was almost holy looking.

We twisted around an inlet, where the boat stopped near the warehouse and was tied off. A ladder was joined. The lady who hired us came up with our draw money. We were getting four hundred dollars until the next day when we could pick up our checks. She said there would be a drawing to decide who would stay and offload. Andy and Ben and I made a pact that if one of us would have to offload the others would volunteer. They were chosen. I was not. They went upstairs to their room to change clothes. I looked out at the city and the water and the road. None of us had drank a beer since we stepped foot on the boat. I thought about twelve more hours. I thought about fish, then about the city. I ran upstairs.

"Hey, guys. Sorry, she won't let me work since I on-loaded in the beginning, plus they're full up."

The guys were cool about it. I ran back to my room and grabbed my backpack. I felt bad for leaving them hanging. Then it passed. I grabbed my money and walked out of that motherfucker. I walked the ladder. I had already seen a few people hit the ground with their sea legs and stumble. I was the last one off the ladder. I stood there for a minute before I stepped off. I had been dreaming of this day all summer. I jumped to the ground. It was like having jumped on a trampoline for hours then landing on pavement. Some people knelt and kissed the ground. I jumped into a cab.

15

I sat downtown in the bar while Grant served me for free. I sat there and drank. I was rugged, bearded. I was looking at the people who had not seen the sunrise in the Bering Sea. I smelled like fish. I became drunk, telling this woman next to me about Alaska. I stepped over the line and stuck my tongue in her mouth. She walked out. I drank until I could physically drink no longer and left Grant a fifty. I laid out in the alley and looked up at the windows, obsessing over the fact that they were liquid. I passed out.

A cop kicked me awake. I stood while he ran my license. I told him I had just come back from Alaska. He told me to move along. It was still early. I walked up Second and paid for a room at the Moore. It was weird laying on a solid bed. I saw the crew on the boat. Everyone blurred sideways and I was gone.

After the warehouse, Ben drove Andy and I to the bank downtown. They had just finished off loading when I stepped out of the cab. We were the first ones to get our checks. The teller was an asshole.

"Sir, how would you like this cashed? Do you wish to open an account with us today?"

"Cash in hand, please."

He took my license. Then he took my social security card.

"Sir, do you have any other form of picture identification..."

"Cash the check, please. Now."

He didn't want to. I had always looked like a criminal to people like him. A manager was called and the company was called. They were out of excuses. The little twerp was laying hundred after hundred in my palm. It killed him.

"Come on. Keep it coming, twinkles."

He laid the last hundred out and bitterly told me to have a nice day. I folded the roll and shoved it in my pocket. I nodded at him.

"Nicer than yours, that's for sure."

Ben and Andy had no problem cashing theirs. Soon a bunch of us from the boat were at the bank. Some of them cashed their checks, then no one could. The company had to put more money in the next day.

We stood out in front of the bank and talked, shook hands, said goodbye. Ricky was going to set himself up in a hotel until his laundry woman came back and they were going to stay there for a night of hot ass, as he put it. Andy, Ben and I stuck together and walked around Seattle. It was similar to Midtown in New York City in the way that you could walk anywhere within an hour.

Andy's sister was living on Queen Anne Hill, and we stayed there that night. His sister was still in the faith. Her roommate was a tall, meaty chestnut goddess. Andy's girl. She walked around in these tight white shorts and when she bent over the counter to grab the phone or write something down she reminded me of a prize mare. She was another Mormon renegade, though once Andy had bitched to us that she wouldn't let him fuck her. She was still brainwashed. He slept in there with her, but in the morning when she walked out and saw Ben and I on the balcony watching the city, she would return the greeting with a sheepish wave, like she was embarrassed about sleeping in the same bed with him. I thought about how sickening religion was. It stuck with people forever. Ben watched her walk back to the room.

"Damn."

We watched the traffic. Ben mentioned that it was weird yesterday, seeing the crew in the real world, other people walking around them.

"Would you ever go back up?" He asked me.

"No."

I had everyone's address in one of my notebooks but I knew I wouldn't write them.

Andy's girl went to work and his sister was weird about letting us stay there when she was gone. She wouldn't go to work until we left. That was Ben's fault. He had to introduce himself as Joseph Smith. We went down to Mercer and sat in the Streamliner. Ben took a bus to get his car and Andy and I drank while I looked around in the paper for a van.

We parked by the ferry and bought our passes. The van was in Whidbey Island. I bought it. It was expensive, but I wanted it, a 72 Ford, light blue, sub-nose, pop top, bed in back, clean as hell. I drove by Jared's grandparents' but no one was around. Up near the water Ben took pictures of us in the van. I opened the doors, the windows, popped the top in front of the woods and water there in the Washington summer. I still had money, and the thought of going back to the desert for the heat became stupid. I drove off the ferry and Ben followed me in his car. I told Andy that I didn't want to go back, that I wanted to stay in the Northwest until winter. That night we parked in the college district, the U District, and we slept in the van. That morning we ate breakfast, and Ben walked next door to get his rolls developed from the boat.

I'd never had a camera or taken pictures. Looking at the photos, hundreds of them, was sad in a way. Now we were back in society and the clock was ticking again. Andy bagged out for Tempe to get together with his old band. Ben took off to go camping in the Olympic Mountains and I looked for a place to live.

16

I paid rent for a basement in West Seattle. The people who rented the space were only in town for the summer. I had my own bathroom, my own kitchen and entrance. Two hundred and seventy five dollars a month. No deposit. The lady who rented it to me said they were having trouble finding a taker since there was no phone line and the floors were concrete. There was a desk down there, a mighty Oak. There was a couch and a stereo system and a pool table. I didn't need a phone. I paid her for six months up front. I liked the space. It was dark and I could hear nothing. The upstairs of the house was sealed off from the basement. Then she sold me a small refrigerator for thirty bucks. That day I went out and bought some crude necessities for the kitchen, some bath towels and so forth.

November washed in. The couple was gone. It rained solid for weeks on end. My bike and typewriter had arrived from Phoenix along with the journals. I had met one girl and I stuck with her for a couple of months. She worked two jobs and went to college and I only saw her twice a week. It was perfect. I met her when I was on 4th buying paper, where she worked as a cashier. She sold me a computer and gave me her number. I had never thought about using a computer. It wasn't expensive. I had a monitor and a keyboard and a small printer. It was a used system and I got it for just under three hundred dollars. I was leery about using it. I was used to the banging of the keys from the manuals I had picked up and from my electric. But I was more concerned with substance.

I grew to love that screen. It was magical, pure concentration. The only things I didn't like to use it for were the short pieces. I wrote my days away in that unreal darkness, under the shield of heavy, grey rain. I had it made. Lisa came by twice a week and stayed over. She had a body. She found me intriguing, for some reason. I had her around for sex, but I had learned how to be tactful, what to say and what not to say with women. All I had to do was deal with some conversation, some jokes, some understanding. Then she would let me fuck her and she would be out of there for another five days.

I had no clock. I figured I had enough money to live on for at least four more months. Down there I wrote compulsively. Lisa would bring over incense from her second job and the place smelled of coconuts dipped in wet concrete. There was always coffee ready. I would lean over the keys and write, leaning back in my leather chair, watching the sweet smoke climb the damp walls, reading my words. I was a king. I was so far away from hard death, so far away from the labor fields and the fights and the poorness and the disgust. I thought I had really made it.

Lisa had skipped her usual first night. I wasn't aware of it since I wasn't aware of time down there. I wrote in long shifts. Sometimes I would sleep for a few hours, from how I could judge it, then I was back at the machine. Sometimes I would sleep in excess and write for just a while. I was always reading my work. Whenever I got burned out I would take my bike out in the rain and ride in the parking garage down California St. or I shot some pool. I'd lost touch with Grant, and Jared and his lady were MIA.

Lisa walked down and woke me up in the morning, saying she was sorry she'd missed last night. She told me that she had met another guy and that he wanted her to be with him, that he had goals and he was well off with a nice house. I told her to go for it. She was upset. She wanted me to get angry or worried. I told her that life is a motherfucker and people had to go with what made them comfortable. She stormed up the stairs. Apart from a few more nights of her popping by to repair her ego, I never heard from her again. Beyond that, when the compulsion for sex struck me I walked down to 7 eleven and bought a porn mag. At least the pictures of them were honest. I could wipe out my desires within minutes and get back to what was real: writing. I had long since tired of ridiculous little games. I wanted no part.

February came. I mailed out two months rent to the couple in Florida. Apart from my weekly walk to 7 eleven for supplies I had not touched civilization, I had no television and I didn't listen to radio. I was doing real work down there. I was creating. I was not working for some asshole and I was not punching a clock or dealing with morons doing the same thing. I wasn't at the movies with my girlfriend. I wasn't hanging out with friends and barstool buddies. That was for the rest of them. I had seriously developed a hatred for the outside world.

I had to breakdown and leave my basement for a printer cartridge. I went ahead and bought a few of them. I drove back down the freeway in the rain. The rain was starting to bother me. It had rained for five months. It was strange getting out of there, craving sunlight out of nowhere. I suddenly missed the desert, intensely. I had so many pages backed up to print, and I couldn't put it off anymore. So I drove in the rain, back to my palace, the rain gnawing on the windshield, beating against the wipers and my brain. It was like piss.

I saw three figures on the shoulder of the freeway. They were dressed in garbage bags, and they stood next to duffel bags and suitcases. They looked like grim reapers. I calculated them and decided they were harmless. I pulled over and honked. They ran at me in the rearview. I reached back and unlocked the side door. One by one I saw the luggage fly in. Then there was this head coming out of a garbage bag. It was beard and teeth. He sighed.

"Fuck, man. Thanks for stopping. We've been out here for three hours."
I nodded to the rearview. Then the other two piled in. I told them to be sure to slam the door otherwise it wouldn't latch. The shorter one sat back in a corner by the bed, silent. The two who had spoken were around my age. The bigger one took the passenger seat. The one in the back finally looked up and around. A short, fat girl. She breathed deeply.

"Ahh, shelter. Fucking shelter!"
The guy next to me nodded.
"Appreciate it, dude. Seriously."
He stared over Harbor Island.
"Man. We just got off the boat. Alaska. Fuckers gave us some draw money and they just told us that they'd mail the checks to us. Six to eight weeks." I looked in the mirror at the other one. He sat against the door, his arms around his knees, looking up to a picture I had on the wall, a National Geographic photo of a vulture standing in back of a baby in Africa, watching the baby crouch in the dirt, dying. I asked the guy next to me where they were headed.

"Austin. How far you going?"
"Two more miles." I laughed. I couldn't help it. The girl groaned. The other guy

kept looking at the photograph.

"The photographer who took that committed suicide sometime after." I said.

The guy next to me took off his jacket. His arms were covered in tattoos. He looked back to the picture.

"Gnarly."

I told them I would get them down to Tacoma. The guy next to me told me his name was Nick, then he told about Alaska.

"I've heard it's beautiful up there," I said.

"Oh, man. The sunsets. You would not believe how amazing they were."

"Any sea life?"

"Lots of sea lions. We fed one at Dutch Harbor."

"Nice."

The girl ran her hand over the blanket on the bed.

"Ohhh. A bed, comfort, warmth..."

She looked at me from the floor.

"Go ahead." I said.

"No. I couldn't."

Nick turned in his seat and spoke, sharply.

"Lana. You fucking WHINE about everything. You drop a hint, the man takes it, and offers you a bed. You'd better take him up on it. It's a long way back home." He turned in his seat.

"Sorry."

"Don't worry about it. Your family?"

"She's my little brother's girlfriend. He's locked up. Craig here's my buddy from Dallas. Went to school together."

I thought about my other sister. She had moved to Dallas a month after my mother died. I hadn't seen her since. Her husband pulled down big bucks working with computer programs, writing them. He was a coke head and he ended up leaving her with the kids. He had a fling with some older broad, and he bought a motorcycle during his mid-life crisis. They were riding back from Lubbock, her home, when he dumped the bike and she flew off into something and was nearly decapitated. He suffered a few broken bones but was not charged with manslaughter. Instead he received a different charge and was locked down in minimum security prison. My sister stayed in Dallas and worked her way up in her company and was making serious cash. I felt bad for not thinking about her until I heard the word Dallas. Thoughts of her started to depress me so I played one of my tapes. Nick stared at the tape player and nodded to the fast tribal and the guitars and the sounds of violins and pianos and bagpipes and screams.

March of Time and Skin

"Who's this?"
"Northern California's finest," I said.
"Man. These guys aren't fucking around."
"They're from hell."
We made Fife, a pit stop before Tacoma. I needed coffee. As I paid the cashier I saw them out there in the rain, getting money together for my tank. I wasn't going to take their money. They would have a hard enough time getting to Texas. They had only received two hundred dollars each for their draw. They were stretching their limbs and other cars were driving by giving them shitty looks. Nick paid no mind to the people. I knew how he felt. Alaska was a mindjob. Now they were back and they probably weren't going to get paid for their season up there. Somehow the rain picked up even more and the girl and his friend jumped into the van. Nick walked slowly through it and stepped inside. The cashier beamed at him. He handed me a few fivers.

"Here, man. For the trouble. Those fuckers out there better get used to it. They better learn how to take it. We got a long haul. They haven't seen anything yet."
I watched him pay for his smokes. He walked back out through the rain and stepped in the van. I bought a gallon of water and shoved the fives in my pocket.

We neared Tacoma. In the bed she was sleeping. His friend sat there, still fixated on the photo. We passed the sign and Nick stared to the big dome,
"Tacoma. How anyone lives here I'll never know."
We passed the Tacoma exits. Craig stirred the girl awake harshly. Nick put his smokes in a backpack.
"Yeah. If you can get us a ways outside of here and let us out near an exit with a station we'd appreciate it."
I looked ahead at the greyness,
"Here's the deal. I'll take you guys in but you're getting the gas and eats."
Lana sat up in the bed.
"We already gave you gas money!"
Nick spun around again.
"Lana! Shut the *fuck up*! He means he'll drive us to Austin. Goddamnit."
She sat back against the doors, "Oh. Oh, sorry."
I glanced at them through the mirror.
"Or you can jump out here and take your chances. Gas in this van isn't cheap. About 80 bucks each from the three of you. That covers my tank there and back."
Craig looked at her.
"There's nothing to think about. We'll take it."
Nick stared them both down.

"And when we get there we'll get up money for your food and drinks on your way back."

Craig nodded, "Oh, yeah. Hell yeah."

Nick put his hand out. "I don't know what to say."

I shook his hand.

"It's not entirely for your sake. I've had rain up to my ears for the last six months. I could stand a small vacation. Why didn't you guys just take a bus or a train?"

Lana pulled a puppy from under my blanket.

"He's why. No dogs on Greyhounds and trains. He's just a puppy. Can't be more than six weeks old. All he does is sleep, but sometimes he whines real loud."

"Like somebody else we know." Nick said.

He talked to the windshield,

"We're at the bus terminal on Stewart. These fucking hippies are giving these dogs away. Here comes Lana with this dog, and it's fucking yelping. The Greyhound guy says no pets. I tell her to ditch the pooch but she tells me to fuck off and she'll hitch back. Craig tries to grab the dog but she kicks him and falls to the floor screaming, holding this dog. Oh, sure, he's quiet now 'cause he was up all night howling. You'll see. So Craig and I figure the dog has like replaced something in her she needed and being how she's my little brother's girlfriend I couldn't let her hitch alone. Craig was all for leaving them behind."

Craig nodded at me in the rearview. Lana threw one of her bags against his back.

"You're such an asshole, Craig."

He began yelling at her. Nick turned, and they stopped instantly. He told them you don't fuck around in another man's car.

Lana looked at me through the mirror, holding the puppy.

"Hey! Can we drive through California? I've never seen it."

"No."

Craig was out on the floor. Lana had gone back to sleep with her pup. Nick was a trooper. I knew he was tired but he stayed awake. We drove across the bridge into Portland.

"This is my favorite city," I said, "I should have moved here instead."

Nick looked out the window, "What's here?"

"I don't know. Something about it."

"Yeah. But if you lived here you'd probably be saying the same thing about another place."

"Maybe."

"So what is it you do, man?"

"Not much, really."

"You have to do something, otherwise you'd be like all the rest of the dead assholes. You wouldn't have stopped for us."

"I'd like to write someday," I said, "You know, for a living."

He looked over at me.

"I fucking knew it, man. There's that something to you, this weird calmness."

He looked at my hands.

"You've had to do something else besides write. Construction?"

"Some."

"Those scars from fighting?"

"What do you do?"

"I work, travel, and fuck. I'm a drifter. Austin is just where my stuff is right now, you know?" He kicked his shoes off.

"But what I'd really like to do is play my bass in a band and tour."

"Good luck."

"I'm really good, man."

"Even better luck."

"Man. You're a negative motherfucker."

"No. I'm a realist."

He laughed. "All pessimists think they're realists."

Just as we hit the southeastern part of Oregon the sun appeared, and it was miraculous. This yellow light in the sky that emitted warmth. I hadn't seen it for half a year. The back roads of Oregon were beautiful. The sunlight came in through the windshield and spiked everything. I drove on through the bright mountains and found a spot to park. Craig and Lana sat up. I noticed Craig had a tattoo of a cobweb from his forehead down to his cheek.

"We stoppin'?"

Nick told him I wanted to walk for a bit and to trade him places. Lana fell back to sleep and Nick took the floor. Craig took his seat and curled up into a ball. I stepped out.

I hopped the rail and sat against the dirt wall below the highway. The face of a mountain stared at me from across a small valley. It was high and snowcapped. I took off my sweatshirt and faced it. The sun hit my face and ran through it like chemicals. Down in the valley a thin stream ran beneath the tall trees and loose rocks, which tumbled down the sides like tears. I sat there and stared at all of it. My face and arms were hot with blood. I was back with life. Birds would land and take off again from the limbs down there. I sunk my hand into the warm dirt and let it fall through my fingers. I missed the road, the dangerousness of no routine. I sat back and thought about everything. I wondered what Helena was doing, and if I still crossed her mind. I wondered if my mother could see me from where she was, and I wondered what she thought of me. I wondered if there were mountains in heaven. I knew there had to be a heaven because she was dead and I couldn't stand the thought of her rotting in a coffin with nothing else for her. Then a cloud passed and blocked the sun. I stood up and put my sweatshirt on.

Craig had etched out a spot for himself on the floor with Nick. I was happy they were sleeping. I drove on, blasting heavy metal with the sun. By the time we hit Jackpot, Nevada, it was dark and I was tired.

I stopped for gas. They were fumbling for money. Lana said she was starting and that she needed to shower. She wanted to get a room for the night. The guys were against it. Lana said she needed a real shower and that if they were able to get a period they would understand. They went three ways on the room. Pets weren't allowed at the motel. I didn't want to share a room anyway, so I offered to let the pup sleep with me in the van.

I gambled ten bucks on video poker and broke even. Nick wouldn't let them gamble. I drank a few free whiskey sours while I played and went back to the van. The pup was on my bed. He was small and brown with a big head. I picked him up and held him in front of my face. Some little creature. Without her he would die. He clamped his gums around my finger. I liked his puppy breath. His little eyes were barely opening and they were dark blue. He was a feisty little shit. We wrestled a bit and he fell asleep on my chest, his head buried under my chin. I didn't mind at all. During the night he would whimper so I stuck my finger in his mouth and he sucked on it until he bonked out again.

In the morning I heard the van door slide open. I had forgotten to lock up before I went to bed. I looked down. I had my hand over the pup. Lana looked in.

"Are you decent?"

"Yes." She climbed in and saw the pup on top of me.

"Oohhh, there he is."

He woke up and smeared his nose across my neck. She put her hands out.

"Let me hold the baby."

I didn't want to. I patted his back.

"What's his name?"

She picked him up and nuzzled him.

"His name's Bubba. 'Cause he's going to be big and strong when he grows up and he'll protect his mama."

March of Time and Skin

The guys piled in. They smelled better. I was glad we'd stopped there. We drove through Nevada all day. The plan was to cut left at Flagstaff and go down through New Mexico. It was dark when we hit Vegas. I pulled over and called Greg. His machine said that he and Stephanie were in San Diego. We passed the big dam and made Kingman. I saw the hotel where I had met Julie and her boyfriend. Nick offered to drive. I told him to wake me up when we hit Albuquerque because the van had loose steering and the weather was getting worse. I bumped Lana to the floor but kept Bubba with me. Craig was bitching about the dog holding them back. He had a real problem with her. He was bitching a lot about everything, the gas station food, my music not being "punk" enough for him, the length of the trip and the money it took. He was getting on my nerves. I told him from the bed that he seriously needed to shut his mouth. Nick was quiet because they were buddies, but I knew they wouldn't be buddies when they got back home. Traveling together will make or break people.

I woke up to the sunlight. We were far out of the mountains. Nick said he didn't want to wake me. I sat up and gave Lana the bed. I handed Bubba over. I told Craig he could have the floor. He took on a pissy air.

"Finally."

I was ready to pop him one. I couldn't stand whiny, precious assholes. We hit a gas station and I drove from there. We made Texas by the late afternoon. Craig wanted the bed. Lana said she was having cramps and that she needed to lay down on something soft. Craig then told her that they wouldn't be in this mess if she hadn't taken the dog. They were arguing again. He wrestled the dog from her and threatened to snap its neck. I couldn't slow down because a trucker was tailgating me. I finally got over to the right lane. Craig held the pup to the side window and threatened to toss it. I told him to give the pup back to her and to shut the fuck up. Nick didn't say anything. Craig told me I could go fuck myself. My blood boiled. There was someone like him everywhere I went. We were 8 hours from Austin. Lana reached out for her pup but he tossed it. I heard him yelp, and in my side mirror I watched him hit the freeway and tumble and break until he was stiff. My heart sank to my stomach. Lana buried her head into the pillow and sobbed. I pulled onto the shoulder and stopped. In the rearview Craig asked me if I wanted a piece of him. I jumped out of my seat and grabbed the back of his hair and punched him right in the mouth. Blood sprayed into my eye and he went down against the door. I hit him hard across his body. He curled up into a ball and swore at me. Nick did nothing. Lana was still sobbing over her pup. I jumped out of the driver side and walked around to the sliding door. When I opened it, Craig almost fell out but he caught himself. I grabbed his bags and threw them as far as I could into traffic.

Then I pulled him out by his belt and the back of his shirt and swung him to the ground. After he hit I got a running start and kicked him in the back. And then, just for myself, I rabbit punched him in the back of the head. He wasn't swearing anymore. Nick got out and stood by his door, eyeballing me. I walked up on him.
"You got a problem with this, Nick? Fucking silent partner."
He put his hands up. I told him I would get Lana to Austin and if he wanted to stay with his buddy or even take her with him I didn't care. He did what I thought he would. As we pulled away I saw Craig's body struggling in the rearview, getting smaller and smaller. I wanted to turn around and run him over. Lana dug into her backpack and licked a clean sock and dabbed the blood from my eye. Nick shook his head,
"I fucking knew this day would come. I always told him he was going to say the wrong thing to the wrong person and he would pay for his mouth. But he always said that everyone was a pussy. Man."
"If I see him again I'll kill him," I said.
Nick told me that he knew Craig had warrants in Texas, and that he knew a cop would stop him on the highway and that he would go to jail. He also told me that he hadn't seen him in a few years before they set out to Alaska. I considered Nick to be smarter than I had thought. He was simply waiting to see Craig get his. He was having a good time with it. I spoke to Lana's reflection in the windshield.
"I'm sorry about Bubba. He was a good one. I don't think he felt any pain."
Nick shook his head, "Nah. He didn't feel a thing."
We both kind of looked at each other. Lana cried. After a while we were quiet. I kept thinking about the pup, picturing his big head and little face. It was horrible. Something so beautiful and innocent and undamaged being destroyed like that. If the trip had been any longer than it was and if he hadn't have been killed, I would have fell in love with him.
We stopped for caffeine. In the diner she was quiet. Nick tried to talk some cheer into her by promising a new dog. I felt a little sick over Bubba and I couldn't eat. Thoughts of Craig being raped in prison helped me get the coffee down. We made Austin later than I thought we would since I drove like an old woman. The cops in Texas were worse than anywhere, and after seeing at least fifty of them writing tickets since we crossed the state line I figured going five miles slower than the signs couldn't hurt. I didn't like the way Texas felt and I didn't need to deal with its patrol.

The sunshine was still a new world. winter in the Northwest changed it to a different planet, always grey, always wet. I knew I would have to get a job soon after I drove in and that thought stuck in the back of my mind all the way down through Texas. When I woke up to the warmth against my side I was glad I was there.

It was a big house shared by people like Craig. To the side of the house a small river ran, and Nick, Lana and I took a canoe up the river for two hours to a cafe named after a flower, where Nick's lady worked. It was a nice trip. We drank and drifted in the warm light, surrounded by trees and small animals. Nick left the canoe at the cafe and his girl drove us back where we ate and shared a joint and hit some bars on 6th street. In the morning I got their number at the house and took off. In Dallas I phoned my sister but there was no answer. I walked around downtown for a few hours and tried again.

I left her a message but I didn't tell her I was in state because I didn't want her to feel bad for not being there. After two false speeding tickets and an hour long search through my van for drugs, I was out of Texas for good.

The trip back was nice. I was driving across the country back to my own place for the first time. I took it slow, nearly four days. I drove up through Washington on a different route, and just before I pulled out of Cle Elum the van snapped under the hood and lost a lot of power. I was only an hour and a half from home but it was past midnight and it was freezing. I sat in the restaurant all night and drank coffee, sleeping in brief cold spells in the van.

The mechanic said something about a piston or a shaft or something fatal. He adjusted something so I could maybe get back to the basement. The van was loud and sick but it brought me in. After I parked in front of the house it would never again move on its own. Downstairs I counted the rest of my money. I had enough for one more month's rent if I didn't want to eat. I had a little over two weeks to get the rent. I knew the couple would be understanding and let me slide a bit, but I didn't want to play that game. The next morning I found a job as a cook in a half way house.

I worked for a week then quit. Then I was a graveyard cook at a busy, trendy, young angst type of hangout. It was a shorter bus trip than the other place. The pay was bad but I ate for free and met my first vampires.

These kids would glue fangs onto their existing teeth and grow their fingernails out, wear ruffled sleeves and order rare meat. In the day you could see them working in video stores or rolling burritos. They would come in late wearing make up and 1800's stockings. Their faces were painted white, their lips black. I first thought they were young theater kids, but one of the other cooks told me they were a serious clique. After a few nights they started to get on my nerves. One night on the chalkboard above the bar I insulted the vampires with a message I chalked in bold letters: REAL VAMPIRES ALWAYS TIP.

This offended the creatures of the night, and my manager had a sit-down with me. He spoke though a neatly groomed goatee:

"Look, man. The vampires are our main source of nightly revenue. They say they won't come back as long as you work here. I told them you would apologize tomorrow night."

"I'm off tomorrow night."

"Well, then apologize to them when you get back."

"I quit."

17

I worked in the big, famous market in a cafe that looked out on Elliot Bay. From the piers the cafe stuck out of the upstairs level of the Market like a new boil on an old face. The bosses were Afghani, and they were both perverted. Their father owned the place but they were in charge. They were my age but they were balding and they were out of shape from over-eating the cafe food. They loved the young girls who worked the Market. The girls did not like them, but they were never rude to them. Seattle for me was easy. I could not see anyone having hard times there by submission. It was a free for all.

Every morning I caught the 55 bus in front of 7 eleven on California. There was a small pause at the junction then we were on 99, curving around the bay into downtown. The rain was finally defeated and springtime up there was nothing but beauty. The green came out in so many shades it went beyond green. I would sit in the cafe and drink coffee before my shift, watch the water and gulls in the bay, and remember things that made me feel far from them.

I worked with a few characters like Eric, the cook. He was a short guy with baby blonde dreads and sideburns. He was constantly stressing, throwing shit across the kitchen. He told me he had grown up on the road with his parents in a bus, that his father had hung out with Dennis Hopper. He never went to school. He had hitch hiked around the country and landed in Seattle at the age of 29. He was still 29. Like everyone else he played guitar in a losing band. I liked him.

There was Graham, a 28 year old who was on the fat side and wanted to be a comedian. He felt shafted because he'd once had the tools to be a great guitarist, but gave them up for a woman. He would bitch about having gone to high school with the latest Seattle bands that had made it. He would tell me of the people he used to jam with. A real name-dropper. He and Eric had these status wars at the cafe. Though he only made around six bucks an hour, he was proud of his job and it sickened Eric. They would argue it constantly. I'd heard the first back and forth on my second day there, when Graham asked me how I got the job. I told him I was hitting a new low. Eric laughed. Graham looked over my shoulder and pointed at him,

"Fuck you."

"No, no no no no. Fuck *you*." Eric said

They stared each other down. I walked off to the side and let them have their time. It became a routine.

Eric was the smarter of the two, so he usually broke the silence.

"Look at you, man. You're always buzzing around here running your mouth and kissing ass. You could make this money anywhere."

"Whatta you mean?" Graham said, "This is a world famous Market!"

"So. McDonalds is world famous. Why don't you work at McDonalds?"

"Man. Fuck you."

"No, no no no no. Fuck *you*."

The couple that rented me the basement came back, and after a short meeting it was made clear that they wanted the basement. Something about the husband needing a workshop for his newest business. I didn't want to leave. I had spent months down there alone. I was comfortable with it. I had clocked in thousands of hours behind the keys down there. I wanted to grow old down there. This always happened at the worst times. I didn't have enough money to move into a real place. The wrong things happened at the worst times. When I had money I was fine. When I ran low a tooth would ache, a contact lens would tear in half, the flu would hit, I would need shoes or work clothes...

When the month was up I moved into Eric's studio until the next payday. I gave him some money. All of my things were easily hidden. I was there on the sly, because his landlord was ruthless about company staying longer than a couple of days. The bulk of my belongings were the machines and the pages, all carefully boxed and taped. Eric was all right but I didn't like living so closely to another person.

He had offered the floor and it beat the alternative, an alternative I was sure I had beat forever. I walked around during my nights off or I rode. I would go back to the place only to shower and sleep. When he asked me what was in the boxes I told him I had a lot of pornography saved up. I had learned not to tell anybody I worked with that I was a writer.

Eric was a big reader. He had shelves full of Bernstein and Kerouac and Burroughs and philosophy from the middle-east. He liked Krishnamurti. He had a few Bukowski books and a couple by Brautigan. He liked to play records. One night we closed a bar on 2nd and we were back at his place, drunk. He asked me if he could take one of my porn mags in the bathroom with him. I told him he couldn't but he grabbed one of the boxes and ran to the bathroom, laughing. He was a short guy and he ran like a dwarf. I could picture him dropping his pants to his ankles on the toilet and opening the box and seeing a heavy stack of typed words. I played an album without reading the cover. Duke Ellington.

His place was bare. There was a small fold out table for his record player and a cheap ten speed and an electric and acoustic guitar. His window faced another window on the opposite building but it was painted blue and you couldn't see who lived there. He was in the bathroom for a while. He came out and plopped the box down on the floor.

He nodded, "You're a real asshole."

I didn't say anything.

"Why didn't you tell me you wrote?"

"I don't tell anyone."

He kicked the box across the floor, "I thought we were friends."

He took some quick steps toward the box and kicked it against the wall. It was like someone kicking my child. I told him if he took one more kick, he was out the window. He wasn't phased. He kicked the box again and spoke.

"I fucking hate secrecy, you hear me? I told you I played guitar!"

He put his hands out and shook them in front of his chest.

"I mean, what the fuck do you think you are? Some *genius* who works with the *little* people and observes them, and then goes home and crucifies them with his mighty wisdom!? Like you're better than they are, better than other people!?"

I let him carry on with a few more insults then I answered.

"So I take it you don't like the work."

He put his hands in his dreads, "Jesus Christ!"

I asked him why it mattered.

"Wait. Stand right there. I have something to show you."

He walked four feet back into the kitchen and dug through one of the two cabinets. He ran over and slammed two notebooks on the folding table. It skipped the record and nearly collapsed the table. The guy next door banged on the wall. He walked up with his plastic chair and set it in front of the table.

"Read!" He yelled. He was passionate about the notebooks. I sat and read. They were pages about his life, overly-written dramatic similes and bleeding heart, heart break poetry. It was awful. I read about ten pages while he stood and read over my shoulder, silently. I closed the book. He took four more steps into the kitchen and made another drink. He walked in and offered the drink to me. I didn't take it. He set it on the table.

"Well?"

I didn't know what to say, what he wanted.

"I'm waiting. Let me have it."

"What the fuck do you want from me?"

"The truth, Goddamnit."

He sat against the floor.

"You've heard the tapes of my band. They were shit, right?"

"Yes, but it had nothing to do with your-"

"Can the pleasantries! My writing, what do you think?"

"Eric, come on, man. You're drunk. I've only read a few pages, I can't really..."

"But from what you've read, it was shit! I know it was shit! Fucking tell me it was SHIT!"

"All right, it was shit."

He jumped up and finished the drink.

"All my life I was bent toward the arts! My parents, the bus, Dennis *fucking* Hopper! I was supposed to create greatness! And you! So calm, so cool, all of that creation you keep to yourself because you are such an asshole. You make me want to vomit. You probably get off on the privacy and then at a moment like this you feel superior! Pornography! Why couldn't you just say that you wrote? You think you're special? You are a fucking fraud!"

Then he left. I didn't know if I should pack my things and get out or go to sleep. The only part that bugged me was the fraud accusation. How could a man be a fraud if no one knew his business? I realized he was out of his mind, talking to himself. He was the fraud. He was like so many others. He tried to use the context for the center, never noticing the context was wrong for him to begin with. He wasn't meant to write or play music and that was fine with everyone except for him. He saw himself as something he could not be. I wanted to tell him that many others had not been meant for creation but they went ahead and made a lot of money doing it anyway. I drank a few, put my writing back together and slept.

I had not heard him come or go. He worked the early, early shift. I walked into the kitchen and strapped on my apron. I could see him cooking out of the corner of my right eye. Out in the bay a large boat caught my attention. I watched it lurk across the water. It was going to Bainbridge Island. I saw Eric nod. I looked over.

"Hey, man," he smiled.

I nodded back and finished prepping the sandwich bar. There was already a line of tourists out the door. I hated them. Graham was all smiles and jokes as usual and there was a new guy I had to train. He was a gay guy named Frederick. After I showed him the ropes I told Akmal I was taking a break.

Downstairs I watched the guitarists and beggars sit on the bright concrete and smoke, watching the gulls swoop down and gulp up bits of bread. I saw Eric on a bench smoking, watching girls. I walked over and sat next to him.

We watched the same girl.

"Damn," he said.

"I know."

He kept his eyes on her ass, "Sorry about last night."

"Forget it."

"I didn't mean what I said about you being a fraud."

"Thanks."

He flipped his smoke onto the sidewalk. A young, arty girl stepped on it without looking over. He leaned back and stretched.

"Shit, man. You're good. Did you go to any kind of school for it?"

"I dropped out of high school."

He shook his head at the water.

"The smart ones are always the fuck ups."

He told me he was enrolling in an autobiography class in the fall at the community college. He said he wanted to tell his life story.

People came and went quickly at the cafe. If I would have been younger I would have come and gone myself, but I knew every job was a nightmare and at least at this one I could blow off steam and see the water and eat for free. I would never have a real career and the job was basic. Eric's landlord turned up the heat on my being there and when payday came it was do or die. I would have over four hundred dollars saved by then and I knew it wouldn't be enough to live on my own.

Through words and the turn of events, Frederick told me he had some space open in his place on Capital Hill. Thrill Hill, the gay strip. After work I walked with him up Pine and we cut over to his apartment. I liked the building, the old style elevator, the structure, the feel. It wasn't a room he had to rent. It was a walk in closet. His place was a studio with this big closet.

"How much?"

"Oh, I dunno. Two fifty?"

"Right. One fifty."

"Come on. Okay. Two flat, and that includes everything."

"I'll give you two."

I paid rent and bought a mattress. It was a twin mattress. It took up most of the floor. I had enough room for a small desk and a chair. I went back to my typewriter. I had to run an extension cord from the living room for power. He worked at the Market for three more days then quit when he was assigned his own chair at a trendy, gay salon. He was a good roomie. I hardly saw him until late at night. He would have guys over and since he slept in the living room on a futon I could hear and smell the sex.

In the mornings he was alone and naked. I would walk from the kitchen and pass him naked there, on his back.

"Nice cock."

"Sorry about that," he would sing from the other room.

"I'm sure."

He was a nice enough guy. He was fickle and moody and he talked about his boyfriends. I met a young college girl named Beverly who lived down the alley, and we were together for 3 months, until she discovered who I really was. I didn't see her for a week then I saw her walking out of her place with a young college boy with a future.

Sometimes Frederick would get drunk and try putting the moves on me. I took it in stride. He never stepped over the line. One night Beverly called and wanted to talk. I asked her why she was calling me. She said she missed me. I asked about her little boyfriend. She told me he was a jerk. I hung up. Frederick looked at me.

"You're going to fuck her."

"If all goes well."

He leaned forward.

"Let me watch."

"Come on, Fred."

"*Frederick*. Listen. I'll let you live here for free next month if you do it."

"She'd never go for it. She's too sheltered." I said.

"Leave the door cracked, play some music."

"We'll see."

March of Time and Skin

All she wanted to do was talk. Back at her place I listened to her whine about me wasting my potential in life. She wanted me, but she wanted me to have a good job and a new car and a home and a solid financial base. I told her that those things were nothing. She argued and I pinned her against the sofa and forced my way in. She really got off on things like that. She was all body. After we finished she told me she thought it was wise to never see each other again.

I went back up the alley, into my closet. Frederick and I drank like fish when he came in from work. I passed out on the couch and when I woke up his head was on my chest and he was snoring. I pushed him off and jumped to the hardwood floor like a cricket. I felt at my clothes. I was fully dressed. I was worried that he might have tried something on me while I slept, but I scanned the insides of my body and I was untouched, with the worst hangover I had ever felt. I had to work in half an hour. Frederick turned over and smiled at me from the couch. I moved in with Beverly the same day.

I finally got a hold of Jared. He asked me where I had been.
"Living in a homosexual's closet."
"Heavy."
He told me he and Sylvia were leaving for Fiji the next day to get married. He asked me if I would be around in a few weeks. He gave me their new number. I hung up and jumped on Beverly as she stepped out of the shower. I lasted with her through the summer. Just before fall she moved back to Newport. I found an expensive room on the hill and stayed there for a month, when the girl who rented me the room and I had a fight over the noise of my typewriter and I got the axe.

Fall came and then late fall and then the rain again. I was living on the floor of a big Russian girl who worked in the Market. I could not believe I was still working there. Eric was on his last week and he was off to Minneapolis and Graham made a dramatic walk out and tried to get rehired after the rush but was turned away. A lot of other world famous places were hiring. I had sex with the big Russian only because I thought I had to. She had a large ass and she smelled from behind when I was back there.

She wouldn't let me pay rent and I was back to the computer. She would read everything I wrote when I was gone. She wasn't a bad person. I wasn't tied down or anything. I felt invaded living there but I had gotten bad at saving money. In mid-November the rain came full swing. I buckled down and started saving again. I could not stand another winter in Seattle. I missed the sunshine, the desert. I decided out of nowhere to go deep into Mexico and begin a novel. I had heard that you could live down there dirt cheap. I thought of the beach, cool water, my old typewriter and smooth, Mexican women. This motivated me.

One day at the cafe a woman came in with her sister. Some small talk was made. She told me she was a playwright. She lived in New York City with her husband. She had long dark hair and wore a long silk skirt with cowboy boots. One of the Afghanis told her I was a writer and nudged me with his elbow, like he was helping me out or something. She wrote me a poem and left her name and number in the city. She said that she knew people in the business and that she was interested to see what I wrote. I watched her walk out. She wasn't bad for her age. That night at the Russian's I was thinking of Helena. She was the only real person I had ever been with. I became drunk and called her mother in Phoenix. She told me Helena had moved to Portland and was working at the Sheep Exchange, some store that bought and sold used clothes. I couldn't believe it. Three and a half hours away.

The next day I called the number in Portland. It was her voice. This grim familiarity. I didn't know why I was calling. I told her I had been thinking about her every day since I last saw her. She was completely floored that I called. But she was still with the other guy. We talked for a long while and I hung up, feeling like a pile of nostalgic waste. I still loved her. The fact that she was so close to where I was only made it worse. Before, she was across the country and it was easier. I was mad at myself for finding her. It made the time in Seattle that much longer.

A week before I got my last check I called the number in Manhattan. I thought if this woman had connections I should try to make something out of it. I wondered if it would be impossible to get a publisher through her. A man answered. I asked for Kara.

"Who's this?"

I told him. She was happy that I'd called. I asked for her address so I could mail her some of my work. She gave it to me. I hung up and packed away my things. I had a week left to wait. I would take a bus to Phoenix, see my sister and the kids then head down into Mexico, where I mapped out a small town on the beach about two and a half hours southwest of Mexico City. There I would get away from America and I would write the book, come back and send it off and see how I fared. I was excited for the first time in years. Soon I had a day left. I walked through the rain. Each drop hit my skin like acid. I endured the big Russian one more night and 11 hours later I was on the bus.

I sat in the back. We stopped at every place possible. In Portland we had a 45 minute wait. I sat outside and looked around. She was out here somewhere. I sat and missed her, saw her face everywhere. My heart was a thousand of Eric's poems and I didn't care. A drifter from the bus bummed a dollar off me.

He mentioned that it was Christmas Eve. It all hit me. I was 26 years old with nothing but a lot of pages and a bicycle and a heavy heart. Some people might have observed the course of my life and been impressed by it. I felt a slight sting of shame. I did not want to die unheard. I couldn't understand why I would be concerned. I didn't want to face up to the part of me which gave a shit about the world, the part which still held hope. I didn't like that part. It was capable of love and it was brave. It was the only beautiful thing that remained. I tried to destroy it but I could not.

I had around seven hundred saved after bus fare. In the place I was headed to write the book, seven hundred would last me a long time. I didn't know or care how I would get back. The bus rolled out. I had been awake all night before the trip and I was shot. In Olympia I faded out.

We had a stop in Medford. I woke up to get a coffee. In the station I reached for my wallet. Nothing. I ran back to the bus and checked my seat and the floors. It was gone. It had either slipped out at the last stop or someone had swiped it when I was sleeping. All my money was gone, Mexico was gone, the novel was burned down before it began. I felt sick. It was useless to report the wallet. Anybody on a Greyhound would not return it. Some bum was happy. I beat myself over and over when I thought about not putting the money somewhere safer. At least I had my ticket paid to Phoenix. Some asshole stole the backseat from me. I rode next to the aisle. I was so depressed I fell asleep sitting up in the chair.

It was Christmas morning. The whole bus was silent. A black guy screamed from behind me.

"Spendin' my Christmas on a *goddamned* bus!"

A few bums laughed. We were coming into Los Angeles, where I had started out eight years ago. I had to sit in the station while the busses were switched over. The same station. I wanted so badly to be that young again, to be waiting on a security guard to run me into Venice, to meet Kim and do it all over. Then it passed and I realized I was being sorry. I took a seat and waited like everyone else.

18

I called her number and told her. She was there within 15 minutes with the girls. She had a new truck, said the payments were murder but it was the first nice thing she had and she was keeping it, no matter what. I saw Helena's face again. I was home for Christmas. I was broke with no I.D. and no money. I walked in the door and saw the couch and my stomach twisted.

The next day was better. I'd slept well and Christmas was over, and the sun was high and warm. I sat out back and wrote the woman in New York and told her I was sorry I hadn't mailed her anything, but here was a short story and some poems. I left my sister's number in the letter and asked my sister for postage.

I had the house to myself during the day after New Year's. My youngest niece was in school and my sister went to work. She had landed a job working for the electric company, entering data and filing new accounts. My older niece was in the process of packing her things to move in with her boyfriend when their apartment opened in a couple of weeks. I felt embarrassed when I heard them leave in the mornings, on their way to do something. I would try to ride in the day or write in the garage but I was too worried with money. I was waiting for my birth certificate to arrive from Peoria so I could get a state identification card. Some of my unpaid traffic fines caught me and crippled me. I could not get a license until I paid them.

March of Time and Skin

On a Wednesday, Kara called from Manhattan. She said she loved the story. I asked her about her own writing. She told me that she had written a few plays that were made in Seattle and the city. This began her chain of lies. She talked a good game. She was five years older than I. She kept me on the phone for a long time, and a phone relationship began. She would mail me a young picture here and there and many letters. Her writing was awful, but a lot of writing was awful. Being down on my luck with no prospects at the age I had reached, I looked forward to her calls and letters. I had failed the road and I had failed my heroes. I had hope with this woman. I was another sheep in the herd but I could not see it. I had gotten older and afraid of my life and I was wrecked.

Everything I had done out there on my own dropped away from reality. Now I was living back with my sister and I was broke and lost. Nothing helped anymore and I couldn't write anything good because I was not steady.

I found a job that would pay me without any I.D. It was one of the old pizza places where I was once a driver. It was an hour long ride from my sister's, and I was working for minimum wage in the kitchen. I felt good about doing it. I had a nice long ride through the road which divided the mountains, and I was doing something to make my situation better. The writing was there in my blood though the edge I thought it gave me was gone. It was good to know that I had my writing but it didn't mean shit in the outside world.

The job was easy enough. I wasn't the top pizza slinger or anything. I did my share. My boss was cool enough to pay me in cash until I was on my feet again. A lot of fine young girls worked there but I was already too old for them. I was beaten and tired out. The only girls their age who even looked remotely interested in me were freaks and sluts and I was too shot to do anything about it. A week went by.

One night I was sitting outside in the back of a supermarket at the halfway point to my sister's and I thought about it. The years and miles and days, a whale against the sun. I had been such a badass when I was a kid. I went long and hard and I took what I saw. Now there I was, taking a break behind a supermarket halfway between a fifteen mile ride between a minimum wage job and my sister's couch. I was a disgrace to my youth and I felt weak.

That thought hit me hard in the jaw, and I pedaled fast the rest of the way, sailing over curbs and flying into traffic, missing cars by a hair. I stopped in a parking lot a block from the couch and rode feverishly, working on new tricks and coughing up phlegm. I rode all night without stopping to drink or eat. Then I went back and sat in the garage and typed out a 34 page short story. It was about a midget who made a deal with the devil.

The next day I called and quit the job. I had a little over sixty bucks and my birth certificate hadn't arrived. I called the courthouse in Peoria and gave some lady hell over it. It arrived two days later. I went out and got a picture I.D. and applied for a new social security card so I could present any employer with the receipt. I hated losing the card and having to go get that lousy receipt. I looked in the paper and found a job down at a beer warehouse in Glendale. They were interviewing for someone to work in breakage, someone to repair six and twelve packs and repackage them. The interview was in four days.

Kara had been calling. One night she told me that she wanted to leave her husband and come live with me. As gone as I was in my head I was all for it. It was weird for my sister. Her daughter had just moved out and I had the room, and soon a woman would be living there with me.

The interview went well, and the manager told me he'd let me know within a week. Kara was due in two more days. At the grocery store with my sister I ran into Robles again. He was nearly bald and he had this huge belly. He was living with some friends in an apartment right behind the store. He followed us home and ate with us. He was driving a box van for a home improvement center and making good money. We sat out in the yard and drank after dinner. He laughed at my long hair and my beard.

"You look like Jesus."

"Go forth, my fattest son, and get me another beer."

We sat and talked well into the dark. I told him about Kara and he offered to drive me to the airport. It took a big load off since I couldn't drive.

It was good hanging out with him again. Sometimes it brought on sadness because of Helena but overall it was good. He took off and I hit the machine all night. The next night we were waiting at the gate and I was nervous. She was the last one off. I had forgotten what she looked like. I was worried about it. If I had mailed a woman pictures of myself when I was seven years younger and showed up at a gate looking like I did she would have hit the door trying to run out of it.

She had some tits and her face was cute. She hugged me and we grabbed her luggage and drove back. Sean thought she was perfect. There was something about her that I didn't feel comfortable with. I didn't know what it was but something was off and I ignored it.

She met my sister and my youngest niece. It was just past ten at night and my sister had to sleep. My niece snuck into our room and we hung out until midnight, when she fell asleep on the floor. I carried her to her room and tucked her in. Kara jumped in the shower and I sat on the bed. I stared at her luggage and understood that I had a girlfriend. I was excited to have sex again but I thought I saw her luggage laughing at me. I laid back on the bed. I heard the shower turn off and I wondered if I'd made the right move.

She was straddling me in her bathrobe. I opened it. They were monstrous. I had never been a huge breast man. I've always looked at the ass. She said she didn't want to have sex right away. She then said that there was something she had to tell me, that it was something she hadn't told anybody, and she kept hesitating. I pinched her large nipples. She didn't want to say. I pinched harder.

"I fucked my cousin," she said.

I let go.

She was in Seattle and she had sex with him the night before she'd met me. She said it was dirty because it was forbidden. It didn't bother me, except that she was married at the time and when I asked about her husband she would say that they had stopped being a real couple years ago. She leaned down and kissed me and guided me in. We went for a while and I pulled out and shot across her stomach. She wanted me to come inside of her. It started an argument, and I told her that maybe the whole thing was a bad idea. She folded and apologized and we fell asleep.

I woke up early. I sat behind the glow of the screen and typed softly. I didn't know where the inspiration came from, had nothing to do with her. I worked into the middle of a short story about a painter living in an invalid's closet. I had started it at the big Russian's. Kara turned over and watched me write. I ran dry. I made us some coffee and we sat awake in the room and talked. That morning she sat on my lap and snapped pictures of me in my chair in front of my words.

We walked to the store. She bought a box of wine and I drank all day while she laid out in the backyard. My sister was leery of her. Women could feel out other women better than men could. I sat out front on the tailgate of the truck and drank the wine, watching cars round the corner. I was trying to filter out all of the signs and demons and temptations that changed a man from a man into a goat, into a coward. I had some more chances, it seemed, to redeem myself.

That night, Kara made dinner. We had chicken and wine and she played some standard classical music. Robles and my sister were uncomfortable. Not with the setting or the music, but with the contrivance. We weren't in New York City. We weren't in some restaurant. She was in our home and Robles had known me for 16 years. Life was not a fucking metropolitan movie. People ate and talked and contrasted each other with the less fortunate and also with better ideas. I stood up and killed the music, played some Johnny Cash. Kara beamed. Robles remarked that he never understood classical music. I squeezed his shoulder,

"Can't lose the genes. You were born with them."

Kara gave me a filthy look. She had spent a long time making the chicken. I slammed my glass of wine, and stared at her. My sister broke in and asked her questions about the city.

Out back I sat and popped a can open out of the twelve pack Robles had brought over. He was in the kitchen helping my sister clean up and catching up with her. I turned the radio on, found the classical music station. They were playing Mahler. It was good. Kara walked out and sat next to me. She stared over the fence, dramatically.

"I worked very hard to make a nice dinner."

"You're in Phoenix, babe. Blue collar."

She nodded. I gave her some advice. "The worst thing you can do is introduce difference to a family."

She told me I was being drunk and ridiculous. I thought that was fair. She had flown all the way out to be with me. But something in my gut told me that she was running from her own life and that I was the least painful escape for her. Robles came out and we drank and joked around. Kara went inside and fell asleep, and we sat in the back yard and finished the twelve pack. After he left I stayed awake in the backyard, listening to the music, watching the turquoise light shimmer beneath the water of the deep end of the pool, and I sat there until sunrise.

I got the job. The warehouse was 12 miles south of my sister's. It was a long ride. My sister cut all my hair off and I shaved. Kara liked it. She said it made me look more respectable. I started to realize who she was. She landed a job making heavy money being some kind of rep for a construction company and part of her job would be driving around the state and taking orders for brick fences and cheap southwestern style walking blocks. She would have to get a license and a car within a few weeks after her training was completed. She'd never mentioned that she hadn't had a license or a car.

I started the job with a guy named Burt and we were talking about women. He had some real horror stories. Now he lived with a woman 20 years older who gave massages at their place. He called it a full release, but all it came down to was a long, expensive hand job. Kara had a thousand dollars from New York. She wanted us to get an apartment together. I was all for it, because my sister could have her house to herself and her daughter, and meet a guy and have a shot at a life again. Burt was in with the people who ran the complex where they lived, and we moved in to a small one bedroom place. It was close to my job, but it was in west Phoenix, and I knew I wouldn't last there.

19

I was promoted to night-loader at the warehouse and my hours changed from 8 to 12 to 16. It was a lot more money but it wasn't a job, it was a lifestyle. It was long and hard and hot and I stuck with it because I was making good money, though I never had time to do anything with it.

One afternoon I woke up and thought of my sister in Illinois. I hadn't talked to her since last spring. I felt bad about it. I called her right away. She'd had another girl and everything was fine. I filled her in on the last year and gave her my address. Pictures came of the girl. She was beautiful. She was in the backyard in a dress with a bow in her hair. I mailed my sister some originals of my poetry and a picture of me that Kara shot with an instant camera.

I started to notice other girls, their curvy bodies, their kind, gentle voices and features. Kara picked up on it and became hateful. I couldn't help it. I did not want her anymore. I was with her for the ideal. The thought of going back out on the road exhausted me for no other reason than I had no desire to keep finding jobs, and that at least at the apartment there was somewhere consistent to write. I had become soft and I knew it, yet I wouldn't break loose. I thought about leaving, but there was nowhere I could really go. My sister had met a new man and my niece was going through a bad break-up with her boyfriend and she had moved back in.

My brother, the cowboy, was out of the question, because he had hooked himself of crystal meth, and was in and out of his family's life and jail.

One Saturday we were drunk in a bar up the road and Kara told me that she had started to develop feelings for some guy at her job. She had brought him up before, and laughed because he liked sports. But she went into a long explanation about how she was in love with me but I wasn't making her feel wanted and that this guy at work really listened to her and it was attracting her to him, so I told her to fuck off. I paid the bill and started walking home.

She caught up to me, crying and screaming that she was in love with me. She fell to the field that cut across to the apartment and started shoving dirt in her mouth. I stepped over her and went home. She beat me to the staircase and ran upstairs and started trashing the place, breaking things I had spent my large paychecks on to keep her happy. In the room I started packing my bags, to a litany of shattering glass and what an asshole I was.

I made it to the door and got my hand on the knob. She ran up and locked her arms around my shoulders, sobbing apologies. I was drunk and almost feeling bad for her, and I held her against me while I cracked the door open. She kissed my neck and dug her nails into my shirt, and she kissed harder and sucked on my neck and dug into my shoulders and then bit into me. I felt my skin break and I pushed her off. She stumbled back with a piece of my shirt in her hand, fell to the floor and smacked her head against the foot of our metal chair and her head split open. Then she jumped up, pushed past me and ran down the stairs, finding a guy in the parking lot and they ran to his place. I watched her legs move toward his door and I hoped she died.

Burt's old lady let me in. I sat down and grabbed a paper towel but she snatched it from me.

"If that crazy cunt called the police you'd better stay just how you are. Trust me."

I remembered Gus and the billy club. She lit up and handed me a can of beer. I cooled off and walked back. In front of the staircase there were four squad cars. They were talking to Kara. One of the cops jogged toward me:

"Hey, hey guy, hold it right there. All right, turn around..."

He threw the cuffs on. She screamed at them to let me go, and yelled to me that she wasn't the one who called the police and so on. Two cops marched me upstairs. As I stood up in the doorway cuffed I looked down to see a man with a bushy mustache and a large glass looking up at me. Her uncle. The whole complex was watching.

The cops took pictures of my wounds and listened to my story. Since she had a mouth they hated her. I was polite and attentive. A female cop went as far as to say that it was too bad Kara needed medical attention because otherwise they would take her in. She undid my cuffs, and told me I should find a new girlfriend. Downstairs I sat on the curb next to her uncle. He looked over at me.
"You know, I don't appreciate anyone hurting my niece."
I gave him a flash of Manson.
"Your niece is a fucking psychotic little whore. You comeback with anymore macho bullshit and you're next, motherfucker."
He laughed and handed me the glass. It was filled with strong liquor.
"Lighten up. Drink this. And keep those cops away from me, I've been driving drunk since Oregon."
I took a drink. It was a healthy amount of Vodka and maybe an ounce of cherry soda. A cop walked over and told me to stay away from the apartment for 24 hours. I told them it was my place and I paid the bills, but they didn't care. Then they were gone. I stood there alone, staring at the staircase. Her uncle pulled up in the new car and asked me where the hospital was. I told him. She was next to him. She looked at me.
"Get out of my life."
I didn't say anything back to her. Bill reached out and patted me on the arm.
"See you later, buddy."
I walked around for a few hours. Nothing made sense. After dark I walked into the place. She was in bed and Bill was watching television. Bill was an alcoholic and a better man than most. He took a real shine to me. He split with his wife and was seeing a Mexican girl in his town. He talked about her a lot. He had a lot of money from selling his ranch after the divorce and I wondered how long it would be before Kara drained him of it. We drank all night and I crawled into bed.
I had to go to work. Three hours into my shift I walked off. I was only working for her. I took a bus to the courthouse the next morning and paid my old fines.

She whined at work and the sports fan said he wanted to kill me. I told her he knew where I lived and that I would shove a football up his ass. Bill laughed. She couldn't deal with our friendship. I almost loved the guy. While she worked to pay the bills for once in her life, Bill and I sat out by the pool and drank and swam. I was sorry to see him go.
Another month passed and I was hanging out with Robles. He had met a girl, and had already moved in with her. I got a job in a cafe making coffee across from Phoenix College. A lot of fine young girls came in and it made Kara even worse.

Sometimes she would stay gone all day on the weekends. I didn't care. When she got drunk she would babble about her husband in Manhattan, how he was a great guy and how she broke his heart and how she missed him, how his rock band was getting huge out there and he was going to be a rock star.

Kara got fired from her job for not doing her job and for wearing skimpy little tank tops to work, showing off her cow tits. She got a severance check. The next weekend she said she was flying to Colorado to visit relatives, and something was wrong about it, but was a nice weekend alone. Her husband called from New York to talk about the divorce papers and we had a small conversation. He sounded like a cool guy. I asked him if she knew anybody in the publishing business. He laughed.

I was working my last two weeks at the cafe. Bill had been calling and he asked me to move up to central Oregon with her. I wanted out of Phoenix. Summer was approaching, and I knew that it was a good chance for me to leave. At this point, it went beyond whether it was right or wrong to stay with her. It was survival, but it wasn't. It had already reached the stage where she could have dropped dead and I would have gone out to eat.

I drove the entire trip. Bill was cleaning his car in the street. We were stopping at her grandmother's, and Bill was out front. He had a haircut. When he saw me he laughed and jogged over. We got out. He hugged me first. Kara bitched about it. Her grandmother was old and near death. She had a lot of spunk for someone like that. We stayed at Bill's apartment that night. He had a small place and we had the floor. We looked around for places the next day. They were cheap out there but so was the pay. I found a job my first time out at the classiest restaurant in town bussing tables for the rich golfers. I quit the same night.

Kara had told me that Bill wanted to live in a house with us. I was all for it. One night he asked us when we were going to have children. She wanted a baby. I didn't. I knew she was sterile. I had been shooting into her for months and nothing had happened. I also knew she was sterile because the Gods had some mercy.

We found a house. It was expensive but she had to have it. She went to Bill for a loan and it disgusted me. I would have been fine in an apartment. They were cheap out there. This house would cost around 900 bucks a month after the bills. The average pay out there was around six bucks an hour. I went with it, knowing it wouldn't last and feeling good about it. After Bill hung out with us for a few days, he decided to keep his apartment. I was glad for him.

20

I was hung over and I poured myself a glass of orange juice. She was watching me from the couch in front of the television. For someone who said it was for idiots, she watched a lot of it and always had to have one. She spoke from her lazy couch:

"You need to ask me if I would like some orange juice as well. You need to work on not thinking about yourself all the time."

I poured her a glass and walked over and poured it over her head, then I threw the glass against the wall and shattered it. I took my glass and sat behind my typewriter. She knocked me over in my chair and slid my pants down and went down on me. To get off, I thought about the girl who worked the coffee shop on the main drag.

Kara's rich aunt out in a small mountain town gave her a part time job in a store she owned that sold children's clothes and toys. Through Bill, I got a job in construction, building complexes on a golf course. $6.75 an hour. It was a joke. The owner of the company was making big money and he paid his workers crumbs and they loved it. The same job would have paid double anywhere else.

I worked the month away. Bill had helped her out with rent and she could barely make the payments on the car he had signed on for her. Somehow it was up to me to pay him back and help her on the payments. But the real pain hit when I would see the fine, young country girls giving me the fuck eye and I could do nothing about it.

One morning she was vomiting. She was already a week late and I was worried. She said she was pregnant. She was happy. The look on her face reflected greed more than the happiness of harboring a life. She dropped me off at work. I was devastated. My life was over. She would never abort it and I wouldn't see a child go without. I saw death tipping his hat to me.

At work I was outside of myself. The rednecks I worked with became more cruel and defeated. The job felt to pay even less, and the rich golfers in the distance swung their clubs into my groin. I was not alive anymore. I had signed the dotted line and the man with the horns was smiling. I shot a nail through my finger and walked off the job, walked nine miles home wearing the tool belt.

I walked past the house to her grandmother's, where we played cards and drank vodka. Kara was working until dark and I needed to drink and I was almost broke off my ass. I liked Kara's grandmother, and she liked me more than she liked Kara. I drank and passed out on her couch. The next thing I saw was Kara yelling at my face about me quitting my job. She had driven out to pick me up and the big, fat man told her I had walked.

She was driving her car beside me as I walked home.

"WHO THE FUCK DO YOU THINK YOU ARE? COMING TO MY HOME AND TAKING OVER AND MAKING MY FAMILY HATE ME? GET OUT OF MY LIFE!"

I kept walking. She sped to the house and locked the doors. I walked to the small store up the street and picked up a cheap 40 ounce and drank on the steps of the house. The grass was high and if you didn't mow it when everyone else did they gave you the Amish shun. They were small town Christians and they lived for church and death and Jesus. I drank on the steps. She opened the door and looked down at me, her eyes wet with her drama.

"You don't even care, do you?"

"No." I said.

A week later I was hired as a bartender. I would start on Monday. Bill got me the job. I went to work with Kara, and walked around the austere mountain town while she worked. It was nice. Old wood and clean air. I heard a famous quarter back lived there. I walked around and drank coffee.

I decided not to drink beer or any kind of liquor for a while, for no other reason than I was doing it out of boredom and it felt weak.

When I popped in on Kara she was talking to her husband in New York. She kept pushing marriage on me when she was already married. She told him we were coming out to pick up her things sometime in the fall. She hung up and looked at me.

"He's always doing so fucking great."

"I'll bet."

She screamed at me and I walked around town some more. When I came back in at the end of her shift, she was crying at the counter. She told me she had just had a miscarriage in the bathroom.

She ran over and held me, sobbing. I held her. I didn't want to.

"Are you sure?" I said. She said she was sure. I told her I needed to be alone, and she told me to be strong. I walked out into a sunny park and looked up. I walked faster, and soon I was running, leaping up and flipping the branches. I would stop and kiss the ground. I laughed with joy. I actually hugged a tree. I looked up to the sky again and saluted. From that day on *I* faked every orgasm.

The job was all right. They only served beer and wine so it was easy. Tips were minimal but I made enough to cover my share. Bill would always be there for Kara because she was a loser. I always ended up putting more in than she would.

I didn't like her methods. If we had a bill for $200 and she only had half she would spend it on bullshit, saying that we were so far from the $200 anyway that it didn't matter. I told her creditors liked initiative and that some money paid was better than nothing. I had to deal with a lot of the payments. She was a leech and I was her vein. I imagined living in the small town with Helena, having Bill for her uncle. I would have loved it.

My favorite night at work was Wednesday, ladies pool league night. These horny, overweight cow town women who loved to tip me well. I could bet and win anything that Kara would show up toward the end of my shift and wait for me to close and leave with her, though she had to be up early. She had landed a job in a town over selling bathroom fixtures. I thought it was symbolic that she sold toilets.

I had weekends off at the bar. Kara wanted to drive into Portland and walk around Hawthorne and shop with my money. I wanted to go. We parked and walked around, then sat in a coffee shop. I felt this weird coldness from the window. I looked over and saw a sign over a building across the street: SHEEP EXCHANGE. My stomach quivered. I smiled a mean smile. Kara asked me what as wrong. She knew about Helena. She had never met her but she was insanely jealous of her. I told her I wanted to walk over and see if she was working and say hello. She was trapped. She couldn't really say no. She followed me across the street. I could feel a fight with her already coming on. In the store Kara walked toward the back and I stopped when I saw Helena writing something down at the counter. Kara had walked behind a clothes rack and was watching and I didn't care.

21

It was her. The same face, the same hair and eyes and neck and arms. I was bearded and rough and she was still amazing. My heart fell back against my spine, its blood running with the wolves of my regret. She was perfect and once mine and I had lost her. She was right there. It was no thought, no six year long dream. It was real. I walked up to her and tapped her shoulder, that lovely shoulder. She turned and looked up at me. I watched her face go through many phases and then she was in my arms again, laughing and holding me. Life returned to my muscles, my arms and soul. It was like a feeding. I picked her up off the ground and held her. I was actually holding her again.

When I put her down she hugged me again and pulled at my beard.

"Wow. Look at you," she said. I took her hands and held them.

"How have you been?" I asked. It hurt.

She said she was fine. I asked her about her life. Kara walked up behind me. Helena looked at her. I badly wanted Kara to disintegrate into thin air.

"Oh. Helena, Kara."

Kara put her hand out with a plastic smile. Helena shook it and nodded to her and said hi. Watching their flesh meet made me ill. Helena was so pure and beautiful, and here I was with this damaged bitch. Kara slithered away as if she had an interest in used clothes. Helena and I talked, and I walked over and told Kara that I was going to spend Helena's lunch break with her. She played it off coolly, but told me she'd be at the car in half an hour. If I wasn't there she was leaving. She had recently had her hair cut short by Bill's girlfriend and she'd dyed it to bright yellow. I watched her walk out of the store, and she moved like an angry dyke. Helena looked at me and in one look I explained everything and she understood.

We sat in the bar around the corner. She ate and I drank coffee. I reached into my backpack.
"I have something for you."
She smiled. I pulled out a stack of my poems and short stories. They were originals. I had no other copies.
"What's this?"
"Some of the things I've written."
She read the first page slowly and shook her head, smiling her smile,
"I knew you'd fall into something like this."

I told her about the years behind us. She told me she was still with the same guy and that he had to go back to Phoenix for a couple of months to make some money. I knew if I had been there alone I would have been with her again. I would have driven her home after work and we would have another chance. I sincerely wished Kara murdered. My timing would have been perfect if she hadn't have been there. Helena saw in me what people like Kara never could, regardless of how we ended. She saw atonement and hard work. Kara simply saw jewelry. We talked and I told her that I still loved her and she started to cry. Then Kara walked past the window and gave me the finger. Helena looked at me and laughed,
"You're out of your mind."
I saw her car drive past the window and she gave me a shitty look from behind the wheel. Helena watched her disappear, "God. What a psycho."
We looked at each other more than we talked, and her lunch was over, went by like no time at all. I also asked her if she missed me, or knew that I had missed her. A strong silence followed, and she gave me a hug outside and I watched her walk into her store and the earth grew as cold as a casket in a cemetery in Moscow.
It started to rain. I walked up Hawthorne with no jacket. It was getting windy and frozen out there. I looked up. The clouds were moving in. I watched the sky bleed its grey blood. The clouds were grinning. They had no tolerance for life. They simply bled where they told themselves to. I reached up and felt my hair and my face, the lines about the sockets. My bones were back there, blocks away in her

store and I was powerless, stuck in Portland with no coat, no money, no love. A horn honked and I jumped in.

She was quiet until we reached Government Camp. She told me that when we got back to town we were through. We would only live together until I saved enough money to leave on. I looked out the window and watched the soldiers maneuver tanks and long, heavy green trucks through the gates of the base.

"Deal."

She pulled over and screamed at me to get out. It was snowing.

"Listen. If I get out, and I'm not afraid to get out, you will never see me again. Do you want me to get out?"

She screamed and floored it. I reached over and turned on the radio.

Back at the house I sat behind my typewriter and read my own poetry. She was in the room packing. She came out and told me she was leaving. I kept my eyes on the page.

"Good riddance. Wait."

She turned and stared at me.

"You put yourself exactly where you are right now," I said, "Just like I did."

She closed the door. I heard the car pull away. I reached for a sheet of paper but the drawer was empty. I walked up the alley behind the house and waited to cross. Her car in the parking lot, and she was on the payphone. I crossed and walked up behind her. She was telling him that she had a nice home and asked him if he ever got the present she mailed him for Thanksgiving. When she was asking him if Arizona was still beautiful I walked by without looking at her. The phone came down immediately. She was on me like a shadow in the store. I paid for the paper and walked out. She stood in front of me, so I stepped around her. She started screaming. She told me it wasn't who I thought it was and that she had mailed her old boss' kid a present. She hated her old boss, and he hated her. She told me I was insane and paranoid. I pressed the cross button and looked at her.

"You're embarrassing yourself. I have writing to do. You should call him back. It's rude to hang up on people."

As I crossed the street I felt her keys hit me in the back. I stopped and picked them up and tossed them to her easily. She caught them and stared at me like a confused dog. Or a rat.

I was sitting at the desk when the front door opened and I smelled alcohol.

"Hi, Bill." I said to the smell.

He sat on the couch behind me. I didn't turn around.

"I wanna know why my niece is at my place in tears.I waved him off and kept reading, making marks in the margins. He raised his voice.

"Look pal, I'm not fucking you and you're not mad at me. So don't be sitting there treating me like some bitch."

I turned around.

"You're right. I'm just so sick of this shit. She's a fucking soap opera and I can't act."

He held his glass over to me. I shook my head. He drank and looked at me.

"She really loves you. Hell, I love you. I don't know what the problem is."

He held the drink out again. I took it from him and set it down, "I don't like her anymore, Bill. She's a liar and a con artist and a cheat. I don't know why I put up with it. I never have before."

He looked at the drink on the desk. I went ahead and drank some and handed it back to him, "You know I like you, Bill. You know I like your mother. But I can't hang around this scene much longer."

He said he understood. I told him what was said in the room stayed in the room. I asked him to keep her at his place tonight. He shook my hand and left.

I packed everything. It was snowing out there. She would be gone all night, and the next bus left the station at 6 in the morning. I laid down and went to sleep.

I felt her crawl into bed with me. She was sobbing and telling me how sorry she was. Bill must have talked to her. I was completely unattached and not attracted to her and had been for months, and when she took her clothes off and started touching me I thought of other girls. Nothing was harder than getting it up for her, then I would jerk inside of her like I had finished, then I would go into the bathroom and run the water and finish with my hand, or I wouldn't finish at all. Either way it was hell.

The next morning I awoke to her unpacking my things and putting them back in their places. I stared at the ceiling and did the same with my priorities, figuring out how much money I would have at the end of the month. I decided to move to Portland.

I told my boss at the bar that I was leaving in two weeks. Payday was once a month. I had wondered why I hadn't received any checks for three weeks. I was living on my tips, and so was she. She put an ad in the paper for a roommate and a young, obese blonde girl answered. Her name was Erica and she was a virgin. I didn't like her. She and Kara hit it off. Figured. I was 27 years old and Kara was 32. It was my Venice Beach girlfriend all over again, only a more psychotic, dependent version.

22

One night at the bar she stopped by and gave me a dozen yellow roses. I didn't know how she afforded them. I set them in the trash. When I came home the two of them were on the couch, and I noticed a small black and white ball on the floor. I thought it was guinea pig. I was tired from the rush of rednecks. I looked down.
"What is that?"
"A puppy." Kara said.
We weren't allowed to have pets. It was on the lease. I reached down and picked up the ball. It unfolded in my palm. A little puppy with a big belly and a tiny face, which peered at me through these black eyes. I smiled. I kissed the pup and it clamped onto my beard and growled and wrestled with it. I talked to it gently. Erica was shocked. Kara laughed and nudged her.
"See. I told you."
I ignored the bitches and walked into the room with the dog. It was a little girl. I laid on my back and she fell asleep with her little head across my cheek. It was love. Kara and fatty walked into the room.
"Where'd she come from?"
"These kids were giving them away at the drugstore. She's only four weeks old. She was the smallest one."

I looked down at her and told her that papa would make sure she had a good life. The two gargoyles giggled. I didn't care.

"What should we name her?" Kara asked, excitedly.

"I don't know. Run some names by me."

They ripped off names. I held her up and stared at her while the names came, and the names weren't any good for her.

I held her over my chest and looked at her belly and her face. I knew who she was.

"We'll go with Meg." I said to the idiots.

The dog was a clever move on her part. Now she had a hook in me. I loved that dog. She was with me constantly. At work she fit into my shirt pocket. At night she was on top of me while I slept. She always had to be touching me in some way. I didn't know what drew her to me. She was never concerned with Kara and she wouldn't listen to her or eat if she fed her. I had to feed her. She was all belly and when I fed her I had to be right there or she wouldn't eat. She was so excited to eat she would shake. Bill came over to meet Meg. He said she was a Border Collie, Blue Heeler mix. A white stripe ran from the top of her head to her nose. When Kara would hold her she would whine for me and Kara would get sour. Dogs are instinctive. They're ruthless judges of character and they are never wrong.

I spent more time with Meg than with Kara. At night she would try to keep Meg outside of the bedroom door but Meg would howl and Erica would take her to her room, and I would get out of bed and knock on her door and take back my girl. Kara grew jealous, and Meg hated her guts. This created more fights in the house. Kara threatened to give her away and I told her if she did then I would kill her and I meant it. It freaked her out. There was something about that damned dog that I loved. I had never really been a dog person or a pet person. I couldn't figure it. I thought of the dog in Texas. Maybe I secretly wanted a dog. This one was a little angel, so innocent, so in need of care. Kara was a bad person and a bad provider. She was too selfish to love anything. After two weeks I finally had enough of her bullshit and I filled the cook's tank at the bar to give Meg and myself a ride to Portland while Kara was at work.

23

In one day I had a room and a job downtown. My job was waiting tables in a dead hotel lounge. My room had three huge windows which looked both ways down Burnside. There was a bathroom down the hall and visitors were not allowed after 10 p.m. I had a bed and a small basin and a medicine cabinet. The landlord was a cool black named Leon. He had a desk down in storage that he let me borrow. Rent was only $240 per month, but I paid him an extra hundred to keep Meg in my room, because they had a no-pets policy. I had a phone the next night. I called Kara to tell her that I was disconnecting my phone service at the house. She was crying. She told me she couldn't believe I was actually gone and then she started swearing at me and hung up. She kept doing the same until I unplugged the phone and awoke to a dozen nasty messages in between a few apologies.

On one of my days off I took a bus to Helena's work to see her. I passed the window and looked in to see the guy from Phoenix in there, talking to her. They were laughing. I slipped by and never called her.

The job wasn't bad. I worked nights. Tips were small but I worked with a fine, young redhead. Kara called me at night sometimes, but I was basically free from the bullshit. I was on my own, and in my favorite city.

Jeff Stewart

24

I began my first novel. It was a random idea for a short story that exploded into a full book. The manual was loud but the old man next door was deaf and the girl across the hall had multi-personalities. Sometimes I would see her sitting on the edge of her bed naked, arguing with herself. On a few nights before, I had thought of walking into her room and leaning her back on the bed. But I already had one schizophrenic on my hands, let alone having another one living right across the hall from me. The book started out with three friends walking around Portland. The main character took over and the other two stood back in his shadow. He was a drifter in Portland, trying to be writer and dealing with his ex-girlfriend up in Vancouver who played bass in an all girl band. It was narrative. I wrote 40 pages the first night. I would work my shift and come home and write until I was so tired I could no longer see the page. I was going like a psychopath. On the weekends I did nothing but write it. Kara kept calling. I told her to go ahead and consider us broken up.

The little redhead asked me what I was up to that night. I asked her if she would like to come over. She asked me where I lived. I told her. The Ace Hotel, Room 308.

She was off after I was, so she had to climb the fire escape to my window. I had already bought the beer and the condoms. She climbed in. It was a dangerous walk up the stairs because they were icy. I helped her in. Meg came out from under the bed, looked at her, then went back under and slept. She said she couldn't stay long because she had to work at six the next morning, since the morning hostess had quit. I was off for three days. She saw my typer and the pages.

"Are you a writer?"
I handed her a beer from the sixer I had chilling on the fire escape. I had no fridge.

"I'm trying."
"Is that a novel?"
"Yes."
"Wow. I couldn't imagine writing a whole book. It seems difficult."

She was such a sweet, sexy child. We drank and played music. When I could take it no longer I ripped her clothes off. I had been with a demon for so long that I forgot how great it was to have a body like hers, so young and tight and clean and curvy. Her ass was a new world to me, so high and pert and bubbly, that curvy lower back and flat stomach, those young red lips I ran my tongue over. I was cannibal eating flesh again after decades of eating wilted leaves on a dismal island. I really let her have it. I threw her around the room like a gorilla throwing an infant. It was pure atonement, an escaped murderer feeling the knife after being in solitary for 44 years. I kept it going for hours. She was wrecked.

I woke her up with my typewriter early in the morning. She jumped up and got her things together and climbed out after she kissed me. I watched her little body move across the street down there to her car from my chair. I was a king again.

One of the cooks was selling his old four-door for 300 dollars. I took the bus across the river and bought it after my shift. It was long and light blue and clean inside. I parked it a few blocks across Burnside where the parking was free, went home and worked on the book.

The phone rang. It was Bill, begging me to come down there and see Kara because she was losing it, making his life a living hell. I told him to drive her up to where I was but he had to work. I owed Bill some favors, well, she did, but I knew he would never collect from her and I felt for him. I told him I'd drive out the next afternoon and stay for a night. Really, I just wanted to drive the car somewhere.

In the bedroom Kara took her clothes off and got on all fours:
"Make love to me!"
I shuddered inside but I did it. I pulled out and shot across her back. She started crying. She asked me if there was someone else.

"No."

"Why didn't you do it inside of me?"

"I forgot."

She started sobbing. I told her maybe this was a bad idea. She jumped up and held me, telling me how much she missed me, needed me. I stayed for two days, and she behaved like a little girl. Erica was a bitch but she didn't matter. I spent most of my time with Meg. Bill took us out for drinks and we stopped by to visit his mother, where we played cards and drank vodka. I had to leave that night, and I couldn't help but feel like it was my last time being there, seeing any of them. And now that I was away from the whole situation, everything was less evil, and I had found a sense of peace with all of it, even her.

I stopped on the way out of town and bought some snow chains for the pass. I had made it all right getting there, but it was sketchy. When I was leaving the store, the car quietly died. I called Bill from the station and he brought one of his mechanic buddies with him. The engine was gone, he said. Kara was more than happy to give me a ride back to the city.

She was off work for 2 days. I slid Leon a bottle of Scotch to let her stay in the room with me. She liked my room, the green shag, the windows. I took her out for dinner then I went to work. The redhead was there and I told her what was going on at my place. She was with it. Halfway into my shift I had a phone call. Kara. She was drunk and screaming, and I heard my typewriter hit the floor. I hung up and punched out early.

She had gone through my garbage. I opened the door and saw her holding a pint of whiskey wearing one of my work shirts and her panties. The used condom was on my desk. I sat down and put my typewriter back on the desk and put the condom in the trash can. Meg walked over. I picked her up and set her under the desk with her favorite t-shirt of mine to sleep on. When I sat back up the bottle hit me on the eye. I looked at her and she gasped,

"I am so fucking sorry. I was aiming for the can, I swear to fucking God I was!"

I shoved her out of the door and tossed her clothes at her. Before I could close it she charged back, in and I fell over. I sat there. She was standing next to me. She pointed to her vagina.

"YOU SEE THIS? THIS IS YOURS! HOW COULD YOU?"

I looked at it and told her to get out. She moved on me but I grabbed her hand and twisted it, bringing her down on both knees as I stood.

"You shed any more of my blood and I'll break your neck."

I threw her hand away and she fell back sobbing. She argued with me and sobbed all night. She wouldn't leave. Every three hours she would have sex with me and sob the whole way through it.

It was a tense day. When the cooks at work asked what happened to my face I told them I was jumped in Chinatown.

I worked Christmas day and made a lot of money. Kara was nourishing the hope that I would be there for the holidays. Christmas night Bill called my room from the house. I heard Kara in the background screaming, Erica trying to calm her. She was yelling that she was carrying my baby and she was going to have it alone. Bill said she had been up drinking for two days. I told him I was sorry about what was happening at the house. When he started questioning me about the redhead I told him it was none of his business. He asked me to come down and live there again.

I kept at the novel. The day after New Year's I hammered out the last sentence. I had 675 single spaced pages. I was off on the 3rd and I sat in a bar and read it. It was awful. Writers are escapists anyway, but this book was all escape and it was just plain bad writing. I liked the prose in parts and the character's voice in parts, but it was a bad book. I had never been so depressed.

Back at work it was late. The redhead came back and told me I had another call. She rolled her eyes.

"Hello?"

"Is that her? Is that the girl you fucked?"

"Yes."

She screamed. I told her to stay out of it, that the girl had no idea. Kara wanted to talk to her. I hung up. She called back and began harassing the girl. She called again and the redhead begged me to answer.

"You know what I'm doing right now, baby? I'm packing. I'm moving to Los Angeles. My friend Glen is down there. I'm getting out of this fucking cold. If you want to come you'd better be here before Friday."

I went home that night and tried to rewrite some of the book, but I decided to let it go.

The next day before I went to work, I was halted by Leon and the owner of the building. Some of the tenants on the floor had complained about the noise from the fight with Kara, and when the owner had done a walk-through, Meg barked at him. Leon gave me a look, and I went with it, because I knew he had to play dumb to keep his job, and I owed him for breaking the rules for Meg. I was served with a 24 hour notice to vacate, but Leon called me at work later and gave me an extra day. I had recovered my 300 dollars from the cook who sold me the car, and I decided to keep that for a rainy day, one even wetter than this one.

That night was Wednesday, and Kara called me at work, bawling.

"I've changed my mind. I'm leaving tomorrow. Fuck you!"

She hung up. I looked out at the snow. Los Angeles. My novel was horrible and I was stuck in the snow with no motivation and nowhere to live beyond Friday, anyway. I knew nobody in Portland, and I had Meg. I asked one of the girls who bused tables if she wanted to make fifty bucks.

The door was locked. I had all of my things on the porch. Los Angeles sounded good to me. There was something about it this time. I knocked and Erica let me in. She wasn't happy to see me. She told me it was their house now. I called her a lesbian. Meg jumped up on the couch and fell asleep.

I stood over the bed until my presence woke her. She looked up at me and wrinkled her brow.

"You're here."

"Los Angeles, huh? You're not even packed. More bullshit?"

"I'm still going. You?"

"I'll go."

"We have to talk first."

"No talk. It'll just change my mind."

"Fine. Don't go."

I walked out of the room. She was on me in nothing flat. I sat on the couch. Meg was chewing on my shoelace and Kara tried to kiss me from behind the couch. I told her to start packing.

I drove the whole way again. On the freeway I looked over to the old beach where I once rode and lived in the beach house. I wanted to point things out to her but I didn't want to share anything sacred with her.

She had no money. I had some in my pocket and the three hundred dollars hidden away, in a side pocket of my wallet. In Hollywood off Western, I talked a landlord into letting us move in with what I had up front. It was a big upstairs studio with a courtyard in the back for the tenants. Everything was on my shoulders again.

25

A guy I had met while walking Meg told me I should go on welfare, like all the artists who move to Hollywood. He said welfare was just an artist's grant. I thought about it. I told her I was going to do it, and of course she had to do it. It took a while to get it, a lot of returning and waiting. I didn't see any artists in the line. I saw poor Armenians and bums.

After a bunch of bullshit, we were each granted two hundred and twenty eight dollars a month, and one hundred twenty dollars in food stamps. There were other things involved, job sheets that had to be signed by potential employers, phone calls, etc. I had a phone connected and had my last check from the hotel in Portland mailed to the apartment. It started a fight when the check came. When I was out with Meg she actually called the hotel up there and talked with the redhead, trying to get some dirt on me. The redhead was nice to her but there was nothing left to talk about. When she told me she had called the hotel I wouldn't talk to her for a few days.

Times were lean. If I wanted to get a beer or some cheap wine I had to go through the line and make small purchases with the food stamps save the change up. Rent was 400 per month but Kara spent half her check on bullshit and we were short.

The landlord was a cool one. He barely spoke English but he could read what I said to him. The whole complex could hear my typewriter but no one complained.
Except Kara.

Her friend Glen was a pansy. He was tall and skinny and he looked like James Dean with a beak. We drove out to meet him where he worked downtown. It became clear to me that the plan had been for her to move out there and live with him by herself. They had gone to high school together. He had moved there to be an actor, but ended up parking cars in his father's lot.
I had Meg in the car. When I stood to meet him he looked at Meg and cocked his head gravely at Kara.
"I can't live with a pet."
I let go of his hand.
"No one here's living with you, pal."
He stepped back and sized me up. I looked at his tight jeans and pointy shoes and gelled Elvis hair. He asked me if I had a problem with him and stepped up to me. I shook my head.
"Don't even try it, motherfucker."
Kara jumped in and did him a favor. I could already feel his gel on my knuckles. Kara tried to make peace and suggested we walk around together. I nodded at him.
"I'm not going anywhere with this pussy."
He started to swell. I told Kara to let him go. He was everything I hated: vanity, conceit, softness, an awareness of his hair and clothes. It figured they were friends. Kara knew better. On the freeway she yelled at me about her friend. I told her he was just another one of her believers and he had no moxie. He was the shadow of a shell. She became quiet, then close. Back at the apartment I wouldn't touch her.
I rode my bike to Venice Beach. It was a long ride down Santa Monica. I checked out the old haunts. Kim was long gone. Her place was a bead store. I rode in Venice behind the courts and checked out the girls. I stayed at the beach all day. I made Century City by dark. I didn't like it or Beverly Hills. They looked planted. When I walked up the stairs I heard her on the phone, laughing. I stuck my ear to the door. She was talking to the sports fan in Phoenix. She told him she missed him and she wanted to see him again. I heard the conversation. She was using words verbatim from the calls she'd made to me from New York. She told him she loved him and I opened the door. The phone came down fast. I shook my head. Here came her tears.
I sat on the floor and played with Meg. She looked down at me. I asked her how

the Raiders were doing this season. She ran to the bathroom and locked the door. When she came out I was undressing to take a shower.

She tried a new angle.

"Where have you been all night?"

"I rode my bike to Venice. That better have been a collect call."

I didn't care. I was numb toward her. She was only around to pour Meg food and take her out while I was gone, anyway. That's as high as I held her company.

She told me she thought I had left her. I kept undressing.

"So the first thing you do is call that guy and tell him you love him. Oh, I liked your stories. Imaginative and original."

Her face turned yellow. She told me that she thought I was over her and she panicked. She said she couldn't be alone. It was the first honest thing I'd heard her say. I took off my boxers and ran the shower. She tried to touch me but I blocked her. I told her I wanted to be clean and my shower would give her time to think of some more good ones. When I finished my shower she was curled up in a fetal position on the carpet, sobbing. I stepped over her and took Meg for a walk down the boulevard. When I came back she was still like that. I hit the machine. Loudly.

The next morning I was far from her on the floor with Meg. A knocker woke me up. It was early. I looked out the peephole and saw a hairdo. I opened the door. A Mexican woman in a business suit. I asked her what she wanted. She asked me if I was the writer. Kara sat up from the floor. I asked her again what she wanted. She gave me a card: Glitter Productions. She said she was old friends with the landlords and she had heard my typewriter a few times and the landlord told her I was writing constantly. I was tired and impatient.

"So what are you, lady? A publisher?"

"Not quite. May I come in?"

I opened the door. I was in my boxers. Kara covered herself and gave me a dirty look. The lady was embarrassed.

"Oh. I'm sorry. Your wife?"

"No. That's charming, though. Come in."

I found a shirt. Meg growled at the lady. I picked her up. I had the only chair so she sat on the edge of the table.

"Do you have something I can read, something short, maybe?"

I looked at her.

"I can read it here." She said.

I asked her again what she wanted. She asked me if I'd ever written a screenplay. I told her I hadn't. She said she never did this but something told her to meet me. She said she had seen me before.

"Where?" Kara asked like a bitch.

The lady was cool and calm.

"I have seen him walking past with the pooch. I said hello to him not even a week ago. I told Juan he had crazy eyes. Juan told me he was always making noise with the typewriter."

I carried Meg into the kitchen and grabbed a bottle of water from on top the fridge. I brewed some coffee. The lady stood and asked me again for something to read. She told me she was working for a subdivision of a famous three-lettered network and she had a shot at a pilot and she wanted to see if she liked my writing, that something told her to meet me, something in her stomach and it is never wise to not listen to her stomach. I liked that. I walked to the closet and hauled out a huge box full of pages. I plopped it on the table next to her.

"You have written all of this?"

"Yes."

"A big box."

"I have eight more just like it."

She raised her eyebrows and nodded to Kara. I glanced to Kara's face. It showed fear. I went through some folders and gave her a few short things maybe four pages long then a long short story. I offered her coffee. She accepted. I dressed while she read. She sat there for a long time. Kara watched her like a hungry man watching a pig turn over a fire. This would never happen to her. The lady finished.

"Very real. Very heartbreaking. Solid work. Published?"

I laughed. "No. I'm a loser. Ask my wife."

Kara hung her head. The lady asked if I had anything less serious, some comedy. I thought to a short story I had written with a lot of dialogue. I pulled out another box and found it.

"I have this."

She read it and laughed. She told me I was talented. I said thank you. Kara didn't expect me to say that.

"I have read many, many, horrible manuscripts by writers with agents. Would you like a job?"

"I don't know."

The screenwriting had done Fante in and Algren was fired from his own movie. I didn't know anything about screenplays. She left me her card and asked if she could take some of my things with her. I refused. She dug into her purse and put a fifty on the table. I told her to keep her money, that I still had to think about it.

"Nonsense. I, too, have starved for my dreams. Consider this a fee for letting me browse and not buy. The address is on the card. Tomorrow, at let's say eleven?"

"All right. But no commitments."

She laughed shook my hand. She told me I was a good man and together we could be rich. She nodded to Kara before she left.

"It was nice to meet you. You are a lucky girl."

I locked the door behind her. Kara stared at me from the floor. She was speechless. I held the fifty in front of me and looked at it.

"Fuck. Let's eat."

We had a Cajun breakfast on the boulevard. Meg was tied to the table where we ate outside. Kara had not said a word the entire time. She wouldn't stop looking at me. I wasn't excited about this. I didn't like sitcoms and any sitcom I would write would not be viewable. But it was nice to eat a hot breakfast again. She watched me eat and told me she thought I was amazing.

"Now you do. Sure."

Here came the tears. She told me she knew I was going to make it and she was sorry for the things she had said and done to me. I told her not to be hypocritical, that it didn't suit her. I told her I didn't want to talk about anything to do with stress. I asked her if we could have one good day. She touched my hand.

"Of course, baby."

We drove to the beach. Meg loved the sand. I stretched out on it and thought about the deal. I closed my eyes and drifted off. When I awoke it was grey out and getting cold. I sat up. Meg was curled around my leg and Kara was gone. I sat up and watched the ocean turn over. It was good. It was good to be on the beach with my dog. I heard footsteps in the sand and turned. Kara with a big coffee for me. She said she loved this beach.

"I was sitting on this beach nine years ago about this same exact time with my first girlfriend," I said.

She asked me who broke it off. I told her. She leaned her chin on my shoulder.

"Why did you leave her?"

"She had no spine."

That night at the apartment I drank some cheap but decent red, and wrote. The phone rang. After a few rings I picked it up and answered. There was a long pause and a hang up. I dialed *69. It was an Arizona number. Kara looked at me.

"Your boyfriend," I said and unplugged the phone.

She told me how sorry she was, that she must have been out of her mind. I shoved her off. That night Meg and I slept in the kitchen.

Jeff Stewart

26

Her office was on the boulevard, down near La Brea. It was on the seventh floor. Behind her left shoulder through the window I could see the Hollywood letters on the mountain. It was already like a sitcom. She told me she wanted a screenplay about a Hispanic family in Manhattan who lived in a high-rise apartment. Their apartment floods. Everything is soaked. They throw everything they own into the water in hopes of getting a large insurance settlement, but at the end of the episode it turns out that they didn't have insurance and they had lost everything. She explained some things and gave me a copy of a screenplay she had written for references, the camera angles and the interior/exteriors and the pans and the zooms and the number of pages. I told her I'd start it when I got home.

    I turned the key. Kara was eating.
    "How'd it go?"
    "It was dull."
    "I know about screenplays. Want some help?"
    "No."
    I wrote the screenplay in three hours. I had the family knee deep in water the entire episode. I threw in some dark humor and some morality. It was easy, child's

play. No wonder there were so many screenwriters. The phone rang. Kara answered and gave it over. It was the lady.
"How is it coming?"
"It's finished."
"You're kidding."
"No. It was easy."
"Can you bring it down right now?"
"No."
"Mind if I stop by and get it..."
"I'll be here."
"Do you need anything?"
"A big, fat submarine sandwich and a coffee, double shot, lots of chocolate."
I could hear her writing it down. I smiled at myself from the phone. Espresso from an agent. Kara must have been proud.
"Got it. A sub and a coffee. What would you like on the sub?"
I told her and she hung up. I was waiting for Kara to mention that I could have asked her if she would've liked some coffee as well, but the ice she was on with me was so thin even a wrong look would drown her.
I took Meg to the courtyard to do her business. Kara sat down and read the screenplay. I didn't have fun writing it and that wasn't a good sign.
Upstairs Kara was halfway through it. She said it was brilliant.
"It's crap," I said, "But maybe."
Half an hour later she was at the door. She handed me my coffee, I poured some in a glass for Kara and she smiled. I had surrendered my chair to the lady and she was reading intensely. She had also bought me a bag of good coffee. Kara sat on the floor. I stood. The lady was quiet. She turned the last page and held the manuscript to her chest.
"Beautiful."
Kara's jaw dropped. I didn't say anything. The lady hugged me and told Kara I was a natural. I asked her about the money. She said they still had to shoot the pilot. There would be a few months to screen actors and she would have to get a budget from her corporate headquarters in Mexico City. She said there was no way we could lose. I asked her again about the money. She said until they got they ball rolling she would pay me ten dollars an hour as office help full time but I wouldn't have to show up or work. She said I would have to go under contract after the pilot was accepted and that she could get me around thirty grand to sign my name. Then there were royalties and contingencies but they might not want to give me them right away. I understood it could still possibly be bullshit. She was flying down to

corporate after she'd made some minor edits on it. She asked for a short story to add to her presentation of her new star writer. I gave her the ten pager I had written about a one legged vacuum salesman who commits suicide by alcohol after he demos a machine for his ex-wife and her new, wealthy husband. He was a recovering alcoholic and he closed the sale then killed himself. She thanked me again and left me another fifty. I locked the door behind her. Kara ran up and hugged me.

Four days later the lady called me and said that her people liked the script but they wondered if I could tone it down a bit. They thought some of the dialogue was too involved for the viewing audience. Still, they loved the work and said it showed promise and she said they were never that kind, even with good writers, they just had to get some power in. I told her to change it how she saw fit.

That night I was drunk. I looked at my typer and around the apartment. Kara was on the floor reading and Meg was under my chair. The phone rang. Another hang up. The same number. It happened at least once a day. I was tired of it.

He answered. I called him by his name, and I asked him why he was hanging up on me. He tried to deny it, but I had the proof. Kara stormed into the bathroom. I asked him politely to hold on. I opened the door. She was holding a kitchen knife to her wrist. I told her to cut the veins vertically so no one could save her. She shot me an ugly sneer,

"I *mean* it. Get away from me or I'll *kill* myself!"

"Do it." I said.

I closed the door and got back on the phone. I asked him to level with me, and I told him I knew about them. He told me they had only had sex a few times, and also once in Colorado. I thanked him and told him she'd be there shortly. I also wished him luck. She came out of the bathroom. I stayed in my chair. Her tears came rolling. She tried to get close to me. I asked her about the time frame, besides Colorado. She told me. The first time was within a week of her working the job, before any trouble had really started. I was so mad I was calm. I told her I wanted no violence or damage or words, I wanted one complete night of silence.

It was three in the morning and I was drunk. Kara was sleeping. I poured Meg some food. I thought about the offer, the screenwriting job. I looked at my boxes of work and at my typewriter and my bike. I took the three hundred out of my wallet and shoved in my pocket. The years of wreckage and waste and slime and blood and work. Thirty grand was nothing compared to the compromise. I did not want to be an old author of my words, heard or unheard, with a motherfucking sitcom on my record. I dialed the number and left her a message. I told her that I respectfully resigned from even the chance and to keep the screenplay for the hundred bucks she flowed me and to please return my story. I hung up.

Kara jumped up from the floor and stared at me. I stood up and smiled at her.

"You are scum," I said.

I pulled the roll of bills from my pocket and peeled off three twenties for her. She saw the roll, and her face sank.

I hooked Meg's leash to her collar, and laid the money on the desk. "Gas money. In your car getting to Phoenix will take half of it." She tried to say something, but she stopped.

I led Meg to the door. I spoke sincerely.

"You have half an hour. Goodbye."

I left her there sitting like that. I walked Meg up the hill to Griffith Park and we walked around the path. Up at the observatory I stared over Hollywood and Los Angeles. It was a good place to sell your soul for scraps.

Back at the place her car was gone. Upstairs there was a pile of her old clothes in the middle of the floor. She had left me a note on the table. It was filled with a bunch of sorry bullshit. I noticed she'd kept her key. I trashed her clothes and went across Sunset and bought a new lock. Downstairs I gave Juan the hundred and fifty slack in the rent and explained to him with my hands that she was gone and she was by no means allowed in my apartment. He laughed and patted me on the back. I borrowed some tools from him and changed the lock. I unplugged the phone and spent four wonderful days in peace.

Jeff Stewart

27

I was writing beauty again. Being in the same area as Fante and writers of his ilk inspired me. I was really going at it. I reworked some of the short stories and got back to the poems more than ever. In the day I walked Meg up to the park and ran her. I still had food stamps and rent was covered for most of the month. I got a letter stating that I was no longer eligible for access since I had not complied with the worksheets and reports. The same letter came for Kara but I burned it. When I plugged the phone in I had no messages.

I had to get a job. It was hard to find work in Los Angeles. I had applied everywhere, even the places where I knew I would hate it and those that would never hire me. I was finally hired at a bagel shop on Melrose for five-fifty an hour.

It was a lousy job. Mornings to afternoons. All of the Melrose people came in with their special orders. Movie stars would come in, and they were short and ugly, with narrow shoulders and large craniums. The camera was kind to them. I hated everything about the job but I had bills to pay. Food service was nothing but aggression.

I vowed to keep in touch with the people I cared about. I called Robles and Greg and my sister in Phoenix. Everyone had my address and number. I didn't really like Hollywood but I was writing a lot. I mailed Greg some poems and stories and he mailed me some drawings and a book, titled Gashuffer. It was an anthology of fiction, and Greg's art was in it. He wrote that I had to mail it back after I read it. He said he knew the guy who put it together, a friend of his named Mick Grasso, who lived in the valley. He suggested I mail Grasso some of my shorter things. I called him to thank him by voice.

"It's cool, man. I like your new stuff. So does Steph. You've really come along with it."

"Thanks, Greg."

"Mail Grasso some shit. He's a cool dude. Have you read it?"

"I just opened my mail and read your letter."

"Man. He put in one of my drawings and he ran some post Buk shit. They corresponded before Bukowski died."

"Good."

"Grasso actually called me in '94 when he died. He was bummed."

"I know. I was living somewhere in the south when I heard."

"Anyway, man. I'm outta here. Want Mick's number?"

"No."

"You take good care. And the next time you wait almost three years to call me we're gonna brawl."

"I'll call you in almost three years."

I wanted to tell him that I'd tried to call when I drove those hitchers through Vegas, but I didn't. I sat back and read through the book. It was good, a little light in places, but a few old men in there were good. Greg's artwork was ever there. I wrote down the address and sent the book back out to Greg the same day, along with some originals.

I walked to the copy store and ran off some things I had written recently and mailed them to the P.O. Box from the back of the book. I wrote Grasso a short letter letting him know how I got a hold of the book and I left my phone number under my address. I mailed him nine pages. I didn't want to overwhelm him with a bunch of shit from a stranger.

I rode to work the next morning. I was feeling all right about mailing my stuff to Grasso. I had never submitted my work before, but I felt all right by doing it. Then I was hit by a car. I flew over my handlebars and landed out on La Brea. There was no oncoming traffic. I looked up. An angry Turk in a white mini van. He was yelling at me, pointing to the dent my bike had made. He didn't care that he'd hit me. I picked my bike up over my head and threw it against his van and stalked toward him. He peeled out and sped off.

At work, my boss saw my shoulder and sent me home. It wasn't broken but it was swollen and after a while I couldn't lift my arm. It didn't really hurt. I rode home slowly with one arm, typed poems with one hand. I called my boss the next day and told him I couldn't make it. Two days later I was fine. I still told my boss I couldn't make it. He said to take the weekend off and he'd see me on Monday. I could not afford the time off but I was writing and I was in a zone and I needed to be in that zone.

The phone rang. There was a long pause, and then some sobs. I hung up. She called back. She told me she really needed to talk. I realized she was calling from his phone so I let her talk. She was saying how she missed me and how much she wanted to come back to Hollywood. I couldn't take it anymore so I hung up. It rang again and I grabbed it.

"NOW WHAT?"

It was a man. He asked for me. He cleared his throat and read some lines from one of my poems, then broke out laughing. He continued:

"...and the music smiled
and the sky told truth
and all of our hands
showed promise."

He laughed again.
"Grasso?"
"Yeah, it's Mick."
"How's it going Mick? You got the folder."
"You are a fucking madman."
"I didn't know if you'd like it."
"Sure you didn't. You know Greg, huh?"
"Yes."
"Listen, where do you live?"
"Off Sunset and Western."
"Rough."
"It's not bad."
"So what did you think of Gashuffer?"
"I liked it. It had guts."

"You think so? I mean, you didn't think it was too intellectual?"

"Maybe for some. But fuck them."

"It went better than I thought it would. It actually sold. I'm doing another one when I get around to it. I just finished my own book."

We didn't talk for long. He verified my address and told me he would mail me some things he had done and my own copy of Gashuffer. We had talked on Thursday and his package arrived on Saturday. I read his poems and a short story and a flyer for his novel. It wasn't bad. He left his number in the letter but I didn't want to call him right away. I had things to write myself.

On Sunday I took Meg to the park and went riding. My shoulder was stiff and I knew I had to loosen it. Sunday night I wrote and Monday I was back in hell. I had two weeks pay coming and a hundred left in my pocket. I wanted to quit but getting a job out there was tough and I didn't want to go through it again. My boss switched me to the eleven to seven shift, and that made it better. Kara started calling in the mornings, every morning for three days. She would cry and sob and I would hang up on her.

The next night I brought home a girl from work and we had some fun. She was young and her body was Melrose, fake breasts and all. She left but I was worried that she might like me.

Kara called in the morning. She asked me what I did last night, that she had a strange feeling. I told her she was instinctive, because I had sex with a flawless body. She hung up. Here came the call back.

"Yes?"

"You could have waited for me, you know."

"Meaning what?" I said.

"You should have given me these two weeks away then let me come back. You know we are meant for each other. Shit, he just pulled up. I should go. I love you. Don't you miss me at all?"

I spoke the last words I would ever say to her,

"You're just a whore."

I hung up.

Friday from work I checked my messages. Six were from her and they were erased instantly. The seventh was from Mick. He called me by my last name and told me there was a party in the valley and to call him when I got home and to plan on crashing at his place tonight, or somewhere else, if everything went smoothly. The next four messages were from her. I called the phone company and had the number placed on caller rejection.

Jeff Stewart

It was always good to come home to my dog. She would leap up and scratch her paws on my legs and wag her tail and screech. She was constantly happy to see me. I could never get mad at her. She was smart naturally, and I had her trained well. It takes a lot of time to have a good dog. I called Mick, and he answered.

"Grasso. Got your message."

I gave him the directions. He told me he'd see me in an hour, tops. I hung up and walked Meg down the stars. She took a big dump on Robert Redford.

28

I opened the door. Grasso was tall and gangly with long dreads. I had never seen a white guy with dreads that good. He had this chin scruff that sat on his chin like a cotton ball. I shook his hand. He looked at me and nodded. I wasn't what he was expecting. I was tall and big with a full beard and the continual look of a man just out of bed. On the phone I sounded like a person who had a nice appearance and glasses and a clean cover. I sounded studious. I sounded intelligent. People were normally shocked to meet me after they'd spoken to me, mainly employers. They felt tricked.

He looked around my place and smiled. Meg didn't bark at him. He put his hand out and she pranced over. He played with her.

"Man. What's your dog's name?"

"Meg."

"She's beautiful. I can't have a dog where I live."

He looked out the window and at my typewriter.

"This place has potential."

I asked him where he was from. Vermont. We talked about back east and I told him a little about my time there. He said we should stay at my place for a while because right then the freeway was murder. I brewed some coffee. He pulled out a baggie and some papers, rolled a joint and lit up.

"You smoke?" He held the joint out.

"Here and there. I'll have a small one."

I took a hit. It was smooth. I walked in the kitchen and watched the coffee. I was glad I had bought the maker. Coffee was a rule. I would give up water before I gave up coffee. I asked him how he took it. Black.

"Black." I said. I was perfectly buzzed. I loaded mine with milk and sugar.

I wasn't going to bring up the writing first. In the living room he was playing tug of war with Meg and a sock I'd surrendered to her after she'd chewed a hole in it. I handed him the mug and I pulled up one of my boxes and sat on it. I asked him if he had a woman.

"I did. You?"

"Same here."

"You scare her away?" He laughed.

"Long story."

He flipped through some pages by my typewriter.

"You mind?"

"No."

He asked me if I ever wrote on a computer.

"Yeah. But the one I had got damaged during one of the moves, so now I use an electric or a manual. I like using a computer for length."

"But the poems run truer on the others." He said.

I showed him an ancient Underwood I had restored from an antique shop in Oregon. It was small. He rolled a sheet through and worked the keys.

"Good action."

"The print's cool. Times New Roman."

He asked me about the box I was sitting on. I was stoned, and showed him the closet with the other eight. He looked down at them and shook his head.

"That's a lot of product."

I had to leave Meg at the apartment. I poured her two bowls of food and water. Mick felt bad that we had to leave her. The house we were going to was in the Valley and we stopped for beer. Mick worked for a salary editing a famous skateboard magazine. He told me he never smoked or drank during the week or when he wrote. He said weekends were holy to him. We bought some liquor. When we got to the house it was full of people who knew him. There were only a few girls and they were with groups of men. Mick introduced me to everyone. After a while I found a seat on a picnic table outside. I watched Grasso make his rounds and shake hands. I put him at just under 30. He saw me at the table and sat across from me. Soon others sat around him. He was talking about getting something to eat, that he hadn't had anything in his stomach since the day before. A guy walked over and handed him a big glass of Guinness.

"Here you go, man. Here's supper."

Everybody was already drunk. Mick stared roughly at the glass and muttered.

"The Last Supper."

I laughed. Nobody else seemed to get it, or nobody else thought it was funny. He saw me laughing and put his hand up over the table at me for a high five. It became clear that we weren't going to make it out of there before morning.

I lost Grasso somewhere during the end of the party. I sat on the couch and watched the people. I heard him looking for me. Then I saw him. He was wrecked. He handed me a large manuscript in raw form.

"I forgot I had this in my car."

"Your book?"

"Damn right. When I finished that bastard I went through the worst depression. I wrote it by hand sitting in parks around my place then I used the computer to copy it, you know, do the fill-ins and make it legit."

It was a heavy book. He said he had to get some sleep.

I sat on the couch and read the book. It was a fast read for so many pages. It was put together like a collage of happenings. It was about a guy and his girlfriend and his buddies failing out of life. It was a good book. He had made it good by using a lot of suggestion. I laid the book on the table and stretched out and slept.

The couch felt good. I had been on the floor since Hollywood. I sat up and looked at the clock on the wall behind me. 11:00. Outside it was sunny. I stepped over a few bodies and walked out back and stood in the sun. I wasn't too hung over. The air was warm, and I watched a lizard scramble up the fence. He stopped, looked at me and ran over the top. I used to pull their tails off when I was a kid in Phoenix, and the lone tails quivered like a rattlesnake's. The pool was covered with a tarp and in the middle of the tarp where it sagged there were beer cans floating in a puddle. I heard the house rising mournfully. Bodies were slowly standing and stumbling into their cars. Grasso walked out back. He appeared unaffected.

"Morning." He said.

I nodded. I asked him if he wanted to get some breakfast. In the house I pulled the book from the table and handed it to him on our way out. He took the book and looked at me.

"How did you get this?"

I shook my head.

"Did I give this to you last night?"

"What do you think?"

He stopped and fanned the pages by the hood of his car. He gave me a stare.

"Well. Let me have it. How was it?"

I laughed at his face then pulled it together. "It's a great book, Mick. You've done it."

I put my hand out. He shook it.

"Good. You're the first person to read it. That's a good sign."

We got in the car. The sun reached in and punched him in the face.

"Goddamnit. Reach in my glove box and hand me my shades."

At a stop sign he asked me if there was anything about it I didn't like. I knew it was coming. I told him it was vague in parts but it had to be, he had no choice. I told him I thought it was ready to go.

We ate fried eggs on toast in a Spanish diner. I liked the feel of the Valley. It was desperation without care. Grasso had a nice apartment. He had an entire closet full of books he'd read. There were hundreds of them. He rolled another joint. I didn't partake.

Back at my place Meg had gone on the carpet and I had to scrub. Mick offered to take her out in the courtyard. It was getting dark and I had one message. My boss. I was supposed to work. I barely caught him at the shop. He told me it wasn't my fault, that he was late in posting the new schedule and I wasn't there to see it. I asked him if I was off tomorrow. He said I was.

I knew I had to work. I'd just spaced it. I had seen the schedule. I hung up and noticed Meg hadn't eaten or drank since I'd left.

We hit some bars by my place. We stayed in the Mahogany room in Hollywood. It was good drinking with Mick. The bar was full so we sat at a table and talked about great, dead men.

We moved to the bar. Mick was sitting next to huge black man straight out of 1930. He was smooth. They were talking low to each other. I was sitting on the corner next to Mick. I knew what they were doing but I didn't know what they were doing it over. Mick leaned over to me,

"Hey, man. Let me borrow twenty bucks, I'm a little short for this."

"For what?"

1930 opened his big palm under the bar. I looked under casually. A large black egg of hash. Mick looked at me and nodded. I gave him a twenty, and the deal was made under the bar, and Mick was happy with the deal. He kept giving me sly looks. Back at the booth we talked to a couple of girls but nothing was going to happen with them. Before we got to my place he hit an ATM and gave me a twenty. Upstairs he sat on the box and broke the hash apart, drunk. He looked like a giant squirrel maneuvering a black walnut.

"Man. 125 bucks for a two golf ball chunk."

"That's a good deal?"

He kept breaking the hash. "Hell yeah, it is."

Meg rose to his lap and sniffed the hash. She sneezed and crawled under my chair. Mick mixed in some of the egg with some weed and rolled it. He lit the end and inhaled. He held it out to me.

I took a hit.

"You don't get high that much, huh?" He asked.

"Not really."

I passed it back. He took another hit and handed it back over.

"You'll be good and high tonight," he said.

"Fuck it," I said, "When in Rome."

We heard gunshots and he laughed.

We finished the rollie. He said he had to get back and call some girl he'd met at the party. I wondered which one he was talking about. He broke me off a bit from the egg. We shook hands. I told him I'd send him some hash-induced poetry.

I smoked the rest of what he'd left behind. I was normal for a while then it hit me. It was good. I sat behind my Underwood and went for hours. Everything was all right. Everything was weightless and friendly. I ran out of typing paper. I was putting my shoes on when I heard somebody knocking. I hoped it wasn't who I thought it was. If I had to see her how I was I didn't know what I would do. I looked out the hole. My Melrose girl. The paper was erased from my brain. I opened the door. Nothing, and I mean nothing is better than intercourse and hash.

She took me out for breakfast. I had slept hard and I felt like a million. After we ate we drove Meg to this placed called Dog Park. You could unleash your dogs and let them roam. Border Collies are herders, and it was good to see her running circles around the other dogs. This big, fat golden lab started sniffing her from behind and she turned and bit him away harshly. I was proud.

We stopped and I bought some paper. She stayed over again and gave me a ride to work. She was working the same schedule that day. I saw a pattern. I didn't want her hanging around all the time. When she took me home she came up and ordered a pizza. I let her stay.

The next morning she left early for work. I got up and read the hash pages. They were insane. They weren't very good but they were colorful. I went ahead and mailed Mick a few pages.

Jeff Stewart

29

I quit the job because I could no longer deal with those people. A couple of weeks had passed and my Melrose girl was history. I had talked to Mick a few times. He had gotten involved with the girl from the party and they were now official. I remembered one of our conversations about women. He had said that he needed companionship. I thought about it. We all needed it. It just came with such a high price.

I had rent covered for the next month. I sat on the floor and went through all of my writing from Seattle. I ran across a story about Eric I had written at the big Russian's. I sat back and read it. I called information in Minnesota and gave them Eric's last name. It was a strange last name, and there was only one listing. I dialed the number. A girl answered. I asked for him. She said he had moved to Boston. I told her I was his buddy from Seattle and she gave me his number. I dialed it and got the machine. I left him a message.

I didn't want to be in Hollywood. I needed to break loose from that place. The pay was low and the apartment at times still reminded me of the whore. And the lady with the office had not returned my story. I tried to get a hold of her here and there but she was gone. When I asked Juan's wife about it she said they had not heard from her. In the afternoon I walked down to the building but she wasn't there. I sat in the apartment all night reading over my notes and stories.

The next day I took Meg to the park then I rode. I came back, made something to eat and sat in the tub. Hollywood was boring on your own. The phone rang. I grabbed a towel and answered it. It was Eric. He said he was shocked that I called him. I told him I was thinking about him a couple of nights ago but it passed. He accused me of selling my ass on Hollywood Boulevard. I said I'd cut him in on my business but there were already too many gay elves on the boulevard. He laughed.

"No, seriously man, how have you been?"

I said that I needed to dry off and that I'd call him later on, when the rates were cheaper. He offered to call back. He said it was weird that I had called him because he had an idea he wanted to run past me. I told him to give me ten minutes.

I dressed and took Meg out in the courtyard. It was a beautiful night. It was always loud where I lived but tonight was quiet. The crazy Indian lady who lived downstairs kept this little shelter for the stray cats in the neighborhood. It was a shopping cart covered in old quilts and she always had food and water in there. Meg chased the cats away and ate the food. Sometimes she would be out there and she would chase Meg with her walking stick, but she was very large and Meg always thought she was playing with her so she would jump on the old woman and lick her dress.

Eric told me he was taking a screenwriting class. I told him about the screenwriting where I was. Bit by bit I filled him in on what had happened since Seattle. He asked me if I would be interested in coming to Boston and working on a screenplay with him. He said we could use one of my stories and that he had some serious connections and funding. He asked me if I had anything that was filmable. I knew what to use. I had written a long story about this guy in Peoria whose older brother that he admired wrecked his motorcycle and became encephalitic and he had to take care of him. I told him about it. He thought it was a good idea. I told him there was a problem with money and I couldn't bus it because I had Meg. I told him I could thumb it for a few weeks and I would eventually show up. He was all for it. We talked some more and I said I would think it over.

I walked Meg back down the stars. I thought about a story of mine being worked into a film. It was intriguing. I wondered how it would fair, the dialogue and backdrops. It was springtime and the risks of hitch hiking ocean to ocean with my dog made me nervous. I liked it. I hadn't been challenged like that in years. It would work out. I would get back in touch with my edge. We were two years back from the new century and everybody was at home, getting fat and staring at the internet. All of the children were obese.

It was midnight. I still had some food stamps. Across Sunset I walked around the wholesale bulk food warehouse and bought some chicken alfredo and some fries. I had the groceries in my hand, walking toward two Mexicans out in the parking lot. They were standing in front of a long green car arguing in Spanish. I walked toward the other gate. They were getting loud with each other. I watched them as I walked. One stared chasing the other around the car and they both stopped on either side of the hood, throwing their hands up and screaming. Then one pulled out a gun and shot the other man in the stomach. He fell straight forward over the hood without a sound and died. The other guy looked around. No cars stopped. A few women screamed in the distance behind me. No one came out of the warehouse. He pushed the body off the car and jumped in. He was coming up behind me. I walked a straight line. I wouldn't look at him. He went around me full speed and jumped perfectly into the flow of traffic on Western. He had the light and he shot through. I still remember the number on his plates.

I waited to cross Sunset. Over in the parking lot they were gathering around the body. I got the light and walked. A group of tenants were at the corner looking across to the lot. They were talking fast. When I got close they nodded at me.

"What happened, what happened?"

"I don't know."

I rounded my corner, and the sirens were coming up Sunset. Up in the apartment I threw the chicken and fries in the oven and uncorked the bottle of wine with an inch left in the bottom. I downed it and sat in the living room. It had been horrible. What could be so important that a man had to die? Then I thought about it. Plenty. That guy could have raped the shooter's daughter or fucked his wife or even killed someone he knew. Most likely the gunman was burned over drugs. And the neighborhood had something to talk about again. They wouldn't give each other the time, otherwise. I grew bitter waiting for my food. Nature breaks down animals in the food chain and nature gave humans murder for their own eradication. I had a nice dinner.

He answered. I told him I had decided to do it. I only had a hundred and sixty four dollars. It would cost me most of that to ship my bike and the rest of my things to Boston. He offered to wire me a couple of bills and I told him I didn't know when I could pay him back.

"Don't worry about it, man. I'm glad you're coming out. We need to work together."

He gave me the address and told me the money would be there tomorrow. He was taking it off his credit card. The password for Western Union was Meg. I hung up and called Mick. He told me I was out of my mind. He said that Boston was a hellhole. Like Hollywood wasn't.

In the morning I walked over to the home improvement store and bought some tape and asked the manager if he had any large boxes in the back. I boxed everything I could. It was still early, and someone was knocking. I saw Mick through the peephole. I unlocked the door. He walked in and looked at my things.

"You're really doing it, huh?"

"Yeah."

"I took the morning off. You'll never get a ride on these freeways."

He picked up my backpack . It was heavy. I had a sleeping bag tied to the back and a few days' clothes and a lot of my writing, my favorites, because I was paranoid that the boxes would get lost in the system. I was nervous about all of my other pages getting lost or stolen. I could always get a new bike or a new stereo. I had a few small backpacks tied to the sides with food and water for Meg. Mick dug into his pocket.

"Here, man. I got you something for the mission."

He tossed me a harmonica. I laughed. He said every hitch hiker needed one to complete the uniform.

We dropped my boxes off at a UPS and I picked up the money. We jumped on the freeway. He was getting me to the Nevada border. I offered gas money but he refused. He was pissed because he had to show up at the magazine before the end of the day. He wanted to take me into Vegas and see Greg. I realized I had forgotten to call Greg to tell him I was coming. I called him from a truck stop. I told him I was hitching to Boston.

"Fuckin' cool, man. You and your dog?"

"Yes. Mick's here."

"No way. Is he bringing you in?"

"He can't. He has to be back at work."

"Let me talk to that motherfucker."

Mick was looking through the postcards. I called him over.

"It's Greg."

He took the phone and shook his head. I stood back and watched the truckers fuel up out the window. I heard Mick defending himself. I knew Greg was giving him shit over not coming out. I could imagine him calling Mick a pussy and asking him what the difference was between showing up at work for ten minutes or calling in. They joked around for a while and Mick hung up.

On the freeway I could feel his brain working. Meg was curled up on my lap. He shifted angrily into fifth, staring at the road.

"Greg called me a pussy," he said.

I laughed.

"This fucking job is eating my soul. I don't even care about skateboarding."

"Will they fire you if you call in?"

"Hell no. I have to be there tonight to okay the final cuts. Motherfucking deadlines."

I thought about having a job that important. I never would. He flew around a semi.

"Fuck it. I'm taking you to Vegas."

We drove into Barstow and Mick made the call. I stood outside. Meg was running around the car, chasing bugs. I saw him talking with his hands into the phone. He came back to the car and said he'd pulled it off but he would have to be there later that night and work up into the next morning. I told him maybe he should just drop me off.

"Nothing doing. We're already in Barstow. It's not Greg, man. I *want* to go to Vegas. This fucking job has been holding me back for years. It's the money. I make good money there, like 50K a year."

"Damn."

"Doesn't mean shit."

We hit a drive-thru in Baker. The highway had been empty. We crossed into Nevada. He warned me about going to Boston to write a screenplay. He said everybody and their mother was going somewhere coastal to write a screenplay. I told him Eric had connections and funding.

He nodded, "They all say that."

I thanked him for his confidence. He laughed,

"I don't mean to piss on your parade, man. If I had a fucking penny for every joker that promised me gain from my work I'd be rich. You told me yourself that screenwriting was a fluke. I mean, I know it's your own story and I'm sure it's a good one, but that doesn't matter. Unless your friend is blowing somebody high on the ladder, you're doomed. I'm just trying to save you some frustration."

I fed Meg a piece of my jerky. Mick looked over to her then back to the road.

"I don't know why you're fucking around with this film garbage. You're a writer, man. If I had the time I'd help you get your stuff going. I'm just too busy with my own shit. And this Eric guy, I know I don't know him, but everybody who can't write and can't walk away from it thinks they're a director, a producer, a screenwriter or a fucking critic, especially the big publishers. I've dealt with the critics and publishers. They're bitter assholes, they're eunuchs rating pornography. The better the pornography gets, the more bitter they become and they ignore it because they can't touch it and it angers them."

It made sense. And I thought back to his novel, which he had written quite a while back before he had been trying to get it published, and I thought it was possible that he'd forgotten about all that now, the drug of writing, and he was quiet for a long stretch. The job was getting to him, the pressures of managing. We watched the highway and Meg fell asleep.

Vegas was a ghetto in the daylight. I told Mick he was going the wrong way. He said Greg had moved. I knew he had been making good money as a garbage man. I remembered back to when he was only working a couple of days a week, to get his foot in the door. Mick said he had an amazing house. Greg already had three years in with the Union and Mick told me that Greg bought a boat so he and Stephanie could sail to Hawaii one day.

There was a black BMW in the driveway. I laughed when I saw it. It was unbelievable to see the house and the car and the Corvair next to the BMW and to think back to when I first met Greg at the pier. I wondered if anyone knew when they drove by and saw those things that one of the greatest painters and artists, ever, lived there and hauled garbage.

He was out back digging an irrigation ditch. Stephanie was in the yard working at the garden. I told Mick it was like a postcard and he laughed. Greg turned around.

"Holy shit. Look at these dubious motherfuckers."

He speared his shovel. Stephanie waved. He came over and gave me a hug.

"How you been, man?"

"Good. You and your yard work."

I let Meg out of the car. She ran through the back and plowed into the garden. I called her over. I told her to sit and she sat by my leg and cocked her head at Greg. He laughed.

"Is this Meg? Look at Meg."

He knelt down and she went to him. He squeezed her ear.

"Man. A little heartbreaker."

Stephanie came over and met Meg. She let their dog out. I hadn't met him. A big guy named Theo. Meg ran him around the yard. He was beautiful. I asked Greg how old he was.

"He's about two. Don't stress, he doesn't have his nuts."

Mick laughed. Greg closed the gate and we went inside. Beers were passed around. We sat out front on the chairs. Greg looked at Mick's car.

"I can't believe you fuckers are here."

"Been too long," Mick said.

Greg asked him how long he was in for. Mick said he had to leave in a few hours. It was good to be there with Greg and his girl. They were the only ones I'd know to the end. Greg asked Mick if he owed him an apology for getting him mixed up with me. Stephanie looked at me and smiled. I was wondering how long it would be before he gave me shit. He stared at me,

"Look at that fuckin' beard. He looks like a rapist."

"I rape painters." I told them.

"So where's this boat?" I asked.

"Over at Steph's mom's." She said her uncle was doing some work on it. Across the street an old lady yelled over to Greg that he had done a good job on the front yard. "Thanks, honey."

"Unbelievable." I said. "A Beemer, a garden, a boat. What's next? Golf?"

"A few kids." Stephanie said.

Greg laughed. Mick suggested he dye his hair white and finance a Lincoln. I suggested he take up cocaine. Greg said one of us had to grow into manhood and buy a house and get stable. We threw some more things around and decided to eat. I suggested we have a barbecue in the backyard. Mick laughed, but Greg knew I wasn't joking. He said he had some steaks in the house. He walked inside and made a count. He opened the door and threw me his keys.

"We're good on food. You're buying the coals and another sixer."

"Deal."

I jumped in the BMW and backed out. I had never driven a car that expensive and I knew it looked wrong with me inside. Mick looked at me from his chair and said it was a dark day in hell.

He was right. People looked at me with respect when I drove by them. It was funny to me how a car made you a good guy. The bad guys drove twenty year old engines and had no wives. I liked the way it handled. It was quick and it had balls. I got the coals and the beer. They were still out front when I pulled in. I stepped out with the stuff and tossed the keys to Greg.

"Like it?" Mick asked.

"It's all right."

The food was perfect. Mick had to leave for the Valley. We walked him out. I thanked him for everything and he put his hand out. I looked at his hand.

"Fuck off." I gave him a hug. Greg did the same and Stephanie waved goodbye from the window. She was on the phone. We watched his car round the corner and Greg said something about the clouds getting darker. I looked up. It was grim. He wanted me to stay for a few days but I wanted to get the trip over with. We were watching a movie with the dogs when the phone rang. Stephanie talked for a few minutes and hung up.

"Shit."

"What is it?" Greg asked.

"A houseful," she said. "That was my brother. They just pulled into fucking town."

Greg told me her little brother was in a band in Reno now, and whenever they played Vegas they stayed at their house. He said her brother always brought the band and their girlfriends down and they destroyed his house every time, and he hated to be there for it. He turned the movie off.

"You're taking 70 or 80 all the way across right?"

"Yeah."

"Shit. I was gonna to get you into Utah anyway. Looks like now's the time. You up for it?"

"I'm up for it."

I said goodbye to Stephanie. She said she was sorry. Greg said he wasn't, he said this was a good way for him to avoid his own anger. I grabbed my backpack and my girl and we left almost right afterward.

I was already having a good hike. Mick got me to Vegas and Greg was getting me into Salina. I wasn't used to people coming through for me. It was a fun ride. I jumped out at a truck stop just before midnight.

Jeff Stewart

30

It took me 23 rides in total, 2 homosexuals, a lot of unstable maniacs and Christians looking for recruits. The trip was uninteresting for the most part. There was the band of car thieves on the back roads of Indiana who picked me up and carried me into Michigan, and Highway 20 in Indiana was the most beautiful part of the whole three weeks. There was the overweight lonely man who talked my ears off for six hours. The others were simply people who wanted company. They all were, really. I stayed with my brother in Peoria and then with my sister up near Chicago for a week. It was heartwarming to see my new niece and the way she made the lives around her better, easier.

There were some problems with the cops but I expected them. We did a lot of walking during those weeks. Sleeping outside felt best in Pennsylvania. I kept no journal of the hitch hiking because I was taking a break and because it had been recorded by too many others and I did not want to spoil the experience. I only put my thumb out to keep my dog. I made up lousy songs on the harmonica and Meg learned to catch a frisbee. It was not a rough trip and there was no danger involved. I was tired when I stepped out in Cambridge and I knew I had made a mistake by going there.

I called Eric from Harvard Square. It was a long walk to his place. The backpack was heavy and the nylon belt around my waist had rubbed it raw. I crossed the stupid Charles River and made a right up Boylston and drank a bottle of tea in Fenway Park. Everybody gave me shitty looks but Boston was a shitty place.

Everything fell through like Mick said it would. Eric tried to hit me up for half his rent right away. He told me whenever I found a job that I would have to pay half of the $850 he paid for the dive on the basement floor. There were no dogs allowed in the building so it was all stress. The next day when I brought up the screenplay he flipped his computer to a screenplay format and told me to let him know if I got stuck. He flipped on the television and laid on his bed. Where were his connections? Why was everybody so full of shit? All of my boxes were in the living room and I didn't touch one of them.

Jeff Stewart

31

I was stuck in Boston. I walked around for two weeks looking for a job. And I had thought Los Angeles was tough. Eric's friends were assholes and the girls he brought home were even worse. I was finally hired at a porn shop next to a gay bar. It paid seven dollars an hour. I was required to sit behind the counter and greet the perverts. I usually liked porn shops but this one had a bad feel to it. The people were so lascivious they made me ill. No personalities. I got a break when this guy came in with his lady and asked me if the place was hiring. I didn't think it was but I gave him an application, and after we talked he said he had a basement for rent in Cambridge for 50 bucks a week. He told me it wasn't much of a place. There was no electricity and I could only come upstairs to use the shower and kitchen when they were home.
    He was right. It wasn't much. There was a damp mattress down there and a candle. He said it stayed reasonably cool in the summer. He was fine with Meg. I lived in Cambridge in that hole during the day, walked the bridge over the stupid Charles River and worked nights at the porno shop. You could not read or listen to music while you worked. There were cameras everywhere. The closing duties at night were wiping the counter and vacuuming and it took about 20 seconds. In the morning I would take Meg to the park and run her so she would sleep while I

was at work. It was a lousy life. I saved up my scraps from the porno shop for the summer. I had only been working 25 hours a week and Meg had to eat and I had to stay alive.

I decided to go back to the Northwest for the small remainder of summer and for the entire fall. There I could make money fast and at least the people and humidity were tolerable. I dug through one of my notebooks and called Jared. I felt bad for not talking to him for so long and now I was calling for a favor. He said it would be no trouble, that he had a basement and my boxes would be safe. I shipped everything back this time and kept only a small backpack with Meg's food and water dish and two days of clothes.

I lucked out on a ride to Chicago from an old man and his wife. It was timing. I saw the RV. They were cleaning it out in the parking lot across from my place on Prospect and I saw the plates. I had my things together and I was ready to hit the freeway. I walked up to the old people and made conversation, telling them I was a student in Wheaton College majoring in literature and my ride had left without me because of some strange confusion I made up on the spot. I offered them gas money but they wouldn't accept it and I didn't really have it. They were actually going to Rockford, over an hour from my sister's. The old lady took a shine to Meg. People trusted dog owners, they liked them. I thought it would be a good hook for a mugger.

I had never ridden in one before. It was pure luxury. I even got to drive. Those people were so nice, they dropped me off in front of my sister's house. I couldn't believe how easy it was. I was fully rested.

My sister asked me about Boston. She asked me if I saw the Tea Party site. I told her it was a small boat in a pond. She looked disappointed. We were downstairs shooting pool. Doug handed me a drink and said that I was just bitter because I was conned into going all the way out there.

"No. My last girlfriend. That was a con. This was just bullshit."

I drank it down. A good whiskey sour. Denise said something about how funny it was that a man as angry as me had written all of these beautiful words. I didn't say anything.

I went to the grocery store with Doug and I bought a phone card. The next night I called Mick. His lady answered. She told me he was in the shower. I gave her the number. It rang within the hour.

"Hey, motherfucker."

"Mick. How was the shower? Do you condition those things or do they repel water?"

"I shaved my head. Where have you been?"
"I made it to Boston and now I'm here, on the way to Seattle."
"How was Beantown?"
"Exactly how you said it would be. And worse."
"Oh shit. Any bodies in your wake?"

I laughed. He told me his book was picked up by a press in the south and he had just gotten the proofs and they were good. He was leaving for the Northwest himself to do some readings with other writers from the same press. He told me he was flying up there. He asked about Meg. I said she was a pro with the frisbee, a natural. She had a six foot vertical. He mentioned getting the next Gashuffer ready and asked for some new shit. I sort of dodged it, and he said I had plenty of time. I had nothing I wanted to mail him for it. I wanted to send him good work and I hadn't written seriously for a while, since Hollywood. There were some pages in Boston from sitting outside but nothing I would send out. We talked a while then hung up. My sister kept me for week and fed me. I was back to my normal weight.

Doug let me out in Milwaukee then drove back to go to work. It was early, still dark. We walked far east up Farwell and cut down a street a few blocks before North and slept in a park behind some bushes for a few hours. I took Meg to the waterfront and let her swim until a lifeguard with a megaphone announced at me that there were no dogs allowed on the beach. It was hot out there, and there were a lot of fine young girls laying on their stomachs in bikinis. They all loved Meg. One in particular.

The next morning she got up and made us breakfast. Her roomies came down and I ate French toast surrounded by flesh. I stayed for three days until she had a day off, and she drove us a good ways north. I wanted to get up to 94 because it turned into 90 and it was a straight shot to my boxes and my bike.

I looked at the state map in a gas station. I remembered Ben from the boat. We were in Madison and Hudson was a couple of hours or so. There was a good chance he didn't live there anymore but it was worth a shot. I didn't have his address anymore. The Hudson phone book only had one listing for the name. Nobody was home but through the screen door I saw a picture of the parents. The woman looked just like him.

She had to get back home. I kissed her and thanked her for the boost. She gave me her number. I trashed it after she rounded the corner. I had my backpack and a portable I had bought for four dollars and sixty cents at a Salvation Army in Milwaukee. I set the typewriter back in the hedges and walked Meg down to the river. I walked this beautiful path while she galloped in the high grass, her back rising and falling next to me. She looked like a porpoise. I let her swim and we sat, watching the water until dusk. Back at the house his mom let me in.

He was living in St. Paul. His mom tried the number but his roomies hadn't heard from him. She set me up in the basement where I typed poems about the old people in the RV and about my new niece and about the people in Boston, the uselessness of them. I wrote about the river and the elephant grass and my dog. His dad came in from work and we shook hands. I watched a movie upstairs with them. She finally got a hold of Ben late at night. It took him a few moments to figure out why I was in Wisconsin, but then it was all questions. I told him I felt guilty because his mom was tired and she was staying awake because of me, that his dad had called it a night hours ago. He told me he was 20 minutes away. I thanked his mom and sat out front and waited for him. Meg looked up and growled. I followed the growl above our heads. A big metal rooster on top the mailbox. I reached up and spun it.

Jeff Stewart

32

He looked the same, a bit heavier maybe. We crossed the water, and I saw the big Minnesota sign. He said he had talked to his roomies and put a good word in for me and they said I could stay for the three weeks they had left on the lease. I told Ben I would hitch out in the morning.

"How's your money?"

"It's low. I'm going to stay with my buddy Jared in West Seattle. He and his wife have a house. You've never met him."

"Oh."

"Thanks, though."

"No. I was just thinking. My roommate's brother owns a roofing company with this older dude. He works with them. The usual shit, tear-off and clean up. He said you could work for a few weeks and get some money up. They'll pay you 12 bucks an hour. Cash."

"I'll do that."

"You'll like them. All they do is smoke weed and roof. I did it for a month. It's pretty loose."

He was laying sod for a living, working 14 hours a day. He said he thought about me working with him but his boss was a real prick and I wouldn't last with him. We gave each other a rough sketch of the last three years. It was raining in St. Paul. He nodded at the rain pelting his hood,

"Good. No work tomorrow. They've been calling rain for the last three days. About time."

They shared a big house. Dogs were not allowed but Meg made such an impression on them that they didn't care. At night we shared the couch, and she slept right on top of me. The job wasn't bad. I hadn't worked manual labor in a while and I was sore the first two days. We worked a lot of hours. Every day there was a different roof, different scenery. I didn't like the Minnesota accent. It was piggish and oafish but I learned to deal with it. By the end of the third week I had some good money and I decided to stay for the fall and leave before winter. I bought a used '87 Vanagon instead of signing a lease or living with people.

My boss let me park in his yard to sleep. Everybody met there in the morning. The couch in the back folded into a large bed and I built a desk and bolted it down behind the driver's seat. The desk faced the sliding window and I could see the trees from where I sat. I'd bought a swivel chair at a thrift store and cut it down and bolted it in to fit the desk. I built drawers that wouldn't slide open when I drove. I fastened my typewriter to the desktop and at night I would run an extension cord from his house to the inside for my lamp. I had laid new carpet in there and when the bed was folded up it felt like a little house. It was funny. One of the roofers told me I should hang a chandelier from the ceiling. They were good guys. They never gave me too much shit because they were afraid I'd write about them. I would shower in the house after work and drive out to eat. It was kind of expensive to live in a van where I was, as far as food went. At night I would hammer out short stories and poems. Some of them were about hammering out short stories and poems in a van.

I stuck through the fall, and it was all right. I had been into Minneapolis a few times but I did not like the conservative feel it had. I had gotten a few raises after I picked up shingling and knowing that I was making that kind of money put me more at ease. I did not like Minnesota but I didn't know what to do after Seattle anymore.

Fall began to recede and it was getting cold. I bought a space heater, and paid a little extra for utilities. The roofs got steeper with the weather. Once we tore off a large roof with a pitch so steep we had to hang from ropes and harnesses. It was burly. We were hanging off the side of this huge face with our pitchforks and these ropes, icicles hanging from our beards. We looked like biblical characters. In the afternoon I quit taking Meg to the parks and lakes because it was too bitter outside. We holed up in the van and stayed warm. I left town soon after, and they told me if

I wanted to come back the next spring I would have a job.

I barely beat the winter. In Jamestown, North Dakota, my clutch burned out and I was stuck there for eight days, and the repair took a lot of money. The mountain passes were icy and fast. I barely made it through one of them. I drove into Seattle, into a wall of rain. I called Jared just after dusk. At his place I had the couch, and Sylvia had changed into a wife. I got the feeling she didn't want me there. They were having problems. Jared told me on the side that she was pregnant and he was against having children. She wanted one. I got my boxes and left there, feeling bad because my last memory of her had been so warm. I decided I would never get married. The odds were only stacked against you. Greg and Stephanie were the only good couple I knew. I think they were the one exception. Every other couple I had met were full of resentment.

I counted my money, $564.93. I had spent Christmas and New Years in Jamestown. I jumped on 5 south and stopped in Portland. Information had her number and I dialed it and she answered. I knew I was wasting my time with her but I was still in love. She gave me the directions and I pulled up and waited. I was a fool for her and nothing could stop me.

I took her to a nice dinner and we ordered wine. I spent a lot of money when I shouldn't have but I didn't care. I was hoping something would hit her and she would ask me to stay with her. She had broken up with the car wash guy but he still came around a lot, she said. I noticed something in her was different, something had changed. She was 28 like I was but she had these concerns about her life. She was surrendered to goals of stability, and it was clear to me that I would never see her again, I would never see her like I used to. I dropped her off, and she gave me this weird handshake. I was glad I had stopped to see her. I was over her for good, but it somehow made me feel down for a while. The dream was over. I wondered what she was thinking after she went inside.

33

Phoenix came mechanically. I didn't stop through Vegas and I didn't call Mick for a few more weeks. I stayed in the van and rode during the day and delivered pizza at night in Tempe. There were a lot of parks with Meg and a few girls, but they were not as exciting as they once were. It was only sex and I started to prefer it by myself. I didn't call any of my family down there. I was a ghost in my own town. I spent four months by myself and I didn't mind.

When I did call Mick he said he and his girl were having problems. We talked for a while but it was tense because his job was getting stressful and he only talked about his relationship problems. He told me he wasn't writing as much as he needed to, and Gashuffer was still in demand but he had to push it back for another year. I told him to hang in there.

It was getting hot down there, too hot to live in a van. The VW was like an infant. I was constantly paying for small repairs. I quit the job and called my old boss in Minnesota. I decided I would roof for the summer and fall out there then move to Manhattan.

Jeff Stewart

34

I was driving down Cave Creek Road for no reason. The sky was overcast and I was having a good time just driving around with nothing to do. I hadn't slept at all the night before because it was too hot. I pulled into a Circle K for a bottle of tea. I walked out and drank, watching Meg panting in the passenger seat. It made me sad to see her suffer like that. I let her out and we sat on the sidewalk in the shade. I put some water in her dish and watched the traffic. A skinny guy with a shaved head and tattoos everywhere walked across Cave Creek and dropped his backpack next to me while he went inside. He came back out and sat next to me and lit up in the shade. He rested his forearms over his knees and wiped his head on his sleeve.

"I'm sweatin' like a whore in church." He said.

I laughed. He asked me what my dog's name was. I told him it was Meg. He stroked her back.

"Man, she must be hating this shit."

"Yeah."

He put his skinny hand out.

"Job."

I shook his hand. He said he was walking back from his girlfriend's. He had some good tats. There were dragons and skulls and pistols and naked women. They were well detailed. I asked him about them. He did tattoos from his apartment. He was trying to quit smoking but he had to have one because he found out that his ex-girlfriend's mother was trying to legally stop him from seeing his son. She thought he was mental. I asked him where he lived. He had a walk. I offered him a ride home.

"You driving?"

I nodded at the Volks. On the way he asked about the typewriter. I told him I was working on some things. He asked if I had ever written a song, and I told him I hadn't. He wanted to read something. I didn't care anymore. He ducked back and read some pages. He didn't say anything about them. I liked that. Up in his apartment it was cold and I wanted to sleep. Meg had found a corner by his tattoo chair and crashed out. It was good to be out of the heat. I hadn't showered in a long time. I was washing up every day in the bathroom at work. I asked him if I could take a shower.

I was in there for a long time. It was beautiful. I was clean again. I walked out, and the cold air hit me like sex. He was sitting on his bed, strumming his acoustic.

"Feel better, dude?"

"Yeah. Thanks a lot."

He talked into his guitar.

"Central cooling is fucking Godly. I never leave here."

"I don't blame you."

I sat on the floor and stuffed the dirty clothes into my backpack. He was still playing. It sounded good. I stretched out next to Meg and listened. He told me I didn't want to fall asleep. I sat up. It was kind of presumptuous of me. I apologized.

"No, man. I mean this is a bad neighborhood. Your van might get robbed."

I stood up and started to wake Meg. He told me if I wanted to sleep over I could, but we had to put my things upstairs for the night, otherwise they would be sold for rock. He was right. In the parking lot there were already two brown sharks looking into the Volks.

"Away from the bus, motherfuckers," I said.

They took off. After we had all of my things upstairs I poured Meg some food. He picked up his guitar again. I laid back on the floor and closed my eyes. He asked me where I was headed. I told him. He started asking me about the writing. I started to answer him but I faded out.

It was dark. I heard the tattoo gun over my head. I looked up to see him working on his leg. It was a weird thing to see from that angle. He wiped some blood from a skull and nodded at me.

"What time is it?" I said. I had a sore throat. The question scratched coming out.

"I don't know. Around one, I guess."

I was a little sick from the change in temperature. I sat up. I noticed his place was clean and organized.

"There's a few beers in the fridge." He said.

It didn't sound like a bad idea. I walked over and grabbed one and sat back on the floor. Meg woke up and stretched and walked to the door. I opened it and she ran down the stairs and went in the grass. She came back up. Job turned the gun off.

"Good dog, man. My girlfriend used to live here with her dog. Fucker shit everywhere."

I looked at his leg. The skull was totally different after he shaded it. It looked even meaner.

"You're good, man."

He shrugged, "You'd be good too, if you did it for fifteen years."

He rubbed some vitamin D into the skull and covered it. He handed me his portfolio from his chair.

"I did these."

I looked at the work. It was amazing to me that someone could do that, make these intricate things on skin, to see what they were doing through the bubbles and the blood. He mentioned he made good money and he didn't have to leave his place to make it. It was all cash, no taxes, no bullshit.

"I liked what I read in the van."

"Thanks."

"You published?"

"No."

"I can't understand how that works, to write something and have it say something, mean something. It's always amazed me. I write songs but they're shit."

"It takes a while." I said.

"Yeah," he laughed, "Trust me. I can't do it."

"At least you admit it."

I walked to the store to get some aspirin. When I came back, he asked me if I had ever thought about doing spoken word to music. I told him about the time I'd read on the boat. He said he had these two guys he jammed with, a drummer and another guitarist. He said the drummer could get studio time.

I wasn't sure about it. The idea of it being private was good. I had been to places where writers read their shit in turn. None of them could write and they each thought they were the greatest. Nobody really listened to the person reading. They just sat and waited like rats to get up there and have their pathetic time behind the microphone, the other rodents looking at them.

The next night Job's appointment canceled at the last minute. He called his friends over. The drummer was Jack, a long haired guy with a pointy goatee and a young girlfriend. The other guitarist was a short kid called Shitter. It was explained to me that he had shit on the floor in 7 eleven when the Iranian behind the counter lied to him and said they had no bathroom. He had to run from the cops.

Job passed around some of my pages. Jack and Shitter loved them. They laughed out loud. Job told them that every page was like that. Jack got on the phone. He told us that we had 40 minutes after set up. We were going downtown to a big studio. Shitter told me about some of the famous bands who recorded there. He made fun of them. It was a rushed deal after the phone call. I didn't take any of it seriously. I reached into a box and grabbed a stack of folders. Jack and Shitter took off first to get the gear ready. In the van we jumped on the freeway. I was quiet. I was still a little sick and I stared at downtown, thinking about my situations. I was sure I had someone looking out for me, someone up there who was lazy and slept a lot, and would wake up to throw something my way once every year or twice, if they were really on the ball.

It was a big place. The producer was a basket case that worked every hour of every day of every week. He was nothing except nerves. He owed Jack a favor for something and I could tell he wasn't happy about paying up. He sat behind his huge slab with buttons and dials and lights and gauges. Shitter had invited a group of his friends to sit in and listen. There were three sexy, slutty girls and a guy and a girl who didn't say much but she was the best one. Jack had his girl there and she had called some of her own friends down. It made me uncomfortable.

We had our own sound rooms and microphones. Mine was an old style silver RCA on a desk stand. We were each handed headphones. The producer liked having the girls there. He hit a switch and we could hear him from the other side of the glass:

"Everybody got their cans on?"

I looked in the other room at Jack behind his drums. He pointed to his headphones. He did sound checks on their instruments then he checked my voice. Jack asked him to give me a slight echo, something ghostly, but without distortion. He did it. I sounded deranged, like a prisoner calling up to a stained window. We had no rehearsal, no time to plan anything. The producer said go and Job and Jack and Shitter opened into a set which was so unexpected and good that it threw me off. I picked a page and read the first line.

Something happened. Through the alcohol we had during set up and through the page I was back in the old hazes. I was feeling every word, every emotion. I could not see the people watching. All of the years and anger and sadness showed in the pages and I was angry that I had lived such a life. It was like someone had turned on something dead inside of me. I read the first piece and looked up. The girls were horrified.

It was a cleansing. I would look over at Jack pounding the drums and sweating, listening to me through the earphones. Job and Shitter had their heads down, strumming to the words and the drums. We could each hear each other and everything connected gracefully, the pauses, the speed which fit the pages, the slowness and mean snare of the drummer when I read something heavy or funny or mellow. I read with the music after a while and waited for them to break into something different before I read again. There were no egos in that place. A beautiful thing was happening and everyone knew it. The randomness had grown into structure and the whole world bended in to listen.

We were ripping the place to shreds. When our 40 minutes were up the producer shook his head and moved his hands over each other, telling us to keep going. After an hour I had no more pages. I had to stop. They kept going and finished with a dam exploding and drowning, an entirety of pain put to peace.

When it was over the studio was dead quiet. Job looked down at his guitar. Shitter shook his head at Jack, and Jack looked at me and nodded, his shirt saturated with sweat. Out there everybody clapped.

It turned out that a few of the musicians who were recording there had sat in and listened to the last half of the taping. There was a famous heavy metal singer from the eighties and I heard he'd walked out on us. There was a woman from a band who had been on top in the seventies and she had been a big solo singer in the eighties. I walked out and the producer shook my hand. Jack and Shitter and Job were walking around hugging people. I stayed back because I didn't know anybody.

The famous singer was fat then and I saw her walking up to me. I almost laughed because of the suddenness of where I was. She said hello in her famous raspy voice. She asked me if I worked for anyone.

"I work for my dog," I said. She laughed.

"All of those things, you wrote them?"

"Yes."

"And you don't work for anybody."

"Right."

"I thought it was incredible. You really need to do something with yourself."

"Thank you. I remember watching you on television when I was a boy. I remember a certain white dress."

She smiled. I liked her. She had been down a tough road. She said she had to get going but she hoped she would hear of the writing doing good sometime soon. I shook her hand and watched her leave.

We had to wait for the producer to burn the CD. It took a while, into sunrise. Back at Job's the whole group was there and I had sex with the girl who had been quiet in the beginning. She really thought I was something. We played the CD and drank until the next night.

Everybody burned out and left. The girl stayed behind and slept with me. Meg kept her from my flesh. She squeezed in between our bodies and held them there. I slept comfortably on the floor. Job's ex-girlfriend had brought the kid over and he woke me up and moved us into his room while he and his lady and their son watched movies. In the morning I looked over and saw her ass up in the air. I slid over Meg and jumped on. Meg found a corner, watched for a second, grew bored and fell asleep.

Her name was Maria. She was fine. Her parents had bucks and she was going over to Italy for the summer to study. She had another week left. She cut out after the sex and left me her number. Out in the living room Job was alone. He was playing the CD. I asked him if his girlfriend liked it. He said he could only play parts for her because his son was there. He was proud of his son, and the battle he was fighting with his ex-girlfriend and her mother weighed heavily on his shoulders. I asked Job if he was sick of the recording yet and he told me he was copying the CD onto a tape for himself and for Jack and Shitter. They wanted me to have the CD and the master studio tape. I told him to give me a tape instead.

"Fuck it, man. The words make it good. You deserve it."

"I think the music is good." I said.

He started bad mouthing his own guitar playing. Self abasement ran neck and neck with Job and his creation, which is why he could truly create. He leaned back in his chair and stared at my arms. I was shirtless.

"You want a tat?"

"Sure."

"I've been thinking about something for you since the studio. I finally figured it out. It goes perfectly with your writing and with who you are. I can't really describe it to you. I drew it while you were sleeping. It would be big, like a half sleeve. You'd have to trust me."

I didn't care. I had always liked good tattoos. I wasn't worried about having one on my body forever. I would never have a corporate job or a good job. I wasn't really into tattoos like some people were. I could never be a fanatic with my skin covered. A lot of those people looked like they wanted you to look at them, to give them attention. It made me weary of them. Still, it was something new to me and new things which involved years of experience intrigued me. I sat in the chair and he began the first few lines.

There was some pressure and some blood and some stinging, especially on the inside of my arm. He would go for a while, spray some alcohol green soap on my arm, then wipe the blood away. I started to like the feel. I wondered if people with a lot of tats got off on the pain. I sat there for a long time. He worked the needle up over my shoulder and down to my elbow. I didn't want to see it. He said I needed to let it sit for a day. My arm was on fire. He dressed the ink and covered it.

One of his appointments showed up and I took Meg outside and threw the frisbee. It was scorching, and Meg was mostly black. She didn't want to stop but I brought her inside and we hung out in Job's room while he finished up with the guy in the living room. It was a piece he had been working on for a week and he finished it. I walked out and saw the work. It was a large back piece of a Japanese fighting fish battling a mermaid. The guy handed Job a roll of bills and split. I asked Job how much it was.

"Nine hundred, plus a hundred dollar tip."

"Unreal."

"Shit. In a shop he would have paid an easy three thousand."

"I didn't know they were so expensive."

"That's why all the dirt bags come here. I'm cheap. And better than most shop artists."

The next day he did some filling on my arm. It was sore. I didn't like the pain this time. I sat in the chair for five hours. Maria came by toward the end of the session and looked at my arm.

"Wow. That's one dark image. Fucking cool."

I walked in the bathroom and looked at it. A biomechanical garden, organic matter but machine-like. It was dark art. I had never seen anything like it. It was pure madness.

Maria stayed over and the next day Job finished most of it. I told him I had to get going to Minnesota to make some money, and I told Job that I would be back in the winter for the rest of it. He wanted me to stay and record some more work with them, and try to sell it. He told me I could pay minimal rent. It sounded good, but there was no guarantee it would sell and I didn't want to be a vocalist or do spoken word that seriously. I wanted to write books.

I took two copies of the session and left the CD with him, afraid that I would break it somehow. I kept the master tape. I stayed for three more days and Maria packed me a cooler full of food and drinks for the trip. She wanted me to call her from St. Paul but I knew better. She was leaving for Italy in less than a day and I told her she didn't need to be thinking about me while she was over there for her 6 months. She gave me the number and address in Italy anyway.

I went to the copy store and ran copies of the things I had read on the album and gave them to Job. He made me sign them. I left that night and made St. Paul in two days. When I was driving through the panhandle of Texas I reached into my backpack and pulled out one of the copies Job had made for me. I wanted to listen to it while I drove. I opened the cassette case and two hundred dollar bills fell out.

Jeff Stewart

35

I was late in getting there, by about a week and a half, and at the house the roofers were in the backyard at the table. Hands were shaken all around but there was this heavy feeling. There was an old man at the table, a man I hadn't met last year. He was the accountant. My boss told me that they had a roofer fall off an eave and he had to go to the hospital. He was a new guy and when he ran his mouth about making cash under the table and having no insurance through the company, it drew some heavy flies. The company almost went under. He said everything had to be legal and the pay would have to be taxed but we would have to set the money aside ourselves and pay it that way. He also said that a wave of Mexicans had migrated up and they were taking the roofs at one third of their cost per square. I told them I would be moving on.

My old boss walked me to the van. He said he was sorry. I told him I felt somewhat responsible because I was late in getting there and if I had been there than they wouldn't have had to hire a new guy and this wouldn't have gone down. He said it was bound to happen sooner or later. I shook his hand and wished him a good life. I counted my money behind the wheel. I didn't have much. If it hadn't have been for Job I would have been hurting.

I drove east. I figured I would land somewhere to make money. Arizona was too hot and the Northwest was too far. I figured I'd try Milwaukee or maybe even Canada.

It was a nice drive through Wisconsin. It was warm and I found an old country station. It was Saturday, and Tom T. Hall was singing about little baby ducks and old pick up trucks and bourbon in a glass and grass. I was a little worried about life. I didn't have nearly enough money to go to Manhattan and I wanted to get started on another book. I had some ideas. I wanted to write a book that would make someone writhe, make them feel the work and the jobs and the women and the places. I wanted to grip them by the throat and shake them loose only when we were finished with each other. I wanted a good book, one which held power in every page.

I passed Eau Claire and popped in the tape again. It was a good time recording it. It made my writing sound new and untried. I thought about Maria for a second. She was such a metaphor for everything in my life.

The next thing I knew I was slowing to the shoulder. Big trucks hauling boats flew around me. I jumped out the sliding door and popped the engine cover in the back. The whole manifold was cracked in half and there was oil everywhere. I looked around. I saw no towns or civilization. I tried to wave a few cars down but nobody cared. I sat there for three hours. Here came a cop. He ran my information and called for a truck.

The tow truck driver looked at the engine.
He shook his head, "Junk."
He towed me into Black River Falls. I kept looking back at Meg in the Volks. She was leaping about the front seats. She saw my face in the rear windshield of the tow truck and sat down. She just wanted to find me. The driver was a nice guy. He was empathetic. At a hotel off the freeway I unloaded my van while he talked to the front desk ladies and explained the situation. They were cool with Meg staying there for a night. They didn't usually accept pets and I had to pay a deposit for her. The driver gave me some garbage bags for the loose ends in my van. I filled four of them. I signed the title over for the tow and watched it go. I was on a sidewalk in the middle of Wisconsin surrounded by my things and garbage bags. I knew I would never be famous.

Up in the room I fell across the bed. The closest thing I could think of was Peoria. I called Ira collect and told him the story. He said Don and his wife were down there and Don now owned his own roofing company. The irony. He said Don was always bitching about how nobody wanted to work. I told him I'd try to get down there. He offered to come get me but he had a DUI. and he was driving illegally as it was. He said I was always welcomed to stay with him and he'd see what everyone could do for me. We hung up.

I didn't want to make the next call but I had to do it. She was in the shower. I explained the day to Doug. He told me I was cursed. I buckled and asked him for help. He had the next day off, said he'd be there by check out time tomorrow. I thanked him and gave him the number.

I ran the tub and let it fill, going through the garbage bags and tossing the useless things which took up space. The phone rang. I went to the bathroom and cranked off the water. It was my sister. She was mad at me. She told me that I was 28 years old and I needed to get my life together. She said I was going to be 35 one day, looking for a place to sleep. I told her I didn't care.

I knew what she was trying to do. It was some tough love bullshit she probably saw on one of her talk shows. A heavy argument brewed. She was right about everything but I thought it was insensitive of her to call me where I was and lay into me like that. I told her that she had no idea what my life was, that I hadn't lived in some wonder bread town and eaten every night without worries. She started to cry. I felt like the devil. I calmed her. She cried and told me she was constantly worried about me. She said I was too talented to live like a bum. She said I was not responsible for any of my losses and that it was time I stopped beating myself over them. She told me I had a future and I didn't have to be so callous all of time. She kept telling me what I meant to her and what a beautiful person I could be if I would only stop hating the world and just took a good look around me. We went back and forth for an hour. She had to take her daughter to bed. I hung up and I cried.

Doug was there right at eleven. We loaded the car and left. He had driven four hours north to get me, and he was driving me two hours south of his house to drop me off. I felt sick over it. He said he had nothing to do otherwise but he wasn't a traveler, and he would have rather been at home with his family on his day off. We weren't going by the house because it was too far off the freeway. I played our tape for him. He listened to every word. Once he almost missed a turn because he was listening closely. After it was over he shook my hand. It made him see me differently. He wasn't used to respecting my life. He said if I ever wanted to do something like that with his band I was welcomed. I gave him the extra copy for the ride. I had tried to give him gas money but he wouldn't take it.

At my brother's I unloaded my things into the kitchen. He met Doug, and while they had a beer I walked out to the car and slipped a twenty into his ashtray. I counted the rest of what I had: $140. Doug drove off and I went inside for dinner.

I called Don. He was overly friendly. He told me had somewhere for me to live and it was free and furnished. He asked me to go out to Bloomington the next day with him and do some side work on this new garage he was framing out there, said he'd be over at six sharp. Ira didn't like dogs. He had the house to himself now, since he and Sally had split for good. She was living in a small apartment above a bar she tended. When I hitched through before, he set Meg up in the basement. It was a concrete floor and it was nice and cool for her. I slept down there with her and it bugged the hell out of him. This time was no different.

At six he was there. I made sure Meg was comfortable in the basement and I grabbed my shoes and ran out. He was fat. He must have gained 60 pounds since I saw him in Phoenix. He had this other chin and he looked older than 42. I didn't say anything about it. I jumped in his work truck and we headed out.

"Heard you was up in Alaska."

"That's right."

"Was it cold?"

"No. It was around seventy the whole season, but we were in a southern bay."

"Think I've gotten fat?"

"I don't know. You've put on a few."

"Quit smokin' five years ago. Bad heart."

"I'm glad you quit, then."

"Louise still smokes."

"How's she been?" I asked. When I thought of her I cringed.

"Same as ever. On my fuckin' nerves."

We turned left onto a dirt road outside of Bloomington. It was a new construction site. I saw the garage he was talking about. It was only a skeleton. He said he had built it from the ground up. A big fat man with a white beard was inside.

"That's Brad. He's the guy who owns the place I was tellin' you about last night. We do projects together. He's a big pussy."

We walked up. He introduced me to Brad, told him I was his little brother and I was the guy who was going to be living at the warehouse. I thought of a warehouse down in industry with a room up high and some rough bar across the street. It sounded good. Brad looked me over and shook my hand. We worked on the garage and drove back to Peoria to the east side, where Louise tended bar. I always thought it was funny that there was an East Peoria.

She was more gruesome than ever. She wasn't happy to see me. We had a couple of beers and went back to Peoria to get my things. "You'll like the warehouse. It's in East Peoria by where we live and there ain't no neighbors. Nearest store is a few miles and there's a bar about six blocks from you. There's a barber shop next to the bar and a vet's office in case your dog gets worms." He laughed.

"It's also got a air conditioner and a icebox and I've already set you up with a small stove, you know one of them ranges, a microwave and you know what else? A tee vee."

"Cool."

"Hell yeah, it's cool. I'd live there."

We grabbed my stuff and headed over. The place was literally in the middle of nowhere.

36

I moved in. It was a room in the back. There was a door to a toilet and a sink. Through the bathroom and out another door was a garage full of pallets and compressors. There was a candy and soda machine in there. Don said that Brad rented it out to a pallet company. They built and rebuilt pallets. To get to my room I had to go through the two glass doors out front and pass a wide, full length mirror and walk down a hall and unlock my door. I had a couch and a table and a large wood stand which held the small black and white television and the range and the microwave. Don had placed some silverware and plates and cups on the range. I set my typewriter on the table. He asked me what I used it for. I told him I liked to write letters. He took me to the grocery store and I stocked up on food for Meg and I. The fridge was small and portable and it didn't hold much. I spent almost all of what I had. The carpet was blue and the wall paper was an annoying state map print. The lights were overhead and fluorescent, so I relied on the small lamp I had from St. Paul.

It was hot and muggy in Peoria. It was summer, and the town grew dark orange and it stank. I worked for a few weeks with Don, and we did a few roofs. He was always late to pay me and he never paid me in full. Work started tapering off, and there was a week without any work. I had five hundred dollars saved. I thought about hitching out, but I was burnt on the idea.

The food ran low and Meg got sick. She wouldn't drink her water or eat. In two days she wouldn't move. It broke my heart. I carried her to the vet's office, where my brother had joked about her getting worms. I thought that was weird. She felt so lifeless in my arms. My heart raced. I had taken her out every day and I thought that maybe she got a hold of something bad in the woods. There was junk everywhere out there. In the office a lady in a white jacket took her from me and I filled out some forms. My hands were shaking. She carried Meg back and laid her on a table and stuck her with an IV so she could get some fluids. I watched my girl on the table and I lost it.

The vet told me Meg may have a mild case of parvo. I knew it killed dogs. Since Meg was an adult now and I had gotten her shots in Los Angeles over a year ago, she said the odds of survival were fifty/fifty. The vet closed at 8 p.m. I stayed at her side the whole time. They had to kick me out. I walked home slowly, my hands in my pockets. She would be on that slab all night. I laid on the couch and stressed. I didn't know what I would do without her, without her little face on my chest every morning. If I lost her I would go mad and kill everyone I saw. The whole night went slowly. I tossed and turned and thought about it. She was my best friend. I wouldn't be able to handle it.

The office opened at seven-thirty and I was sitting out front. They were fifteen minutes late. Inside the lady who watched over the sick animals all night said that Meg had woken to go to the bathroom and she had retained a lot of water. I walked past them and sat next to her. I put my hand on her little head. She smelled my hand and her tail wagged. I told her I loved her and if she died we couldn't play frisbee anymore, and she couldn't swim or chase the ducks in the park. I was choking up. All she heard was frisbee and swim and ducks and park and she tried to stand. Her little eyes were red and she was hot, and she was breathing heavily. I put my head on her back and sobbed like a child.

The lady said it was a good sign that she could wag her tail and retain water without a lot of vomiting. She also told me not to get my hopes up. The vet took my arm and led me out, telling me that they had seen worse cases of what Meg had and they had saved a few. I walked back to Meg. The lady followed me. I sat next to my girl and stroked her. The vet started to say something, but she let me stay. I stayed until they closed. While I was there Meg had stirred a few times and went outside to go to the bathroom. Her food was also tubed into her and the lady said her stool was a little more solid than before. That night would tell all, but she told me to expect the worst. Back at the warehouse I was awake all night.

The next day I was there again and they were late again. Inside, Meg saw me and ran over. The lady said she was lucky. I told her it had nothing to do with luck. I was so relieved that I forgot about the money. It didn't matter. I could starve for a while. The important thing was my girl was going to live. The vet bill was $494. I had to feed her this special food and mix in a pill for a week. I would have robbed a store or cut somebody's throat and stolen their money to save my dog. I would have seriously given a limb and gone without forever to keep her. I walked out of there happy that I still had six bucks. At least the place had been close.

Another week went by with less and less. I had run out of food and once I'd tried to microwave some of Meg's from the bag mixed with water. I poured sugar over the top but I threw it back up. Don never stopped by if we weren't working. I was writing a lot of poems and I never got to fully sleep on the weekdays because the workers next door were hammering wood and running the compressors from 7 a.m. until dark. There was this little, fat, hairy one and he had constant diarrhea. I slept about ten feet from the bathroom door and I would hear him in there every morning, spraying the bowl with his waste. He had already used up all of the rolls I had in there without replacing them, so I started keeping them in my room. One morning I knew he had no paper in there but he was letting it fly anyway and I knew he walked out and went back to work without dealing with it. The worst was when he forgot to flush and I had to wake up and walk in there and see it. He couldn't run the water while he sprayed to hide the noise because there was a valve under the sink you had to turn over to get water and the stupid motherfucker couldn't figure it out.

I was in hell, in hell. Summer was ending and I had racked up over 2 months there already. I was starving to death. Meg had enough food to last her for another month. I sat there in my boxers and pumped out poems with a madness. I had tried to start the book many times but I was so crazed with sickness nothing came out right. I hadn't even a shred of the longevity it would take to write a novel. I pounded out a lot of short stories. My longest one was 27 pages but after that one every story lost power after the twelfth page or earlier. I stuck with the poems. They would not stop coming out of me. I covered every second of every day of my life.

Don stopped by one morning and told me we had a job to do for his landlord. He said the guy owned a used car lot and he might swing me a deal on a beater in exchange for my labor. The house was up in Pekin and after we finished it he took me to the lot where the guy let me put a hundred bucks down on this blue bucket with no brakes and no exhaust. It was loud and I didn't trust it. He gave me a temporary tag for the back window but I left it blank in case I got pulled over and hit for no insurance. I would tell the cop that I had just drove it off the lot and I was on my way to insure it. I never got popped driving it.

The car wouldn't get me out of state but at least I could drive it to Ira's house and shower once in a while. We did a few more jobs but Don somehow screwed me on every one of them. The dealer wouldn't give me the plates or title until I paid it off. He wanted eight hundred bucks for that death trap. Whenever I had to stop the car I would have to pump the brakes and throw it into park and rock the frame. It had no radio and no heater and no air. Summer ran past me, laughing.

37

It was getting colder out and the rodents were coming in for shelter. I could hear the mice running the walls while I tried to sleep. It was not uncommon for me to feel one run across my feet when I brushed my teeth. Meg would chase the sounds of the mice in the walls and I was going insane. I had flies in the room. They would come in from cracks in the light covers and take over. One night I spent six hours killing every fly I saw with folded typing paper. I became obsessed with them. I would crouch behind the big stand after I had cleared the room of them and wait for one to crawl out from the ceiling and I would spring on him and flatten him. I thought I would never get to Manhattan, I thought I would rot there. I had nowhere else to go and no money. All I had was the warehouse and I was lucky I had that. I could feel my mind slipping away moment by moment. It had nothing to do with where I was or the lack of food or humanity. It had to do with the morbid process of my incessant repetition of speeding into brick walls, my travels further into failure. My own brother lived close and he didn't give a fuck. Time came forth and showed me pictures only the dead could see.

Jeff Stewart

38

I was not human anymore. I hadn't used my vocal chords in over six weeks. I was barely surviving. I learned to adapt to Meg's food but that made it go quicker. Ira drove over illegally one Sunday and gave me a twenty. When he walked in and saw me he had to stop and put it together. I was ashen, and my ribs were showing. He took me out to eat but my stomach had shrunk and I couldn't put down half a burger without getting full. He bought me a can of coffee and some groceries. He didn't have much money but I was able to live for a few days off the groceries. All I had was the typewriter. It was all I ever had. He wanted me to come stay with him in the south end. He even said Meg could live upstairs with me. I couldn't do it. I convinced him that I was fine. I had become so addicted to being alone that even spending the day with him was painful.

Another month went. On my 29th birthday I locked the place down. I could see headlights outside of my room and I heard someone knocking but I didn't get up. I was dead and destroyed, wasted, sorry, lonely and fucked. I had once had women and people who believed in my work. I was once a human with honor and strength and muscular flesh. Now it was gone. Everything was so gone I wondered if it had ever existed. Maybe I was born in this room and everything had been a dream, a neuro-chemical hallucination brought on by flies crawling down my throat and copulating as I slept. I had quit masturbating because it exerted me, and it only made me hungry afterward. I was not even alive. I was a cell in a jar and I was being monitored by giants who had painted this life for me to live as though it was real. I inhaled deeply, closed my eyes and refused to breathe. Not because I wanted to die, but because I was bored with breathing. My body went through a cold wave and then it was dark.

I awoke with a headache and vomit on my chest. Meg was on top of me, licking my face. I was naked, and I reached down and counted the thin muscles which poked out of my stomach. I had eight of them. Eight was a magic number right then. I thought of scenarios with the number eight. If I cut off two toes and two fingers then I would have eight of each. If Johnny had ten apples and Susie ate two of them then how many apples would Johnny have left? Eight, goddamnit! Eight was a powerful figure! I drew figure eights in the air with my finger.

Jeff Stewart

39

I was twenty-nine years old and I was a loser. I had tried but I had failed. The world was good and sports were good and careers were good and a job meant success and only fools thought they could write. Brad came into my room and told me he wanted money for the utility bill. It was a total of two hundred and eighty six dollars. I jumped up, and told him there was that number again. I told him I would give him eight-hundred and eighty-eight dollars in eight days. He backed away slowly and told me whenever I got some money, that was good enough for him. He told me to take it easy as he backed out the door. He had his hands up and he bumped his head walking out. I looked at Meg and she cocked her head at me.

I was a freak. I was wasting away by flesh, rotting away by soul. Where were my people now? They were out in the sunshine and they were making love and talking to God and God talked back to them. I was no concern of anybody's anymore. I was now at the gates of my real self. I was born for this room. I was born to write in this room. Without this room I would blow away in the dusty wind.

One night I awoke to the sound of Meg growling deeply. I had never heard her growl like that. I reached back and flipped the light on. She had this huge rat cornered in the room. It was drawn back against the wall, hissing at her. It was horrible. He was big and vicious and his tail reminded me of a whip used to snap out my eyeballs. He took a scratch at Meg and I snapped. He was diseased and hungry and he had the heart of a demon. Then I got it. He was a demon, coming for me to take me away because I had even failed to do that on my own and the devil was fed up with me. He sent the rat to me to gnaw out my esophagus in my sleep.

I stood and hissed back at him. He was watching me with those eyes and he wanted me. I picked up my typewriter and held it over my head and stepped toward him. He gave me a flash of death and I brought the typewriter down and killed him.

Meg jumped onto the couch when it hit. My typewriter was broken and he was on his back, a claw still ready, but the nerves died in seconds. His face showed pain, remorse to his master for not carrying out his work. I scooped him up and carried him out the door. He was heavy. I walked down the hall and saw myself in the big mirror. There I was, naked, holding this rat. My profile was sick. There were my ribs, and I had a six month beard and long scraggly hair. I saw the picture again and my mind rushed back into my skull. It hit me and I took one more look at the mirror and stumbled back against the wall and slid to the carpet, holding this rat and sobbing. I threw my head back against the wall and screamed. I sobbed and heaved and coughed up yellow and blood on the rat. I cried for him and for my life. I screamed for my mother in heaven and for my soul, and for a way to get back into my body and live again. I screamed at the ceiling and called my fate a worthless whore.

Outside I held the rat by his tail and swung him in circles until I let him go. He disappeared in the darkness, and I heard him thump far out in the grass. Back inside I turned the valve and scrubbed myself with hot water until my skin was red and raw and it pulsed. I spent the next hour bending and screwing my machine back to use.

The next morning I felt better. I woke up and hit the typewriter and didn't stop for 36 hours except to piss and read. I had to use the backs of other poems. I passed out with stacks of pages upon the table and the floor, and the next day I walked to a payphone and called my sister collect. I asked her for some money. She wired me forty dollars. The car barely had enough fuel to get to the station. I bought Meg some food and myself some typing paper and a loaf of bread and some eggs. On the way back I realized I had forgotten to buy coffee. I decided to go back to the gas station for a quick cup. As I was waiting for traffic to clear for the left turn I heard a second of screeching and this explosion. My knees were over my head. Meg had fallen to the floor and was trying to make her way back to the passenger seat, and we were spinning. I pulled her into my chest. I thought she had been killed, but she licked my neck nervously. When we stopped we were parallel to a pump and my door was sealed shut. I kicked it open and jumped out. Meg ran out and sat behind the store. I looked across the street and saw a fat woman on her cell phone. Her car looked brand new, and the front of it was bent clear back to the windshield. Her airbag was out.

I was rushed by a group of people who had seen it. Two of them were girls who worked there. They said they had seen the whole thing, that the woman behind me was on a cell phone and didn't see me. I walked over and leashed Meg and sat on the curb. I remembered the cops. I went to the payphone and called Don. He was the closest. He actually answered his phone, and he drove down. One guy asked me if I wanted him to wait for the cops so he could be a witness. I said hell yes.

In the store I called the dealer. When he found out I was rear ended he was happy. We synchronized a story. The cops showed up. I didn't need a witness. Plenty of people ran up to them and told them how it went down. A young cop saw my car and asked me if I was able to walk. I told him I was still in shock but I refused the ambulance. The fat woman was fine. She was crying over there. Don smiled some slime at me, he told me I was going to get a lot of money for this.

The cop ran my license and asked about my insurance company. I nodded to the tag and told him I just made my first payment half an hour ago and it was just off the lot. He bought it and I had no charges. He gave me the police report and suggested I go to the hospital for X-rays. I asked Don for a ride back. He said he had to get Louise to work. He said not to forget him when the money came in, that he had woken up to come see if I was hurt.

One of the witnesses dropped Meg and I off at the warehouse. I didn't need to go to the hospital. Ira drove over the next day and I stayed at his place that night. My back was only a little stiff from the accident. The next day was Thanksgiving and we spent it alone at his place. Meg even ate with us. I couldn't eat much, but the hot food was a nice change in my system.

I had to deal with her insurance company. I called the claims adjuster, and he said he would give me a rental. I told him I had no way to get it and he said it could be dropped off where I was. It was her fault and he knew it. I had him by the balls. He said he would have to go inspect my car for the damage assessment. He asked me how I was doing, like he gave a shit. I told him I was in constant pain. The car came in no time. It was brand new. I drove to the warehouse and slept. I waited for two days to call the adjuster back. He wanted to meet with me. He said he wanted to avoid all legal confrontation and make us both happy. I knew I could see doctors and specialists and draw it out with a lawyer and go for her premium, which was a hundred grand, and all that would happen to her was that she would get dropped from her policy. But that could take years. I wasn't really hurt and I wanted out of that place so badly I could taste it. I looked bad enough naturally, so I wasn't worried about giving him a good show. I was at his office at three sharp. I walked out with a check for 10 grand.

At the dealer's, I paid the car off to keep my word and they sold me a mini van for a thousand. It was dark blue and it was quiet and played tapes. His son followed me to the warehouse with it and I drove him back in the rental. That night I packed. I sat back on the couch and looked at the money. Someone up there had finally woken up and kissed me right on the back with another car. Someone had checked their notes and realized they had forgotten me and reached down and touched me. The next morning I went out and got my plates and insurance for the van. I loaded the van and left Brad his money on the table and took one last look around. I lived there seven months. I locked the keys in the rental and called the place and told them I had locked myself out and gave them directions. I said I was sorry for the inconvenience. I filled the tank and drove to Ira's. I laid five hundred bucks on him and I left.

Jeff Stewart

40

It was afternoon and I was on the freeway. I passed the dirt road in Bloomington where I had gone left seven months ago. I blew past it, playing my music. I pulled off an hour later when I saw a huge pet store and bought Meg the most expensive bone they had. It was one of the best days I could remember.

I drove into Ohio and got a room in Dayton. I showered and ate and slept in a bed. I was on the freeway early. I had to stop in Pennsylvania for gas. Off the exit was a copy store. I spent a long time in there copying the warehouse poems. I got lost getting back to the freeway and ended up on the main street of the town. The air was cleaner than Peoria. I was driving into a college district. Fine, young girls everywhere. I passed a Shell station because I didn't see it soon enough and drove up a ways. I saw a post office sign and turned in, mailed the copies to Mick's P.O. Box. First class.

On the way back to the station I saw a barber shop. I pulled over and locked up, cracked the windows for Meg and got a nice, short cut and a clean shave. It took a while. At Shell I gassed up. Next to the station was an old apartment complex made of red bricks. It had a courtyard. Out front girls walked by and there were two guys sitting on the porch, smoking and drinking beers. It was a nice scene. It was comfortable. I asked the guy behind the counter how to get to the freeway.

I drove the main street and jumped on the freeway. I was on my way to the city to write the book. Parking would be a bitch but at least the sidewalks would be full of busyness and there was an energy. It would be expensive and loud but the city was amazing. I would have to focus a little harder to write the book but I could do it. I looked at Meg chewing her bone and rubbed her head. A few miles up, something hit me in the face. Where was I going? New York City was all hustle. I needed to write the book. The game was over. I needed solitude and an easy, steady mode. I pulled off next exit and turned around.

41

I parked at Shell, and walked up to the manager's door. He answered. I asked if he had any vacancies. He showed me the only one he had. A huge upstairs one bedroom with a big closet and a balcony. He said it was three hundred and fifty dollars a month. He gave me an application and asked me about my credit. I told him it was lousy and they'd never accept me. He looked at me like I was crazy. He said he had a few applicants before me and he would let me know. I asked about the deposit. He said it was one month's rent and the application fee of thirty five dollars, that the total move-in was $750. I looked around the place. It felt good, like I was home for a while. I added the numbers in my head and pulled out the roll. I peeled off four thousand, five hundred and fifty dollars. His jaw dropped.

"What do you do?"

"I'm a writer." I counted the money to him.

"Here. One year's rent."

He held the money and studied me. I peeled off another hundred and stuffed it in his shirt pocket.

"There's your application fee. Are we cool?"

He went down and drew up the lease. I stayed up there and walked around, looking for the best places to set everything up. He came back with the forms and a pen.

I signed the dotted line.

I used his cell phone to get the utilities and gas switched over to my name. The phone company said it would take four days before I could get connected. She gave me my phone number.

I got the keys and brought my things upstairs. I went out and bought a bed and set it up in the big closet. It fit perfectly. It was dark in there and I would sleep soundly. I spent the next few days furnishing my place and buying groceries. I spent a lot. I drove out to a computer wholesaler and bought a reasonable computer and printer, along with a multi-shelf corner desk unit.

I stayed up all night building the desk and setting up the computer and printer. Then I built the leather chair on wheels. The floors were wood and I had another desk on the far wall of the bedroom with an electric and a manual for the poems and shorter stories. I could roll back and forth.

I sat behind the computer and took a test drive. I wrote some lines and printed them out. Everything worked perfectly. I drove out and bought kitchen and bathroom supplies and some toys for Meg. I was set up with a couch, tables, a dining room table and chairs. I had lamps and stability. The last thing I bought was a phone, a black cordless. I still had enough money to live on for quite a while. That night I bought a bottle of wine and got wasted, playing my music on the new entertainment center. I fell asleep on the couch. My couch.

After my family and Robles, the first one I called was Greg. I gave him my address and we talked for a while. They were trying to have a baby. He told me he'd get me something out in the mail. I called Job in Phoenix and a few others. I waited until nightfall to call Mick. When he answered I told him I was the president of the gay rights movement, and I wanted to recruit him. It took him a second.

"Holy shit. Where are you?"

"Pennsylvania. Get my package?"

"Yes. Man. I don't know what to say."

"You can say it's good work. Or you could not say anything and keep it suspenseful."

He laughed.

"It's good work, man. Seriously."

"I'm glad something good was maybe pulled from there, hell, from everywhere," I said.

He was giving me 12 pages in the next anthology. It was almost finished. I said I would mail him a copy of the spoken word tape and a letter in a couple of days. We hung up. I slept in for a few weeks and nourished myself back to normal.

Jeff Stewart

It was the day after Christmas. We would be upon a new century in five days. I took Meg out to do her business. There was snow everywhere and the trees had icicles where they once had leaves. Back upstairs it was warm. I brewed some coffee and made a nice breakfast. I sat behind the screen and turned it on. I drank my coffee and stared to the window. It was covered with snow around the edges. I thought about the book, what to leave out for more short stories and poems. I decided it would be narrative. I began the only way I could and reclined back and read the first line. It looked good. Back out the window was fourteen years of research. Shit, I was just getting started.